LADY IN WHITE

WARLOCK OF ROCHESTER
BOOK FOUR

ELI CELATA

Lady in White by Eli Celata
Published by Hidden Helm Press

LADY IN WHITE
Copyright © 2019 ELI CELATA
978-1-949604-09-2
Cover Art by Book Covers Art

www.elicelata.com

Warlock of Rochester Series

High Summons

Grimm Remains

Smoke & Mirrors

Contents

Chapter One

In Solomon's store, books flew through the air. Their covers flapped like wings. Biographies and larger print dove, hunting the pocket dictionaries that dodged between the shelves. The whole bookshop soared to life around us, and for the first time, magic brought a smile to Tommy's face. Grinning, he laughed as fantasy books hopped about on the floor in series lines with the first book in any series leading the rest like ducklings. Others gathered in circles. A group of horrors stacked pencils in strange free-standing sculptures. Though all of these behaviors stemmed from my and Jordan's mind, I couldn't help but snicker as the Stephen King's novels sauntered through the rest like a gang out of some straight to TV musical.

"Okay," Tommy said. "This is pretty cool."

"Magic has its perks. The whole Hell thing isn't great, but the more you know, the less horrifying it can be." Jordan tossed a bookmark into the air. The romances lunged, scrambling to steal it for their nests. The winner scurried back to its shelf. Stuffing the bookmark in with the rest, the book settled on top of it.

At the table, Solomon sipped his tea. An anthology sat in his lap, preening its pages as he ran a hand along its spine. "A psychiatrist would have a field day with this mess."

"They'd have to parse out who's controlling what first," Jordan replied.

With a snort, I sent the children's books back toward their section. "I think we know who's having the romance novels tear each other up."

"Be polite. We have company," Jordan scolded, stretching to blockade the urban fantasy from the paranormal romance. "Do you have any other questions?"

Rubbing his chin, Tommy hummed. "Magic comes from Hell. Demons aren't hunting mortals. Hope makes you an anti-demon glow stick," he reviewed. As the books filed back to their shelves, Jordan nodded. "I should probably avoid swimming at night."

"Yeah, havfine are horrifying," I agreed.

Tommy winced, running a hand over his shaved head. "Murderous mermaids. Isn't there anything non-human that's nice?"

With a shrug, I said, "Lei's not bad."

Solomon placed the anthology back on the table and took another sip of his tea. His white brows rose, but he didn't argue. Jordan remained silent as well. Both waited for Tommy to respond. Maybe they realized Jordan was a horrible judge of character. Offering Lei showed my failing in the field. Although I aimed at comforting Tommy, I couldn't soften the blow too much.

"Lei – Jordan's roommate?" Tommy's brows furrowed. He glanced at Jordan. "That's weird, right? Living with a demon."

Solomon beat Jordan to the punch. "Yes. Yes, it is."

Sitting down across from Solomon, Tommy studied the shop. His gaze drifted from the books as they stilled to the bookmarks which piled back into their own stands beside the cash register. Bags cradled his eyes, and as he scratched one palm with the other, my roommate slowly nodded.

"Okay, I think…it's not great, but I think I get it." Tommy focused on me. "And you didn't know about any of this?"

"Well, I mean, I saw demons and could…" Holding up my hands, I showed off the sparks. "Just didn't know the specifics."

Leaning against the counter, Jordan asked, "Has this helped?"

"Yeah," Tommy admitted.

Solomon's cup clinked against its saucer as he put it down. "Being mortal in the magical community can be intimidating, but you'll find you have a level of freedom magic users don't have. Though, if you don't mind me saying so, you aren't the usual type."

With a frown, my roommate blinked. "What do you mean?"

"Most involved mortals sought magic out," Jordan noted.

"Adrenaline junkies," I suggested with a grin. "Superhero-wannabes, fantasy nerds…"

"So…you?" Tommy joked.

A squawk escaped as my only defense, sending the less than subtle snickering from Jordan into a full-blown cackle. "Hey!" I exclaimed as my roommate smirked. "I have magic. Any adrenaline addiction I have is not my fault. It's hereditary," I groused, glaring at Jordan.

Jordan fell silent. His eyes scanned my face like my words implied anything more than exactly what they meant. We hadn't confronted that issue yet. Whatever uncle-nephew bond existed between us wouldn't grow overnight. He was still Jordan. I was still me. Maybe my weird awareness of him made more sense, and the way my mother acted around him definitely clicked after the discovery. They had co-raised me for a while.

And that's precisely why I hadn't brought it up again. Our relationship was weird enough without wondering if my mom had loved him and if he had loved her too. Add in the absent father who, as it turned out, didn't even realize he had a kid, and this was way above my current threshold for stress. I'd already almost died once this semester thanks.

Before he could say anything, Solomon pondered, "Perhaps all hunters do. A poorly developed self-preservation instinct could be linked to magical ability."

I shrugged and took a seat beside my roommate. Vibrations had me upright as I tugged my phone from my pocket, beaming as Joel's text popped up. "Joel's got the party supplies for tonight," I said with a grin. Jumping up, I stuffed my phone back into my pocket. "Mind if we head out? Tyson's coming back tonight."

"Take the weekend. Monday and I have a video call with the Daughters' Elder Council early tomorrow. I'd like to preemptively empty my schedule to get blitzed after if necessary," Jordan told me. Solomon's brows rose, but he kept any comments he might've had to himself.

"They're deciding Wolfram's fate, right? Where do you think they'll send him?" I asked. "Didn't that German group want him? Something about him being theirs to deal with because he was from Hamelin or something? Or is he going to end up - ?"

Interrupting me, Jordan forewarned, "They may refuse to move him."

"What?" I gaped.

Jordan gestured vaguely. "It could be too dangerous."

"Then what's the alternative? Kill him?" As I spoke, Tommy flinched.

"Wolfram was Wilhelm, and he killed people," Tommy mumbled to himself as if to calm the instinctual panic at our topic. Murder talk wasn't exactly my favorite either. "This sounds like it's above my – my everything. I'm gonna be outside."

With a small wave, Jordan watched him go. Solomon sipped his tea after saying a short: "Good day, Thomas."

"They aren't going to kill him," Jordan assured.

I glanced at Solomon's face, but he stalwartly focused on his tea. With a frown, I crossed my arms over my chest. "Where would they keep him? Can't keep him in the Grith, and there are no other safe houses around, so he'd be moved somewhere still, right? Like Boston or...or somewhere."

Jordan shook his head. "The Daughters have a facility in Damascus, but the Hunt's stalking the east coast. Warping with Wolfram would be suicide."

"So we're just hoping they hate you enough to let you take that risk?" I asked. He nodded solemnly. "Why aren't they killing him? I thought they didn't take prisoners."

"They don't," Jordan retorted.

Swallowing his tea, Solomon clucked his tongue. "Keeping someone alive is usually the more damaging alternative."

"His life depends on the Elders believing Conall exists, and that he's more dangerous than Wolfram. Kasimira's taking lead on that front," Jordan said. With a wave of his wrist, he dismissed me. "Go! Things should be quiet for a while, and you've got to make your apartment look like the Buffalo Bills exploded in it."

"Well, the Bills and the Avengers. We bonded over Spider-Man," I pointed out. Pulling on my coat, I waved a hand. "See you next weekend."

"Keep your phone on!" Jordan called after me.

I waved over my head, not bothering to look back as I pulled the door closed behind me. Emergency calls weren't the norm. Jordan avoided asking for help whenever possible. Tommy waited with his cell in hand. Frowning at the screen, he furrowed his brow. It was a textbook look of Tommy discontent. Anything from a mass disaster to a particularly frustrating game could inspire it. Glancing at me, he slid his phone into his pocket.

"We gotta hit the store," he said.

"What for?" I asked. "I went last night. Seriously, I got everything on Joel's stupid list." All on Jordan's dime post-hunt, but nobody needed to know that. "When are we even going to use two dozen giant beach balls?"

Strolling toward the main streets, Tommy shrugged. "He's got a plan."

I snorted. "A plan? Don't you mean his vision? He sent us a spreadsheet called 'Epic Welcome Back Party.'"

"Let it go, Jon," he warned.

"Why? Ever since the funeral, Joel's been a jerk. He didn't even know Grandma Scott, but he gives me shit twenty-four seven!" I groused. Running a hand over my face, I inhaled and exhaled slowly. "Sorry. I'm just...salty, I guess."

Tommy snorted. "Just a bit."

I rolled my eyes but held my tongue. Buckling under Joel's bull won me more credit than arguing. No idea why they elected me the 'bad friend.' None of them had to patrol the city hunting demons. I missed a few hang out sessions, and I couldn't exactly tell them about magic, so I had to deal with it.

Tommy led us down University Ave. Luckily, Joel's new supply list wasn't too long. Our party, apparently, wouldn't be the same without sparklers, duct tape, and bendy straws. A light chill swept through the air. Every time we came out of a store, the sky seemed darker and the air colder. By the time we made our way back the apartment, it was snowing.

Tommy waited as I fumbled with the lock until the door swung open. An explosion of blue and red decorated every wall. Streamers and helium-filled beach balls hung around the ceiling. Tommy's university fleece blanket covered the back of the couch. Joel marched from his room. Over his head, he held his beanbag chair, which he dropped beside the couch.

"Chuck the subs in the fridge. I ordered wings for later. Nachos are in the oven. Sparklers with the party poppers go on the counter," he directed. "I'll stick them in the cake instead of candles."

Tommy blinked. "You can't blow out a sparkler."

"That's the exciting part," the quarterback returned.

With wide eyes, Tommy glanced to me for backup. "I think Cameron next door has some of those relighting candles from Will's birthday," I offered.

Eyes narrowing, Joel scoffed. "Trick candles. Plebeian."

"Using plebeian," I drawled. "How bourgeois."

His lips curled into a sneer. "Says the kid who can apparently afford to spend over a hundred dollars on beach balls."

"You said I had to!" I retorted.

Shuffling around us to set down the bags, Tommy pleaded, "Let's keep it civil."

"Whatever," Joel grumbled, storming back to the kitchen.

In anxious silence, the three of us rushed around to get everything in place. I grabbed Tyson's favorite games and movies while Joel finished the nachos and set up other snacks. For all our apartment family dinners, we had never put this much into a single night. As four college students with less than stable incomes, we couldn't afford it. Still, it was worth it. Tyson would appreciate the effort, and he deserved a warm welcome back.

"Hey," Joel called as Tommy and I took the liberty of starting up the game console. "Where's everybody else?"

"Everybody else?" Tommy asked. When he glanced at me, I shrugged, and we both looked back to Joel. "Who else was supposed to be coming? It's a school night."

"The rest of the football team? Tyson's friends that don't live with him? Mike? Chantal?" At our blank expressions, Joel groaned. "Why did you think we got all this food? This was supposed to be a party. All caps on 'PARTY!'" Digging out his cell,

9

he huffed, "We're in college. Skipping classes isn't that hard."

Setting down his controller, Tommy shook his head. "Let's just keep it small."

"I made nachos! We have wings coming and enough subs to feed a small army!" Joel gestured toward the fridge.

I grinned and cheered, "No cooking for a week."

"Yeah," Tommy agreed. "This way nobody has to think twice about food this week. Just grab and go. Keep it low key."

Joel ran a hand through his hair, but with a cluck of his tongue, the drama king shoved his phone back into his pocket. "If Tyson asks why this party is so pathetic, it wasn't my fault." Tommy and I nodded. "And if nobody else is allowed, that means no cell phones! No messages – no tweets – nothing tonight. Going offline, and that means you, Blythe."

"Emergencies only," I promised.

But Joel wasn't to be appeased. "Explainable emergencies only."

"What?"

"If you can't explain why it's an emergency, it isn't one. No running off for Jordan or Canada or whatever," Joel demanded. "If you can't sum it up in five words, it's not our problem."

Well, that wasn't happening. Demon emergencies wouldn't qualify, and even if I summed it up in five, only Tommy would believe me. I rolled my eyes but nodded. Lying to Joel wasn't new. If he asked something unrealistic of me, I had no problem telling him what he wanted to hear. Any disappointment was his fault.

The lock on the door clicked. Stepping into the apartment, Tyson dropped his duffle bag and burst out laughing. "Seriously, guys? I was gone a week."

"Appreciate the gesture," Joel commanded. He smacked Tyson on the back as he passed, ducking sideways to grab the duffle. "I'm shoving this in your room. You'll deal with it later."

Before Tyson could argue, I guided him toward the couch. "You have more clothes than the rest of us combined. I'm sure whatever's in there can stay there for a couple of hours."

"Fine by me," he said, kicking off his shoes.

"Mario Kart? Or something more serious?" I asked.

Tyson hummed. "Battle Royale?"

Nobody could beat him at Battle Royale. None of us had played it with him since the beginning of the semester. With a resigned groan, I said, "Sure."

Joel collapsed into his beanbag as Tommy shuffled around the table. When he handed Tyson a plate of food, my roommate's entire face lit up. "Aw, you guys do love me!" Digging into his nachos, he glanced at us all suspiciously. "How long do I get to enjoy this?"

"Consider this a one and done," Joel informed him.

With his own plate in hand, Tommy sat beside me. "Joel's into big gestures."

"Especially if they get him out of just plain being nice," Tyson joked. Joel shrugged, not even bothering to argue.

With Tyson back, the weird tension melted away. Tyson thrashed me. I handed the controller over to Tommy. After running the gambit of the three of us twice, Tyson benevolently allowed a new game. As they raced on screen, I lounged and debated if I could get away with summoning the rest of the wings from the kitchen without getting caught. Although wings were spicy bits of happiness, laziness didn't justify magic. Lei probably would've encouraged it, but that hardly made it better. With a groan, I rolled off the couch and grabbed myself some wings. My phone buzzed. Fumbling it, I got a single glimpse of Jordan's number before Joel slapped it out of my hand. Before I could move, Joel held a finger in front of my face. His brows furrowed.

"Don't even think it, Blythe," he hissed.

"What the – what was that about?" I demanded. Before I could grab it, Joel kicked it further underneath. "Seriously?"

Tyson sighed. "Lay off him."

Joel snorted, rolling his eyes. He leaned back into the couch, glowering as I crouched to grab my phone. Rude without reason. Honestly, he hadn't been my biggest fan before Wilhelm, but for some reason, he absolutely hated me now. Any time I focused on anything magic related, out popped

Joel. Between Jordan's relationship revelation and my absolute failure, I maxed out my suck quotient. I didn't need Joel reminding me of my friendship failures.

Of course, by the time I had the phone, Jordan had stopped calling. He hadn't even bothered to leave a message. Because, why would he? A message would make this a two-way street, and I was just his confused screw-up nephew. No need to help the family black sheep. A warlock in a family of wizards, I didn't need to be told I lurked in the shallow end of the gene pool. Self-loathing bubbled like acid in the back of my throat. I was being stupid. Jordan cared. He helped with Tommy, and the lessons today went well. Things were getting better. Shoving my phone into my pocket, I sat back down.

"See?" Joel drawled. "Not even important."

"Shut up," I snapped.

Sighing, Tyson stood. Without a word, he retreated into our bedroom. Tommy watched. A frown etched into his face. "Not cool," he murmured when Tyson shut the door.

"See what you've done?" Joel growled, keeping his voice a whisper.

Tommy stood, shoving Joel back into his seat. "This one's on you."

"Me? What did I do?"

"Can't you leave Jon alone for a couple hours? You've been jumping down his throat all week. What's your problem?" Tommy asked.

My gaze bounced between the two. The tension in the room stretched tight. If a gap existed, I considered making a run for it, but they were on either side of me, so escaping wasn't an option. Pressing back into the couch, I kept my mouth shut and resisted the urge to go invisible. However, while Tommy geared up for a fight, Joel immediately shut down. His brows relaxed. The snarl relaxed into a small frown.

With a wave of his hand, Joel announced, "You couldn't even begin to understand."

"If you can't explain it in five words, it's not on tonight," Tommy paraphrased Joel's earlier rule.

Glaring at me for all of two seconds, Joel held up his hand and counted along with his fingers as he said, "None of your damn business."

Before Tommy or I could speak, Joel stormed into his room, slamming the door behind him. All around us, beach balls sunk. They tugged streamers down with them like trails of paper blood. Shoulders drooping, Tommy shoved one aside. A curse escaped him, but whatever he had said, he said in Spanish, so I had no idea what it meant. With a shake of his head, Tommy grabbed the plates scattered near the couch. We stalked around the apartment in silence. Cleaning distracted us for a time, but there was only so much to do. When there was nothing left to clean, we stood in the middle of the empty main room. The weight of my phone drew my attention. Though it hadn't rung again, Jordan wouldn't have called me without reason.

"I'm going to go for a walk," I told Tommy, grabbing my jacket. "Maybe it'll give Joel time to cool…or you three can hang out without him getting weird about things."

Tommy's brows lifted. "You don't have to do that."

"We both know I'm not doing this out of the kindness of my heart or anything. Jordan hasn't called back. I might as well go and see why this whole domino train of stupid happened," I replied.

Though his frown deepened, Tommy nodded. "Text if you're going to be out late."

"Sure thing, mom."

Heading out into the night, the crisp autumn air blew through Rochester. Everything hung on the edge of winter. Dampness clung to the trees, edging toward frost. The scent of dead leaves itched at my nose. Maybe it was the sooty carryover of car fumes or newly laid asphalt in half the potholes in the road, but the metallic twang of iron permeated my senses.

Shaking my head, I stepped a league, racing across the city toward Solomon Morgan's bookshop. While Jordan's apartment was closer, Lei's know-it-all face wasn't something I wanted to see. Down the streets, lights flickered. George's car sat outside the shop. Said psychic sat across from Solomon at the front table. Purple and gray cradled George's eyes. Jordan didn't seem to be anywhere in sight. The two leaned over the table, strangely missing a tea set, deeply engulfed in conversation.

As I entered the shop, I caught the end of whatever pep talk Morgan was giving, "– Wild Hunt in the region, there's hardly a way to be certain."

Before I could back away unnoticed, the doorframe flared. Morgan stood, brushing off his shirt. "I'll leave the two of you to it then," he said.

"Thank you, Solomon," George said. "I appreciate your advice."

With a nod, the older man headed up to his apartment. As he went, I inched closer to the door. "I really got to go. Jordan called, but I guess I should've gone straight to the apartment."

George rolled his eyes. Waving his hand at me, he kicked out a chair. "Come on."

"Jordan could be waiting on me."

"Jon. Sit down," Jon commanded. His voice left no room for argument.

With a huff, I stalked over and slouched in the chair. George shook his head and crossed his arms over his chest. So he was going with the disappointed parent routine. Ridiculous. I had enough of a lecture from my mom over the whole Wolfram affair. Nothing George threw at me would work. Wolfram tricked me. I lied to everyone, and even though I had promised my mother I would stay back and let Jordan get into his own trouble, I had stepped right into the thick of it. Gerhard's death weighed on me. Grandma Scott's too. The timing made me suspicious despite the supposed coincidence.

George tapped the table, drawing my attention back to him. "Great. Now that you're back with me, let's have it."

"There's nothing to have."

"You didn't trust Jordan to have your back, and you didn't trust me to know what was what. Wolfram could've gotten away, and Conall did. We have a half-transformed wizard who-knows-where; the Wild Hunt has spent the last week and a half terrorizing the northeast." George cocked a brow as he leaned back in his chair.

I ground my teeth. "Jordan and I already talked. We're fine."

Frowning, George drummed his fingers. "I heard Tommy came to your lesson earlier today."

"I've had three since the Hunt. Jordan lectured me. Kasimira lectured me. I don't need another one. I'm full up on it," I informed him.

If Jordan had avoided me, I would have understood George's decision to lecture me. He stepped up when Jordan failed, but Jordan hadn't this time. I had my wrist slapped. In Monday's office, I had sat with my head bowed as Kasimira ranted about how irresponsible I had been, and Jordan had watched, listening and adding to my list of failures until they both were content that they had read me the riot act. Jordan hadn't mentioned it again, and sometimes my thoughts got ahead of me, but we were doing okay. I didn't need George poking holes into this. Not when he stood as the one who had the most to lose if I screwed up again.

"You need to communicate. Not communicating put you and Ilea in the middle of a blood feud between rogues," George explained. "If we hadn't arrived in time, you'd have been killed. Best case - frankly. Worse case - torture. Worst case - Wolfram might've felt a little vindictive and put you in a catacomb like Shiloh's. I'm sure at least one member of the Hunt would've been up for trying to digest the Source's nephew."

"I didn't know he was my uncle."

"You knew you were his student," George retorted.

"He already gave me this lecture. I get it. He doesn't trust anybody else to teach me, and nobody else really wants that responsibility either. This is his last resort and mine," I drawled, pushing down the coiling confusion which set my stomach upside down whenever I thought about it. If Jordan decided to leave, my options became ultimatums. Either I gave up my life in Rochester or I end up on the wrong side of the Daughters and massively underprepared for whatever they – or Hell – send after me. "I've gotten this lecture from Jordan. He was the one who called me, so…" I stood, frowning at the floor. "I get your trying to fill in the gaps for Jordan – help him out, or whatever. Don't worry. He actually didn't screw this one up."

Sighing, he slouched further into my chair. "I'm not worried about Jordan. I'm honestly more concerned by you."

"Me?" I blinked.

"This is all new to you, Jon. Things aren't getting easier after this. Wolfram's unique, I'll give him that, but our kind – magic users – we're liars," George told me. "I wanted to make sure you were in a good place."

"Your family had to leave because of me."

Snorting, he shook his head. "After Giuseppe, it was only a matter of time. Now that the Wild Hunt is sticking to the east coast, moving became a win-win-win."

"How?"

"Safer, cheaper, and closer to family," he counted off on one hand.

And this was why I worried. No matter how big my screw-ups, George took the dad route. Somehow, justifying made it worse. Nothing he listed had to do with him or Jordan. He hadn't even mentioned the risk to the Grith. Everything tied back to me. Me putting myself in danger. Me nearly dying. Guilt weighed down on me. Yelling would've been easier.

"You don't have to be nice to me about this," I grumbled and fell back into the chair across from him. "I messed up. People could've died. People did die. If we'd all just trusted each other, maybe Gerhard would still be alive."

His brows furrowed. "Kasimira might've suspected, but nobody knew Wilhelm was Wolfram until after that. Gerhard's death isn't on you."

"But I saw what was coming. Conall showed me. Gerhard told me. I should've pushed more. Something was going on from the first time he

19

showed up in my head, and I can't – I can't even trust that it's not going to happen again," I admitted.

I hadn't had a dream since that night. While dreamless nights should've been a relief, insomnia crept up on me. Rare nights when I got to sleep, I woke up more tired. These strange episodes of pitch blackness came. Sounds like a muted bass underwater echoed, but odds suggested it was just my pulse in my ear more akin to sleep paralysis rather than a dream. Every breath doubled and out of sync. Unnatural didn't begin to cover the experience. Darkness itched at me. Stretching back endlessly, the emptiness exhausted me.

George stared at me. His multicolored eyes bore into mine as if he could read my thoughts. Scratching at the stubble along his jaw, he leaned his elbows on the table's top. "You've flared your soul since then, haven't you?"

"Yeah but he was in my head."

"No, he was in Hell. Anything you saw came up the line. It wasn't real. It wasn't directly in your head," he assured me. "Conall has had centuries to train – just like Wolfram. He's had practice."

Frowning, I glared at the floor. "What if it isn't just that?"

"Then he's an empath."

My gaze jumped up to meet his. "What?"

"Conall is a master manipulator, but he doesn't sound like a psychopath. Maybe – he's a prophet," George suggested, and when my brows knotted, he continued, "He's a wizard, so any

20

precognition is useless, and he's obviously not ordained, which would suggest a family lineage, but it also would suggest his primary ability isn't something Hell can easily manipulate – empathy."

"Because demons don't get feelings?"

Shaking his head, George waved away my comment. "They don't know how to be nuanced about it, but that's not the point. An empath can create connections between people through their magic. He wouldn't be targeting you through Hell but through a sort of stint between his connection to Hell and your own. Most commonly, this connection is used for siphoning magic. While an empath can't cut off a person completely, if left unattended, they can leach strength or negatively influence a user's magic against them."

My stomach churned. "Like the outburst I had before Shiloh?" I asked.

"Maybe," he admitted. "But even if Conall has that ability, there're ways to deal with it, and we can even check it if you're worried." Pulling out his cell, he put it on speaker phone. Lei's name popped up on the screen. It rang twice before the demon picked up. "Hey, Lei?"

"What?" the demon drawled.

"We're concerned Conall might be an empath. Do you mind going downstairs for a while and checking everyone's lines?" George asked.

A groan echoed over the line. "Can't someone else go?"

The psychic smirked. His sharp canines flashed. "It's you or Berith. You really want him back in Jordan's life?"

Several thuds and a crash which might have been a television being upended sounded. "Stupid winged brat! Horrible plot holes everywhere!" After a sharp growl, the line went dead.

With a self-satisfied grin, George lounged back in his chair. "There you go."

"What just happened?" I asked.

"Conall's soul was nearly a void, so flaring your soul would've taken care of any top layer leaching." He told me. "However, if his lines run through Hell, Lei can trace them back. He'll check the basics for yours, Jordan's, and mine."

"What about Wolfram's?"

The easy smugness remained as he shrugged. "He'll be cut off from Hell while the Daughters await transport, and wherever he's headed, his magic will be useless anyways. His connection to Hell will effectively cease to exist until he's out."

A shiver ran down my spine. Even hearing about someone losing their magic verged too close to a limb getting cut off. Sure, a leg falling asleep was closer, but the sudden loss – and likely minimal explanation – would not just be numbness. His magic would be invisible. There one second and gone the next. Like a gaping hole had been opened up inside, and nobody would bother to tell him it would get better because, for someone who had done what he'd done, there wasn't anyone who wanted it to get better. Well, anyone but Conall, maybe.

Drumming his fingers against the table, George said, "That's handled, so back to the point." I held back a groan. The psychic leaned forward, pointing at me as he commanded, "Communicate."

A second passed then another. I glanced aside then back to him. "That's it?"

"Basically," George replied.

"But I attacked Jordan."

With a smirk, he shrugged. "And you're never going to be able to get the jump on him again." He waved his hands as if to wipe the memory from my head that he was the one who told me I could get away with it in the first place. It was ridiculous. Not that I could call him on it. "You're his nephew. Whether he wants to admit it or not, you two are alike. Trusting the wrong person – being overly protective, it's kind of just the way you both are wired."

I snorted. Trusting wasn't one of my top hundred qualities let alone a top ten. Once I trusted, sure – loyal to a fault, but trust wasn't respect. Respect could be given readily. At the very least, I could fake it. Trust was earned. However, as soon as I made my discontent audible, my brain proceeded to list out evidence supporting George's claim. Wolfram fell into the iffiest end, but I had trusted Jordan immediately too. Bonding in the first hour together, Tyson and I failed the reasonable cautiousness test as well.

"I'm selective," I argued. "It's not like I trust a ton of people."

"You slept in an apartment with a stranger you'd met once."

Slamming my hands on the table, I sputtered, "There were extenuating circumstances."

"Sure," George chuckled, shaking his head.

"Besides, you trusted -"

My comeback was cut off as the door swung open and slammed against the wall, sending the poor angel ringer to smash against the ceiling as it clanged. Hair newly bleached, Jordan kicked the door closed. Even his eyebrows were white. His eyes shimmered bronze as he paced, railing in Icelandic. George leaned back. One eyebrow rose, but he didn't speak – just waited for the rant to end. Waving his hands, Jordan growled. He pressed the heels of his palms against his eyes.

"Bad day?" George asked.

Kicking out the third chair, Jordan collapsed back into it. "My presence is required at a video conference with Hikmat. She wants to meet Jon."

"Huh…could be worse." When Jordan's eyes narrowed, George continued, "Basma generally elbows her way into every opportunity possible to berate you."

"She already had her chance. Basma gave us an earful about wastefulness and the futility of chasing after the Erlkonig for what she called 'an obvious fable made up by a thrice-damned blackguard in a bootless attempt to cover his own posterior.'" Jordan rubbed the bridge of his nose.

"Even Kasimira couldn't convince her Conall existed."

Somehow a red-headed wizard from the 13th century had become the Bigfoot of the magical community, and considering it was a safe bet Bigfoot was some type of demon, I would've thought the Daughters would've believed. Regardless, Kasimira wasn't my go-to trusty source either.

George listened to Jordan's rant calmly. He nodded at all the appropriate places, and when the Source finally slouched back with a heavy sigh, he let a few seconds of silence pass before speaking. "Long story short, Wolfram stays for the foreseeable future."

With a sigh, Jordan nodded. "Wolfram stays."

If there was a reasonable explanation, I couldn't think of it. The math just didn't work in my head. A building filled with children, and the Daughters made them the focus of the Wild Hunt. In time, Conall would heal. He would return, and if the Erlkonig had his way, Conall would slaughter as many as it took to put Wolfram six feet under.

Chewing on my lip, I shook my head. "We should just kill him."

"He dies, and we have a bigger threat on our hands," George pointed out.

Jordan clucked his tongue. "The Grith isn't impenetrable."

"Conall doesn't have an insider." Even as he spoke, the psychic's eyes widened. "Shit. They can't seriously think a honey trap will work. Not with that many children."

With a shrug, the Source stared out into the dark street. No demons had passed. While the bookstore had become a hunter hub, demons should have been attracted rather than repelled. I wouldn't have cared, but the Wild Hunt didn't need more recruits. We had no hope against them. If they came for the Grith, the blast radius would decimate everything around Lake Ontario.

"Hikmat has concerns," Jordan said.

George's brow furrowed. Understanding gleamed in his eyes. "Malachi's come to the same conclusion then."

"This…" Tapping his middle finger against the table for emphasis, Jordan shook his head. "Magic is from Hell, but it can be used for good. Prophets run on familial lines – supposedly blessed by the big man upstairs."

"If Conall is a prophet, he won't be the first that went rogue, and he undoubtedly won't be the last. Free will, freedom versus security, age-old argument, and you ranting about it now won't change facts," George said. Jordan leaned against the table, but when he opened his mouth, a raised eyebrow kept him quiet. "Malachi thinks it. I think it. Even the kid's suspicious."

"Not exactly suspicious." George side-eyed me, so I added, "Concerned." Semantics but an important point.

Jordan frowned. His gaze roved from my head to my toes as if checking for injuries, but when he found none, he murmured, "Concerned?"

"He got in my head. Wolfram screwed with my…" I waved a hand at my eyes.

"You flared your soul. You should be fine," he retorted. With a sigh, Jordan pulled out his phone. "I can call Lei and have him –"

Raising a hand, George informed him, "Already done."

"Great – then you can go home, Jon." Tilting his head, Jordan narrowed his eyes. "Why are you even here? I only called to make sure you showed up this Wednesday. I emailed you." He glanced down at his phone. "Crap…I meant to message you. You didn't have to come down here. Text me next time."

Nodding, I drummed my fingers against my thighs. Wolfram already survived one prison. He knew how to bide his time, even while being digested. Still, the idea rolled back around. "Are they going to torture him?" I asked.

Jordan's shoulders sagged. His eyes flicked over to meet George's, and the psychic sank back in his chair. Shifting his gaze to me, Jordan sighed. "Not yet."

Chapter Two

Tyson grabbed his supplies, organizing them into his backpack. His lips remained downturned. Fraternal disappointment summoned a similar look, but he paused every few steps as if his thoughts grew too thick and projected molasses around him.

Leaning back in my desk chair, I asked, "You okay?"

"Getting there," he said, but as he turned to sit on his bed facing me, his frown twisted into a grimace. "What happened between you and Joel?"

"If I knew, I'd have fixed it already."

"Weird."

I shook my head. "It'll sort out eventually."

"Sure, but I wouldn't want him on my case. Joel can hold a nasty grudge," Tyson warned, sliding his backpack onto one shoulder.

"Luckily, Tommy's on my side of whatever this is, so it won't get too bad. Besides, I sort of have other things to worry about," I said, and when Tyson's frown deepened, I added, "Not anything major. Just - I found out Jordan's my uncle."

"Oh."

Scratching the back of my neck, I shrugged. "Yeah, and my dad doesn't know I exist. Apparently, Jordan stepped in as 'dad' for a while, so…weird, but I'm glad I know now."

Tyson chuckled. "But it would've been nicer to know before?"

"Yeah. It would've been," I agreed. "Still, it's Jordan. I don't think it was about protecting himself. I think he didn't want me thinking my dad didn't want me, which is stupid. Even if he doesn't, Jordan's been there as much as he could."

With a laugh, my roommate shook his head. "Your family is bizarre."

"Just half of it."

Rolling his eyes, Tyson snorted. "Sure. Just half."

He wasn't wrong. My mom's parents were pretty fanatical. Though if they had ever met Jordan, he would've been able to confirm Hell existed. That meeting, however, wasn't one I ever wanted to attend.

Begrudgingly, I shrugged. "Mom's normal at least."

"Normal? Ha, your mom's a freaking one-woman army." Pulling on his other backpack strap, he said, "Tommy and I are meeting for lunch, so unless you want to be stuck with Joel, get your butt to campus at one thirty." With a wave, he headed out the door.

"Will do!" I called after him, leaving out the door of our room to salute in jest before the door shut and locked behind him.

Collapsing back into my desk chair, I moved my text to reveal the graded quiz I had hidden from Tyson. He had enough issues without worrying about my grades slipping. If I didn't want to risk losing my scholarship, I couldn't afford to be distracted. Giving up magic wasn't an option. That left sleeping in and video games to sacrifice. With a groan, I shoved the quiz aside.

I needed a 3.5 overall each semester. One B wouldn't kill me. Even thinking that seemed dangerous. If I didn't push myself now it only would get worse in the upper courses.

***

Numbers flooded my brain, and while I enjoyed being back in the logical world of mathematics, marketing kept flying over my head. Definitions were easy enough, but memorization only went so far. Not for the first time, I debated jumping the business ship directly into accounting or a straight mathematics degree. Not like I would use it anyway. Unless Jordan took my magic.

Yeah. That definitely remained on the table. With a groan, I shuffled my newly made flash cards. My books and notes spread out across the floor. Leaning against the couch, I rested an elbow on one knee.

"Maybe it wouldn't darken my soul to put up an illusion and copy off of Tyson," I grumbled.

As if laughing at me, my magic sent a breeze across the room, sending my papers flying. Collapsing back against the couch, I closed my eyes. It was almost one anyway. I would have to head out soon.

The lock in the front door clicked. As the knob turned, I twisted the air, bringing everything back to neat piles before Joel came in. His headphones blared what was probably some indie film soundtrack, so I didn't bother greeting him beyond a wave. He lifted his chin, nodding at me, and went straight into his room. Whatever tenuous, joking relationship we had started to form no longer existed. I could leave it. Our disconnection would rot and compound. If I was lucky, separate meals might mitigate the issue until next year, but Joel's actions affected more than just me.

Gathering up my work, I dumped it on my desk. Everything in me screamed to leave it. Joel wasn't a demon. I couldn't just banish him. I marched up to his door, and it flew open, and I froze.

His bright eyes narrowed. Holding up my hands, I stepped back, but he didn't blink. My heart raced. "Have you heard of the Lady in White?" Joel asked.

The tension drained out of me. "What?"

"Lady in White - apparently an urban legend. This ghost woman searching for her daughter or her daughter's killers or something," he said. Finally, blinking, he leaned against his doorframe. "I've been assigned to 'study the city' for my sequential art project."

"Tyson probably knows."

Rolling his eyes, Joel huffed, "He got enough problems without being a walking-talking search engine."

My brain buzzed with white noise. Creatures beyond paranormal stories haunted Rochester. Joel, however, didn't know I was a demon hunter's apprentice. He had to be angling for something. But what?

"I could check the bookshop for anything," I offered.

Joel nodded. "Thanks," he said and shut the door in my face.

Maybe we were okay after all.

***

We were not okay. Joel was a spiteful little shit. An afternoon in the backroom could've been fun, but instead, I was buried in binders from some paranormal investigators. Covered in dust and

33

having sacrificed two hours of possible study time, I returned victorious.

"Here!" I held out the three binders and two books from Morgan. "He needs the binders back before Thanksgiving, but the books are yours to keep."

Joel's eyes scanned down my arm to the books then back to me. His blank expression remained. "I changed topics."

Falling into the chair beside Tyson, I groaned. "What? But you just asked me about it today!"

He shrugged. "I have the internet. Some old broad and her dogs. Crap story."

"You take that back!" Tyson slammed down his sub. "Nobody in this apartment is going to disrespect the Lady in White."

"What's the Lady in White?" Tommy asked before taking another bite of a chicken wing.

Tyson rounded on him. "A tragedy, that's what it is. Little girl gets kidnapped, and her mother goes out looking for her with hounds to track her, but the little girl gets killed, so she never finds her. Now her ghost and the phantom hounds still look for the spot where the murderers buried her daughter!"

With a shrug, Joel sipped his soda. "And you summed it up in - what? Like three sentences?"

"I thought the daughter ran away to be married, and the mom died while chasing her," I said, glancing down at the books. "I stopped reading after the first few pages of the binders. Morgan has an entire wall dedicated to paranormal activity in and around Rochester."

With a yawn, Joel slouched further in his chair. "It's not that big of a deal."

"That's like one of the major ghost stories. Lady in White around Durand-Eastman Park, and that Ghost Deer further out," Tyson argued.

"Not that popular," Joel retorted. "Everything I found said it was a drowned woman who protects other women. That's three different stories," he said, gesturing at Tyson and me. "What's even the point?" He shoved his chair from the table. "It's just a story, and just because somebody thought it was funny to run around in some stupid moth-eaten dress doesn't make it important. It doesn't make it real."

"Wait – what?" Tommy called, stopping Joel in his tracks.

Running a hand through his hair, the other grumbled, "Professor Mullaney assigned it, so I went to open studio this afternoon. Lights go out. Some jerk in some dusty theater get-up walks by. Group of freshman shrieked and completely upended my charcoals. They're freaking stubs!"

"Did you figure out who did it?" Tyson asked.

Joel collapsed back into his seat. "No idea."

"Then we figure it out," I offered.

Cleaning up his plate, Tommy frowned. "Did everyone get assigned that? Or just you?"

"Just me," Joel confirmed.

Tommy's eyebrows rose. "So you were definitely the target."

"You're like the least superstitious person I know," Tyson commented. "Why would they think some fake ghost would freak you out?"

For a moment, Joel's eyes darkened. The ridges of his cheekbones sharpened as he swallowed. Every muscle in his face tensed. With a scoff, he tilted his chin up, glaring down his nose at Tyson. "As if I'd know what those idiots were thinking."

"Do you believe in ghosts?" I asked.

Rolling his eyes, he stood so fast his chair slammed into the wall. "Forget it," he spat and stormed into his room, throwing the door shut behind him.

"That's not weird at all," Tyson drawled.

We both looked to Tommy, but he shrugged. Whatever Joel's problem was, he would either tell us eventually, or it would go away without us ever knowing. Though it made me a crap friend, I hoped the latter. Joel didn't like me as is. Any failure to help him would only sour things between us further.

**

Tuesday wrecked me. At the base of my skull, my head pulsed. A lifetime without dyslexia gave me no clue what to do when the letters and numbers smashed together and jumped around. Half of the movement came from exhaustion. Whatever inspired the rest lived outside my diagnostic skills. French sucked. Pressing the heels of my hands into my eyes, I inhaled slowly, letting the air expand my chest in hopes my heart would stop racing. I hadn't even had caffeine.

Opening my eyes, I glared up at the teacher's notes. She lectured on in French, and only a collection of long summers of muttered Louisiana Creole French allowed me to follow along. Something about grammar. Made sense. It was a French grammar course. I fidgeted, wiggling my pen and pointedly glaring at my desk anytime her voice pitched higher with a question. If she asked me something, there was a growing chance my response would just be profanity and/or vomit. Speaking in tongues made this course a moot point anyway. As long as I had a mage or higher around, bilingualism wasn't that impressive. It also wasn't necessary.

Forty impossibly long minutes later, I rushed out of class, avoiding the concerned furrowing of Professor Martin's brows. Odds on her trying to talk to me before next class were skyrocketing. Yet another concerned adult. Heading back to my apartment, I pushed down the frustration building inside of me. Like a shaken soda can, I edged closer to bursting. A single demon was all I needed. Something small to take the edge off.

The city had been crawling with them for months, but after the Hunt passed through, I had barely seen a baoht let alone anything worth expending energy on, yet at that moment, I would've been willing to go full kamikaze on even one of those tiny specks of damnation. Instead, I made it home without a single void in sight.

"Welcome back," Tyson greeted from the kitchen table. All his missed assignments were laid out, filling up the surface with paper.

Setting my bag down, I took a seat across from him. "You need help?"

Tyson groaned. He leaned forward, resting his forehead against the table. "A double major never felt more stupid."

"You missed a week. That's three classes tops. Even with your course load, you can totally catch up," I assured him. Scanning the typed notes and highlighted syllabi, I debated the truth of my words. While I had no doubt Tyson could do it, the workload for the next several days would be difficult, to say the least. "When did you add a marketing course?"

"Marketing in Nonprofits is only offered in the fall semester. If I took it next fall, it'd completely throw off my schedule," he explained. Twirling a blue highlighter, he gestured at the associated syllabus. "Professor Grossman pushed the midterm back two weeks, so I missed that." He guided the highlighter to another pile of papers. "Took the midterm in Econ, but Accounting had an essay, and I sent it in – but Dr. Kulkarni offered me a chance to resubmit by the end of the week if I wanted. Is he being nice? Did he see it and think I need it? Or is he just throwing it out there to psych me out?" With a shrug, he grumbled, "No clue."

"Didn't Tommy take a course with Kulkarni last year?"

Tyson's brows rose. "Yes!"

Leaning back, I glanced down the hall toward Tommy's room. "He here?"

"Nah – should be back soon. He had work this morning, but I think he was going to the movies or something with his boyfriend," Tyson said. He grabbed our Econ book and flipped it to the correct chapter. "Do you have last week's quiz?"

"Sure." Digging into my backpack, I handed him the sheet.

Any hope I had that he'd ignore the minus next to the B wasn't happening. "Thought you had the unit on lock," he said, gesturing at the grade with his pen.

"Rough week." Not a lie. "I'm sure I aced today's." Hopefully, also not a lie.

Flipping through his notebook, he wrote down everything in red. While he intended to study the notes, each line felt like weighing my mistakes. None of the Grith kids dealt with this. Any classes they served had a purpose which would help them hunt demons. Nobody expected them to be anything but hunters.

My stomach sank. Every villainous monologue made sense each time I complained – even just mentally – about my freedom. Jordan encouraged me to stay in school. He and my mom worked to keep me out of the community, yet here I was. Complaining about how I didn't get a chance to not have a choice. Gerhard would've loved school.

"I'm gonna leave my folder and notebook for Econ here," I told Tyson. "I gotta go for a run."

"Running?" His eyes narrowed. My heart raced, thundering in my ears, but rather than press further, he grabbed my notebook. "At least somebody has kept their health goal since I left."

"You'll be first string next season for sure," I cheered with two thumbs up.

By the time the door shut behind me, my magic surged. Electricity sparked up my fingers. Running down the stairs, I threw open the outside door, and pulling water vapor close to me, I shifted myself out of view before leaving the city behind.

Not a demon in sight. Every dark and semi-dark corner stood empty. Not even a hook shimmered in the shadows, waiting for the Void Hours. Going south, I traced the streets of Penfield, stalking Fairport before heading further south to round Victor. A few small-time demons popped up. A dorota around the mall inched its way toward the cinema. Movie theaters weren't exactly known for being brightly lit. Giving it a run through, I left, disappointed to find nobody had beaten the dorota to the punch.

Heading north, I hit the lake and froze. Gray water sloshed out in front of me. Some boats still moved along the surface, but no matter how much I strained my eyes, nothing blinked in the darkness. Something had wrecked Jordan's lights. Only emptiness remained. Vast swathes of water and strange shapes moving below the surface. The havfine were back. Around me, the illusion burst. Vapor scattered and rained down on the sand in a perfect ring.

"I'm overreacting," I said, but my feet didn't listen. My body remained frozen. Petrified, I inhaled slowly, reassuring myself, "I can fly. I'm practically Superman. I don't even have to be near the water when I cross it, so…" Feet still didn't move. "Crap."

Pulling my phone out of my pocket, I dialed my mom without looking at the screen. She would be so disappointed. I only came here for her. Normal required a degree. After all she went through for hers, the least I could do was get mine. The line rang, and I managed a step backward.

Every doubt swarmed me. Any pride I had in my intelligence withered beneath the weight of Wolfram's con and my failing grades. I had never believed my ego to be fragile. Obviously, I was wrong.

"Jon!" my mother's exuberant voice came across the line. "How are you?"

"Hi, Mom."

A single breath passed along the line. "What's happened?"

"Nothing bad," I lied. She wouldn't leave it there. Given a lead, she would dig at it until she found out everything. While I had called her, I needed clarity, and I only had one place I could think to find it. "Just not sure how I feel about

42

Jordan being my uncle. Why didn't you tell me?"

"It's complicated," she said with a sigh.

"Complicated? How is it complicated? It actually makes more sense. Dad – my bio dad – didn't realize I was conceived, the Source of Magic did. Dad left; Jordan popped up like the weirdo he is." I shrugged though she couldn't see me. "I mean, two years – that's not like he raised me."

"Wow," my mom murmured; her tone dry and soft. "Then you're doing better than I am."

"What?"

"Jon, they're identical twins. Sure, Jordan's about half a foot shorter than your dad, but he spent almost three years with me. Honestly, it's a lot more complicated than just him being your uncle for me. I wish it wasn't. I wish he could've stayed, and we could've given you the family we never had," she told me. "It's complicated."

Sirens rang through my head. This wasn't where the conversation was supposed to go. Nothing about this made me feel better. My mom had loved Jordan. She didn't need to say it outright, but everything led my brain straight to that point. Complicated was a relationship status. A want for there to be something that wasn't and the call I wanted to make my life a bit easier upended me. On the plus, the revelation wasn't bad. Strange, sure, but definitely more interesting to think about - and less horrifying – than where my mind had been before.

"But why didn't you tell me that my father doesn't know I exist? I mean, maybe he got one of Jordan's letters, or somebody in the community told him, but…is he even my dad then? Or does two years count? Does that make Jordan my uncle-dad?" I scrambled for clarity in the mangled mess of my thoughts.

"I can't answer that for you, baby boy."

Taking another step, I turned my back on the lake and walked south. "Okay, so complicated might be a good term for what this is." With a sigh, I tested, "Maybe I should take some time off. Focus on figuring out the whole dad-uncle-magic thing."

"No."

"I'm not saying I won't go back, but there's a lot to demon hunting, and it really is life or death, so some time away won't kill me," I argued.

"You are staying in school. If you even think of dropping out, I'll come down to Rochester, and believe me, demons have nothing on me," my mom swore, and I believed her.

Leaving wasn't an option, which meant I couldn't give up. I couldn't fail out.

"Don't worry. I'm here for the long haul," I promised her. "Love you."

"Love you too. Now, what's going on with

those roommates of yours?"

Chapter Three

Meeting at the bookshop before sunrise, Jordan and I headed northward. Beyond a nod in greeting, he didn't speak until we made it to Canada. If he noticed the slight stumble getting on and off the lake, he was decent enough not to mention it.

"Don't talk unless spoken to," he commanded. "Keep your face as blank as possible. No eyebrows, no head-tilts, not even a frown if you can help it. Hikmat isn't the worst, but she's still an Elder. If she had a reason to push my training you, she will. Right now, we have the Jaegers backing us, and I don't want to put them out. They've got enough on their hands with Wolfram."

"If they don't believe Conall exists, then why is Wolfram still alive? Nobody thinks he can be rehabilitated," I asked as we walked further inland.

Jordan shrugged, running a hand through his hair. "They're not idiots. The Daughters realize something has the Wild Hunt up in arms. Even if they don't believe in Conall, they might think they can use Wolfram against the Erlkonig or Cernunnos."

"But Cernunnos is Conall."

"Belief might be a weapon for magic users, but blind faith isn't natural to us," he said as the Grith rose before us. "Common sense either."

After Shiloh, Monday had rebuilt, but the increased warding then had nothing on the fortress the Daughters transformed the manor into following Wolfram. From outside, the stone wall remained the same, but after passing through the gate, the illusion vanished, and two more warded gateways came into view. The second was stone as well, but the third, which was still under construction, rose out of a cement block. Entirely iron, wards covered every inch.

Once through the third, the large yard, though diminished, still stretched a good distance around the house. Hurricane windows replaced the old though the rune work remained. With shutters to further guard them, they stood out like a satellite dish on a thatched roof.

"They do realize one of their biggest threats is inside the wards, right?" I asked.

Despite the sun only just breaking the horizon, we weren't the only ones awake. On each corner of the third wall, familiar faces stared out, surveying the world outside as if the passing mortals drifting by posed even half the threat buried within the Grith's walls. The twins, Helena and Leta, took the front corners, but I couldn't see the other pair toward the back.

Jordan ran a hand through his hair. "They know their prisoner."

"And they are more afraid of Conall and the Hunt than of what he can do on his own?"

"He can't do anything. Isolated, warded..." Jordan shook his head. "Centuries in Shiloh's void, and he masters illusions. It tells you something about him, doesn't it?"

"That he's manipulative?"

Shaking his head, he sighed. "He's stubborn and highly motivated. He mastered illusions because if he managed to get out of Shiloh's void, being Wolfram wouldn't save him. If he ended up in Hell, being human would get him attacked. All the other Hamelin children would've recognized him, and he didn't hide his predilections, so that could get him killed," he explained as we walked up the stairs. "The illusions weren't for Conall. As much as he claimed to want revenge, he murdered Gerhard for Conall."

A shiver ran down my spine. Clay and flesh stitched together. All remaining parts of Gerhard had burned thanks to Ilea. There had been a spark. Small but bright, life returned to his eyes as he tried to speak, and any interest I ever had in Frankenstein died right there and then.

"Maybe we should've just told them about Conall's golem-work," I suggested as we stepped inside.

In the entryway, Ros stood with Monday. The space between them seemed awkwardly measured. Glancing at Jordan, I cocked a brow, and he gave me a small shake of his head to hold my tongue.

"Good morning," Ros said. Her pale lips curled into a warm smile. "Kasimira's getting the computer setup, and Theda's grabbing some coffee. Do either of you want anything?"

"Kid?" Jordan prompted.

I shrugged. "Meinhard mentioned cinnamon buns last week. Got any left?"

A small smile twisted Monday's lips, and his eyes fluttered over to Ros as if she were an angel, and he couldn't bear to look away. Though his eyes were on her, he informed me, "Unfortunately, they were gone within minutes."

Swaying slightly closer to the Grith Wizard, Ros offered, "The younger classes made scones yesterday."

Any free food was good. "Please and thank you!"

"My pleasure." She stepped aside, gesturing toward the kitchen. "Why don't we let Jordan and Malcolm gameplan for the call? I think I might also have some cinnamon sugar butter that would go with it nicely."

As I followed her, I angled back to Jordan, mouthing, "Malcolm?"

His eyes met mine then pointed to Monday as if I had asked him to whom she was referring. I knew Monday's first name. I wanted to know why she called him that. Everybody referred to him by his surname. If anything, it had given me the impression he was secretly a superhero. Most alliteratively named folks inspired that assumption. However, the use of his given name surprised me. I couldn't say why. Ros used first names with everybody else. It was a level of familiarity innate to most people who cohabitated regardless of their personal relationship. Joel used my first name, and he was pissed at me. My little shipper heart just wanted to read into it.

"With so many kids, we buy tea in bulk. We have black, chamomile, and peppermint. Any preference? Or would you prefer something else to drink?" Ros asked. "I'm afraid we don't have any sugary drinks. Kasimira's still on her all-natural food kick. I was lucky to convince her not to remove all simple carbs."

"Milk would be fine."

Her nose scrunched up as she glanced back at me. "Milk? With scones? Queen Elizabeth would gasp in horror."

"Thank goodness I'm not British," I replied.

Laughing, she uncovered a tray of differently colored scones. "Blueberry lemon, cranberry orange, and…" She turned, searching around the kitchen. "We have gruyere and bacon somewhere around here."

Grabbing a blueberry, I sat back on the empty counter beside them. "The royal butlers would inwardly cringe at keeping two scone flavors together. Oh dear, the flavors might mingle!"

"Not mingled flavors!" Ros cried, pressing the back of her hand to her forehead.

Two kids crossed through. They gave us a wide berth, and the second they walked out the opposite side, their voices picked back up. So much for being the cool college student.

Ros grinned and handed me a cup. "Hope whole is fine."

"I'm just glad you're feeding me."

"If only all the kids were so easy to please."
She grabbed a scone, sitting back on the island
across from me. "How are you?"

"Curious about if you're dating Monday," I
retorted.

Her pale skin flushed pink. "What?"

"Sorry, Malcolm."

Her lips quirked into a smile. "You know I
have a teaching certificate and a degree in
psychology, don't you? I see textbook deflection
when I hear it."

"Synesthesia then?"

Pressing her lips into a thin line, she reached
forward, tapping my arm. "Are you okay? You've
been through a lot, and though I'm sure George has
talked with you, I'm here if you need me."

Bull. She was a Daughter, and even if she
was my favorite, her allegiance wasn't to me. If
anything, she probably wanted to give me an out
from Jordan. A useful option, sure, but the weight
behind it grated on my nerves.

Smiling, I shrugged. "I'm good, but I'll keep
that in mind."

Though her lips tilted up to mirror my
expression, her brows pinched with concern;
however, if she intended to say anything else, Ros
didn't get the chance as Jordan sauntered into the
kitchen. Grabbing a scone, he glanced between us.

"You give him the download on Hikmat?"
he asked.

"Not yet."

"Suppose there isn't much to say," Jordan murmured. "Come on. Monday needs us all in his office.

Awkwardly, everyone except Theda gathered around Monday's computer screen. While we chatted with Hikmat, Theda would guard Wolfram. Despite his isolation, they had him under twenty-four/seven surveillance.

Jordan pushed me into a chair at the far edge of the camera's view. He glanced at the screen, and stretching out his foot, he shoved me further back, so he sat slightly in front of me as well. Kasimira took the other chair. Unsurprisingly, Jordan and Kasimira ended up front and center.

"It'd be best," Monday warned me, "if you only spoke when directly addressed."

"By name," Kasimira agreed.

Ros, who stood beside him with their arms nearly touched, nodded. "Definitely only by name."

With a swirling ring, the video rang. A click loaded the image of an older woman with tanned skin. Silvers and grays colored her short hair. Hikmat's hooded brown eyes watched us with amusement.

"Nice to see you all," she said in a hoarse voice.

Her eyes slid across us. Massive scarring stretched along the right side of her neck. Shiny burns melded up into a hole where her ear had likely once been. At her voice, everybody – Jordan included – sat up just a bit straighter.

Kasimira quickly took the lead. "Pleasure to see you as well, Elder Hikmat." She didn't bother with any further niceties and said, "We were told you had additional questions regarding the Wolfram matter."

"I do," Hikmat agreed. "There were a number of abnormalities described in all three of your reports. Though the Wizard Monday offered a similar account, the Council found it rather hard to believe this could have all occurred under the watch of a triad, the Grith Wizard, and the Source." Smirking, she sighed. "Perhaps we expected too much."

"Our focus was on the rehabilitation of the Hamelin children. If the issue had been solely Wolfram," Kasimira argued, but Hikmat waved a hand, and the red-haired daughter went silent.

"If Wolfram had been the only issue, he would have still convinced an acolyte to murder an innocent." Tristan deserved more, and part of me wanted to thank her for reminding them that his death hadn't been a suicide. On the other hand, with how they had treated him, calling him innocent seemed insultingly late. "Regardless of whether the other child would have died, a soul became corrupted and another died because of that child. All under your watch." Tilting her chin up, Hikmat shook her head. "I am disappointed in the three of you. We expected more. These children deserved better from you."

Jordan shifted in his chair, leaning forward. "With all due respect," he said, though his tone didn't suggest the phrase was sincere. "They had to fight against a number of prejudices and deal with a hundred and seven children. Seventy-eight without any idea of the modern world who suffered posttraumatic stress disorder and you expected them to do better?" Kasimira tensed beside him. "The miscommunication and distrust – thanks in bulk to you and yours – prevented a coordinated front. Two casualties are nothing compared to other major rogue illusionists. Henri Bordeaux decapitated ten acolytes right in front of the Council of Elders in 1793."

Inhaling loudly through her nose, Hikmat clucked her tongue. "This isn't a trial though it is refreshing to see you defend our members."

"Wolfram had centuries to hone his illusions." With a shrug, Jordan sat back in his seat. "Underestimating his abilities led to a confrontation with the Wild Hunt. We can't afford to pretend the two aren't connected. We also can't pretend he isn't a threat on his own."

"And of that, the Council has no doubts," Hikmat informed us.

Kasimira's brows furrowed. "Then what does the Council doubt?"

"Beyond the existence of this Conall?"

"You can doubt his existence as much as an atheist doubts Lucifer exists, but he's still here," Jordan drawled. Monday rested a hand on Jordan's shoulder, and to Ros's obvious relief, Jordan shut up.

Hikmat frowned, etching deep lines around her mouth. "A magic-user cannot become a demon. There has never been one, no matter how dark they became, who transformed, and no one has reported even an attempt besides you, Source."

"We all saw Conall. Wolfram recognized Cernunnos by that name, and we recognized him to be a mortal wizard. How else would you explain a wizard surviving in Hell for almost eight hundred years?" Monday inquired.

Hikmat inclined her head slightly to the side. "How can we be certain this Conall lived eight hundred years? Wolfram could have easily met him after leaving the void."

"Cernunnos visited Henrietta Scott and was acknowledged by her prior to her death," Jordan explained. "Even if he isn't eight hundred years old, that suggests that he is the same Cernunnos her family died confronting along the Hindu Kush in 1937."

Jordan avoided looking at me, but this was it. If she was going to talk to me, this made the most sense. I had seen the meeting after all. My heart raced. We needed the Elders to appreciate the gravity of Conall's existence, and I could do it. I was ready.

However, she didn't even glance in my direction. "And what proof do we have that this wasn't another illusion?"

And my brain screeched the breaks. I had seen Cernunnos. Grandma Scott had acknowledged him as Cernunnos, hadn't she? It wasn't an illusion.

Wolfram wasn't there. None of that was an illusion. Her words wrapped around me, and I couldn't find a way to prove it wasn't an illusion beyond the fact that Wolfram was elsewhere at the time.

"Wolfram is a mage," Jordan reminded her. "A wizard or a demon would've needed to warp out of the fire that my apprentice unleashed. Otherwise, we wouldn't be having this conversation as our problem would be crispy."

My whole body tensed, but again, she kept her eyes on Jordan when she asked, "Who else witnessed the affair?"

"It happened at the Scott house," Monday responded. "As her family is mortal and strictly out of hunting, no one else witnessed Cernunnos or Jon's response."

"Unfortunate."

Kasimira's eyes narrowed. "Extremely fortunate. There are over two dozen mortals in the household."

"And yet, we're back where we started. How can you prove Conall and Cernunnos are on and the same? Furthermore, even if they were, how can you prove that this Cernunnos is the only one there has ever been? Mythology mentions Cernunnos far before our records. While our records first note him by name seven hundred and fifty years ago, Celtic mythology predates that by centuries."

None of this was serious. Hikmat and the Elders had no plan to listen to us at all. Their decision remained regardless of our answers. We were just a formality, and she was going through the motions before she dismissed Conall's existence.

"But what if you're wrong?" I asked.

Monday squeezed Jordan's shoulder, but his plan to make my life miserable crackled in the air. Whatever he sent my way, if I could get the Elders to take Conall seriously as a threat, it was worth it.

"We don't function on 'what ifs,'" she informed me. "We cannot afford to risk lives to move someone wanted by the Erlkonig. Passing him through Hell isn't an option, which means we have to take the time for mortal transport. Mortal transport risks exposure. If your Conall exists, we may have a new demon on our hand. The Covenant falls into question, and mass panic ensues." Narrowing her eyes, Hikmat focused directly on me. "I don't expect someone raised by a mortal to understand the multitude of variables we must consider. I do, however, expect you to learn." Her focus returned to Jordan and Kasimira. "And with that in mind, we will not acknowledge anything to do with Conall or your assertions regarding Wolfram's connection to the Wild Hunt beyond their desire to have him dead. As a result, his transport from the Grith will be postponed indefinitely."

She knew. None of what she said denied Conall's existence – just the acknowledgment of it. Any shade she threw was measured. The Elders would not take responsibility for Wolfram, so we were stuck. Pulling his hand back from Jordan, Monday squared off, but he remained silent as Ros grabbed his forearm. Kasimira clenched the arms of her chair.

"I will transport him," Kasimira offered. "Jordan can warp us to –"

Again, Hikmat waved her hand for silence. "He will remain at the Grith."

"Surely he could be held at the citadel in Tel Aviv."

"The Grith is one of the most heavily warded places on Earth," Hikmat retorted "We have found placements for all children over the age of twelve. The younger ones will be difficult, but the Sons have connections at a number of monasteries."

Monday's fists clenched. "You expect me to turn my home into a prison."

"I expect you to do as needed." Her dark eyes glimmered. "When we have dealt with Wolfram, you may continue your work."

"I no longer work at the service of the Daughters," Monday informed her. "If they want to go, I will do everything in my power to ensure the transition goes smoothly, but I will not force any of them to go where they do not feel safe."

And my desire to turn invisible was at an all-time high. Monday's voice left no room to argue, but the angles of Hikmat's face and her scars suggested she wasn't exactly a pushover either. Their eyes locked. Neither blinked as their wills battled.

With a sigh, she blinked first. "They have been through enough already, Malcolm. Our only intention is to offer an alternative for those unwilling to remain after the recent incident."

"Then let me move Wolfram," Jordan pressed, leaning so the computer's camera focused on him. "As long as he's here, the Wild Hunt's sticking around. I can't fix Rochester with them here."

"Transportation isn't an option."

Crossing her arms over her chest, Kasimira said, "Then let's kill him."

Silence reigned over the room. Though the Elders refused to admit Conall's existence, I couldn't fathom any other reason to not kill Wolfram. The Daughters didn't seem to shy from murder.

Hikmat cocked a brow. "Is there no further use in the mage being alive?"

"If a wizard cannot become a demon, then no."

Drumming my fingers against my thighs, I waited for anyone to point out how bad an idea this was. We played chicken with our lives. Everyone who mentioned the Covenant pointed that we owed the rest of humanity for what had been done. Our duty laid in defending mortals from demons. If we killed Wolfram, Conall had nothing tying him to humanity. An entirely new breed of demon would form, yet nobody spoke.

Darkness swirled around my head. Like a tightened violin string, my tie to Hell flicked and vibrated. My stomach rolled. Pain flared across my abdomen and down my spine. Clenching around the arms of my chair, my fingers paled as my muscles flexed. As quickly as the pain came, it fled, and when I glanced up, Jordan's eyes were on me.

"We will take that into consideration," Hikmat informed the room. "For now, he remains alive in isolation." Before anyone could argue, she warned, "Children don't always know what is best for them," and the video cut.

Chapter Four

"Well...that went better than expected," Ros said.

Kasimira rolled her eyes, glaring back at her elder sister. "How could it have been worse?"

"She could have ordered Wolfram's execution," Ros reminded her.

Shaking her head, Kasimira cradled her face in her hands. "Maybe they're right."

"They aren't," Jordan cut her off. "Conall is a threat."

"But can he actually become a demon? All we have is your word that Ezekiel, your father, believed and attempted, but he didn't succeed, so we have no way of knowing what would happen or how it would work if it did! This is – we're putting ourselves in the line of fire, and I have no idea what we're up against," Kasimira said. Her shoulders sagged much the same way that Ilea's had upon learning of Wolfram's trick. Though trick seemed to light a word for the murder he had urged. Her hands dropped aside, and she groaned.

Ros patted her sister's back. "We can handle this, Kasi."

"We need to get more information from him." Sitting up, Kasimira stood. "Something they can't ignore."

Jordan ran a hand through his hair. "Has he been talking at all?"

"No," Ros admitted.

"We'll find a way," Kasimira assured him.

"How?" Jordan demanded. "Torturing him? Wolfram spent centuries in a void with a corrupted soul. Nothing you could do to him could match that."

"Perhaps we could bring in a trained psychologist," Ros suggested.

Her sister quickly said, "No."

"His soul's dark, but that doesn't mean rehabilitation is completely off the table. It'd be better to work toward that than to sit by and hope we manage to break through while we risk darkening our own," the elder of the two sisters argued.

While the two went back and forth, Monday moved around his office. He shifted his computer back around. With each adjustment, he went back and forth from the angle of the screen to the exact position of the keyboard and mouse to one another. Of all nervous ticks, an obsessive organization of his environment hit me as strange. My mother did the same, but I hadn't seen anybody else do it.

"Wolfram's more dangerous than he is intelligent, and he's damn smart. He'll find a way through the wards eventually," Jordan added, drumming his fingers across the arms of his chair.

Monday hummed, sitting back in his chair behind his desk. "And his connection to Conall?"

"Lei's already feeling out Jon's connection and Wolfram's," Jordan informed him, glancing up to meet the other wizard's dark gaze.

"Connection?" Kasimira frowned. "What do you suspect?"

"Wolfram has an addictive personality, but his interactions with Conall..." Trailing off, Jordan glanced at me. "Why don't you go visit with the kids, Jon?"

"I think I'd actually like to hear this," I retorted.

Everybody stared at me. Their judgment was nearly palpable, but this involved me, and I wasn't about to be moved by silent glaring. Ros was the first to turn away. Her eyes moved to Monday. The second her eyes landed on him, his gaze jumped to meet hers.

Tilting his chin up, Jordan studied me before shrugging. "George suspects Conall has some inherited empathy and may have bonded to Wolfram."

"And Jon," Kasimira surmised.

"He invaded my dreams, so..." I shrugged. "Not good."

"Not good..." she repeated in a tight voice. "You had a fallen wizard in your head." She stood so quickly her chair rocked on its back legs before slamming back onto the floor. "Did you know?" she demanded from Jordan. "The dreams that Gerhard described. It's the same, isn't it? Conall was already in this house. They coordinated from the beginning."

An explosion went off in my head and I whispered, "He undermined Wolfram from the beginning."

"What?" Kasimira's glare dissipated when her gaze fell on me.

"He warned us. If we'd understood, we would've caught Wolfram, and none of this would've happened. Conall literally told on him," I explained. For all the affection Conall expressed, he had tried to get Wolfram caught from the beginning.

"What would have happened?" I asked. "If he'd been found before Tristan and Gerhard?"

"An evaluation, then rehabilitation or execution."

Jordan tilted his head. Shifting his jaw, he hummed. "Likely the execution as he'd killed Wilhelm by that point."

"Which means Conall wouldn't have had to kill him himself!" I cried, tossing my hands in the air. Blank stares met me all around. "Seriously? We can get Conall by getting Wolfram. You guys saw how they were with the Wild Hunt. Back to back, closed rank – they're a unit! Conall picked the Erlkonig eight hundred years ago, but Wolfram can get him back."

Jordan raised a brow. "Except Wolfram wants to become a demon too."

Entering Hell had been their plan. The two of them plotted their descent, but going after that had torn them apart. Conall treated Wolfram with undeniable affection. As much as he had tried not to, nicknames and jokes passed between them. For all his rage, Wolfram wanted to impress the wizard. He had killed Gerhard for him.

"Let me talk to him."

"Not happening," Jordan snapped.

With her hands on her hips, Kasimira glared at Jordan. "I think it's time you take your apprentice home."

My fists clenched at being so quickly dismissed. Gritting my teeth, I pushed on, "I'm somehow connected to those two. Conall reached out, and even if it isn't an empath bond or whatever, I spent a ton of time with Wolfram. I could get him to talk!"

"Jon, he tricked you. Manipulated all of us. Illusions aren't like other types of magic. I can't even do them as well as he did," Jordan said. "And I would need you to be trained up on them before I let you get anywhere near him again."

"No one is going anywhere near him." Kasimira pointed toward the basement.

"But I could –"

"You think he's some type of lost child, but he's not. He is an arrogant, smug, angry young man who is sitting down in that cell acting like it's a throne! If there's some kind of twisted bond between those two psychopaths, it doesn't make them redeemable! We should kill him. Both of them!" the red-haired Daughter roared, slamming her fist against the wall.

I hadn't realized there was background chatter until it stopped. With a growl, Kasimira stormed out. Ros opened her mouth, but no words came out. Shaking her head, she chased after her sister.

"That went well," Jordan murmured.

Leaning back in his chair, Monday sighed. "Wolfram is a difficult case."

"It might actually be easier if we just kill Wolfram and let Conall go dark. We'll at least learn what happens." Only someone as nihilistic as Jordan would think that was acceptable. Monday and I stared at him for a moment before he added, "He's getting there anyway. I'd rather have him on my hands than the two of them together."

"Are we afraid of a Thelma and Louise situation?"

Monday chuckled, but exhaustion shadowed his features. "Do you need a comparative analogy?"

"It's how he thinks." Jordan held up his hands, and standing, he gestured to the door. "If you decide to rebel, I'm here for you. Otherwise, we'll keep patrolling and let you know if the Hunt heads your way."

Nodding, the Wizard of the Grith frowned. "You can help by being here next Sunday. I want to reinforce the wards weekly."

"Done," Jordan promised before he exited.

"Thank you for the scones," I offered before following.

We headed back through the house, and while only watchful eyes and stray pairs wandered around before, there were children in every nook. Some studied in groups, completely ignoring us as we passed, but others whispered. The whisperers stopped. Their eyes stared, tracking us as we walked down the hallway.

Jordan didn't acknowledge them. He swaggered with his head up and shoulders back, but then again, he was used to the attention. Slouching never helped. I mimicked his posture and hoped for the best. It worked until we hit the yard.

Children ran around on the grass, but while they scurried past us, the guards on the third wall had changed. Leta and Helena sauntered side by side toward the house. They spoke, and something Helena said made her sister laugh, sending her eyes our way.

Leta waved and ran over with her twin at her side. "Hey, Jon! Jordan! Mind if I pick your brain a little bit?"

"Sure, what's up?" I asked.

"Helena and I saw a pack of yeth out near the lake last week. Most retreated to Hell before we could take them out. Another pack – might be the same one – showed up around the east edge of the city," she said, rocking back and forth on her heels.

Jordan shrugged. "Yeth are generally pack animals. Seeing them in large quantities isn't unusual."

"But they weren't common around this area until Giuseppe," Helena noted.

"They often congregate around powerful rogues, so with the Wild Hunt and Conall, I wouldn't be surprised to see more of them around the region," Jordan told her, and though what he said made sense, only Helena seemed convinced. Leta worried her bottom lip. "Yeth are common demons. Anything from draugr to a long winter can bring them about."

Leta's brows furrowed, but she didn't comment, allowing her sister to drag her off. Helena smiled brightly as she did so. "Have a good night!"

"That was kind of weird," I murmured, watching them go.

Jordan rolled his eyes, continuing through the gates and out into the city. "Paranoia after a disaster isn't unusual."

"But, I mean, yeth? They're hellhounds – as in dogs. Why would packs be so surprising?" I retorted as we stepped leagues side by side.

Rather than going over the lake, Jordan guided me along its edge. With the sun up, no havfine were in sight despite the chill to the early autumn morning. The silence stretched over us. Stupid Jordan knew I'd break. Of the two of us, I had the motor mouth.

Searching my brain for an alternative topic, I jumped the second one came to mind. "What are they going to do about Ilea?"

"What do you mean?"

"They sent her somewhere, right? Some Daughters' facility to get her soul all scrubbed and clean after she killed Tyson," I explained. "Why can't they take Wolfram there? Do the – the cleansing or whatever?"

"Need to feel you did something wrong. Wolfram doesn't," he retorted.

"But if Conall wasn't around, would they still be doing the same thing? Or would Wil-," I cut myself off immediately. He wasn't Wilhelm. As much as I had known him by that name, he had killed his brother in Shiloh's void. From the very beginning, he had lied to me.

"You need to separate Wolfram and Wilhelm in your head."

Compartmentalization - definitely something the grudge-bearing Source of All Magic could comment on. Arguing with him, however, wouldn't do me any good. "I'm trying."

He studied me out of the corner of his eye, whizzing around trees with practiced ease while I struggled with all my attention on the ground ahead of me. Ahead of us, the falls roared. "You're going to have to kill someone eventually, Jon. I don't know anybody - psychic or otherwise - who hasn't been in that position," Jordan warned, reaching out to pull me into the air as we headed over Niagara Falls.

"I don't want to see him because I want him to get better," I admitted. "I just want to know…" the truth, the line where Wolfram decided I was a good tool to use.

It was stupid. Nothing he said would make what he did better, and asking him to explain himself would only deepen my guilt. I had introduced him to my friends. They all fell into the line of fire because of me, and there was nothing Wolfram could or even would say to change how dangerous that had been. Even asking presented another opportunity to lie. Manipulation and lies were his forte after all. Just another type of illusion.

"We'll figure out Conall on our own. We don't need him," Jordan assured though he slowed to a normal walk as we hit the edge of Rochester.

"But will it be the best way?"

He shrugged. "There's not really a good way to deal with Conall."

"How did you deal with Ezekiel?"

"Went down and dragged him back up. He'd used Belial, so...not hard when the demon likes me more than him," Jordan explained.

His eyes fell to the ground, and I reached out to pat him on the back, but I just couldn't manage to close the distance. Knowing Belial meant something to Jordan didn't change his demonhood, and none of that mattered now that he was officially obliterated. No heaven or hell waited for him, but maybe nothingness was a relief.

"The Erlkonig owes allegiance to Lucifer, right? Maybe you could...I don't know, like talk to him?" I asked, and Jordan chuckled, gesturing at his hair.

"Why do you think I'm bleached?" Shaking his head, he scratched at the piercing through his now white brow. "He thinks the whole mess is hilarious. If he ate mortal food, I'm sure he'd have a thing of popcorn to sit back and watch the whole thing unfold. It's not like he's got much to entertain him."

Rolling my eyes, I scoffed but didn't say anything. Jordan wasn't serious. Still, the idea of pity for the Devil irked me. I never expected more of him, but his punishment never seemed enough. A deal with the Devil may have sprung the Covenant, but somebody before that had to have left the gates to Hell open, and it sure as heck wasn't a human.

"But couldn't it completely throw off things in Hell? The Erlkonig would have another leg up on Lucifer," I said.

"He could."

"Conall owes nobody allegiance. What if he wants Hell? Seemed the Erlkonig liked him. Maybe even enough to rebel," I argued as we stalked the perimeters of the city. No stray demons lurked, and until the void hours, we wouldn't have much work.

Jordan paused. His eyes lifted to the sky, and squinting at the arch of the sun, he sighed. "Honestly, the Erlkonig could do it. But it would absolutely devastate Hell. Not something anyone up here would be upset about."

With a snort, I crossed my arms. "Maybe Conall's just doing the Covenant after all. Biggest bang for his soul."

"Somehow, I don't think he's that self-sacrificing; otherwise, he'd have killed Wolfram already," Jordan drawled and picked up his pace, changing direction to head toward the center of the city.

A bitter chill crackled in the air with each gust. Winter washed over us, and like a balm, it smoothed the rough edges of my thoughts. While warmth and sunlight dug out the dark, the cold softened the bright intensity, soothing me as if my soul was inflamed.

Like a nervous tick, he ran his hand through his hair. Jordan glared at the white strands as if they were an affront to nature. "Why don't you just dye it?"

"Physical reminders can be helpful. Best way to ensure I minimize my time downstairs," he confessed.

The white shimmered in the early sunlight. He resembled a ghost, all pale from head to foot save for the dark brown of his leather jacket. Like flicking a switch, my brain turned to Joel. He knew how to take a joke, and nothing suggested he was superstitious, yet the Lady in White prank had spooked him.

"Have you ever heard of a demon also called the Lady in White?" I asked. Jordan's brows furrowed. "It's a local legend."

"Doesn't make it real."

"Doesn't make it not."

A slight snort escaped, but he managed to choke down the majority of whatever laughter bubbled up at my expense. "Shiloh's gone, and she never surfaced in this area before Toronto."

"What about Lilith?" I asked.

His brows shot up, and Jordan turned on me with a grin. "Lilith! Shit, Jon, how did I not think of that? She wasn't an angel. She didn't shatter! She took a walk downstairs and – bam! Demon capable of bearing young."

"What about Berith? Maybe he was a human too."

Jordan chuckled. "Nobody wants to be a human as much as Berith."

I shook my head. "Are you going to bring Lilith up with the Elders?"

With a wave of his hand, Jordan brushed off the conversation. "The Daughters will believe what they want. Focus on things you can change."

"Like what?"

"Your schoolwork," he retorted. "I'm warping to Greenland. The Wild Hunt ended up there over the weekend, and I want to see how far east they'll go before turning around."

Guiding me into a secluded alley, he stretched his arms before pinching the air in front of him. While the rest of the magical community seemed to be avoiding warping in and around the area, Jordan had no fear of Hell. The Daughters had no excuse to not let him move Wolfram.

"Wait, the Wild Hunt's out during the day?"

"Best time to hunt," he said, saluting me before he fell into the rippling waves of the warp which snapped tightly closed behind him.

Scratching the back of my neck, I sighed. All these motives fluttered around me, and while I could appreciate sonder like nobody's business, considering everything exhausted me. Hikmat and the Elders wanted Wolfram at the Grith. Whether or not the Wild Hunt remained, Jordan would warp, so they didn't have an excuse to not transport unless they had no place to put him, but they had a number of facilities. The ends explained the means. The Elders desired the children out of the Grith. Add in a preference for a torched Rochester, and leaving Wolfram around made sense.

Berith offered a variety of mysteries. Ones I wasn't really up to feeling out. Stepping out of the alley and away from a possible headache, I headed home. The closer I got, the more people crowded into the street to enjoy the sunny weekend weather.

Crowds gathered around street crossing, and as I tapped my foot, I waited for the light to change. A bright red coat and a greyhound caught my eye. The pair trotted down the street, crossing a man on a blue bicycle, which nearly ran into a gray jacketed older man in a newsboy cap. He wasn't tall. Gray hair curled out from the edges, and with his shoulders hunched, he blocked sight of the majority of his tanned neck. Everything on him was better suited to the 1940s from his hat to the custom leather of his shoes. Honestly, he almost reminded me of Giuseppe.

A chill ran down my spine, and when the light turned, I raced around the street. Dodging around a family, I jogged. Everything in me wanted to league walk, but I couldn't risk getting caught. Arriving on the opposite side, the man was nowhere to be seen. Heart racing, I shook my head. Giuseppe's wife had died. He had no reason to stick around. If anything, he had every reason to run. The Daughters were in Toronto. Jordan and I guarded Rochester. If he got caught skulking, this wouldn't end well for him.

Shoving the thought – another cruel possibility – from my mind, I focused on getting back to my apartment. I had to study. Something was coming, and it had nothing to do with a magicless old man.

Chapter Five

Propping my head up with my hands, I reread the same sentence for the ninth time. It was like a vacuum opened up between my ears. Insomnia encroached, but even those scant hours I managed failed to be restful. Darkness lingered after I woke, the unknown itched at the back of my mind. Aches made my joints creak like an old man. Drumming echoed in my ears. Adjusting my jaw, I glared at Tyson. Bright, chipper, jerk Tyson fiddled with his highlighter, letting its cap and end thud against his desk.

"Can you stop?" I snapped.

Tyson paused, glancing up at me from his book. "What?"

"I'm trying to read. Just – come on."

He glanced around then shrugged, going back to his book. Silence settled over the room. Glorious, beautiful silence, and back for time number ten to the sentence. I managed a paragraph before something squeaked. Leaning back, Tyson shifted back and forth as he read. When he went right, the chair smoothly moved. Every left shift screeched.

"Seriously?" I slammed my book down on my desk. "If you're not going to study, get out!"

Tyson glanced around as if I could be talking to anybody else. "What are you talking about?"

"That god awful sound! Are you deaf?"

Groaning, Tyson kicked up his feet. "You're insane."

I shoved everything into my backpack. Tossing it over my shoulder, I stormed out, slamming the door behind me. Everything itched. Magic crackled all along my skin. It and my irritation fed off one another, leaving me a ticking time bomb before I had even gotten to the lobby. Gray loomed overhead. Rain was imminent. Logic dictated I head back upstairs and bunker down in the living room until Joel ultimately showed up and ruined that. Just that thought sent me out the door.

No matter how lanky, if a man was over six feet and seemed angry, people got out of the way. Intimidation wasn't my favorite. Most days, people crossing the streets hit me the wrong way. That day, I preened with each one. Sidekick or no, I had power. If I wanted to cause an earthquake, I could. I wouldn't, but I could.

My feet led me down Lyell Avenue. Exploding on the street wouldn't end well. I had enough risking my life and sanity over the Genesee, so a bit of fire sounded better, and the worst – and probably best place – to do that was the Delco Plant. Abandoned and damaged, the building was a death trap. Not even the police wanted to deal with the sporadic fires people still set.

Like a skeletal specter, the building towered over a rumble-covered yard. Tossing my bag over the fence, I caught it with a gust of wind. I slipped through a gap near the building. Grabbing my bag, I slung it over one shoulder before heading inside.

80

Charred metal, broken and chipped surrounded me. Ash covered everything, and the smoke-dimmed glass blocked more light than the heavy blanket of clouds outside. Debris covered the wood floors and whatever broken, hollowed out structure remained tied together by threads. Pillars held up the floor overhead. Rusted pipes hung. Some had completely fallen to the ground. Red crusted any metal in sight, and even the scant graffiti tags were charred.

Emptiness leaked out of me, and even as I let my soul swell, the light flickered as the darkness tugged against me. Jordan hadn't called which either meant Lei hadn't found anything, or the eashian hadn't returned. Considering his dedication to laziness, the stretch of time told of more effort than I thought him capable of dedicating to anything. Throwing my bag against a pillar, I screamed. A swirling vortex swelled. Wind slammed into the wall before curling back around on me, softening the noise, but the ash stirred, and black streaked the air.

Enenra swirled to life. Pulled into my vortex, the tiny cyclonic demons stretched. Their voids spread and dampened, one into the next until even the dim light let in through the dirty windows incinerated them. A flick of my lighter and fire cascaded into the tempest around me.

Electricity snapped over my skin, but no matter how much I let out, the itch remained. With a sigh, I stopped. The ash rained down in a circle around me. None of this made sense. Energy buzzed around me, but my bones ached. I had never been so tired. In an empty room, I wasn't alone, but I couldn't say why. Where my thoughts normally buzzed around my head, my brain flatlined. Crouching, I pressed my hands against the wood.

"What's wrong with me?"

Sometimes, when I fell quiet, voices would call out. They were never clear. My attention would be elsewhere, and suddenly, I heard my name. Other times, something touched me, but nobody was close. Having seen monsters, I had once believed in ghosts too, but knowing they weren't real, I couldn't brush off the tingling across my shoulders as if someone had come up behind me and run a finger around the back of my neck. Nobody was here. Ghosts didn't exist, and any demons inside had been torn apart.

Closing my eyes, I willed my heartbeat to slow. "Conall?"

Not surprisingly, nobody answered. I'd be lying if I didn't feel like it was a dial tone situation. Not that I wanted him to pick up the other line. A clean head should have been a relief. No illusions, no weird connections to centuries-old murderers. Yet everything buzzed around my head. If somebody else wasn't causing it, I couldn't fix it. I couldn't even blame puberty.

"Seriously? If you're being silent to screw with me, that is just going to make things worse," I grumbled, cradling my head in my hands.

Claws clicked across the wood. A cold wind swept through the room, and ice crept along the window panes. From the shadows, the hounds of

Hell emerged. Blood and ash matted their fur. Bones twisted beneath exposed sinew. Rising from Hell, the yeth kept their heads low to the ground and their shoulders hunched.

My shield expanded, turning me into a bubble boy, but they didn't even get close. The demonic wolves trotted around the floor. Kicking up debris, they sniffed as if searching for something, and for once, that something wasn't me. Sitting beside a pillar, my bag caught my eye, but none of them went near it. Raising a hand, I sent out a tendril and pulled my backpack into my shield. They didn't even glance my way.

"Is this your answer?" I murmured when a few of the yeth scratched and curled up in a pile of demonic puppies. Pulling out my phone, I snapped a few pictures, but even the flash didn't draw their attention. "You guys here to chill? Or just messing with me?"

If nothing else, my curiosity drained my irritation and the buzzing of magic beneath my skin returned to a pleasant simmer. Shaking my head, I sat down, taking out my textbooks. Quiet reigned through the floor. Outside, thunder rolled. Sleet painted the windows, sloshing down around the building and leaking through the cracks.

Calm settled over me, and I fell easily into studying where I'd struggled. Maybe Tyson had annoyed me. Or perhaps the warding itched. Glancing up, I scratched the back of my neck. Warding didn't hurt. Runes protected magic users. Runes, souls, and prophets – three types of magic which weren't Hell-adjacent and none of them should have bothered me. It hadn't bothered me before, and I wasn't sure why even the idea of it rubbed me the wrong way came to mind. If my headache came back, I decided to bring it up with Jordan, but for now, I would appreciate the relaxation. With just the shield buzzing around me, tension drained from my shoulders. My headache faded.

***

Shoving my homework back into my bag, I stood, and a few of the closer yeth looked up only to snort and roll back over as if I was disturbing them. I chucked my bag over my shoulders. Only Lei acted as lazy. Tightening my shield, I sauntered toward the door. A few hounds rolled over. Their ears – if they had flesh to them – lifted. One even cocked its head.

"Not that it hasn't been nice, but I'm heading out before I have to explain 'a hellhound ate my homework' to a professor – or Jordan," I announced, and sneezing, the head cocking yeth flopped back down on the floor, sinking right through and back into Hell. "I definitely should be worried about this."

Shaking my head, I headed back home. The slush had turned to rain, and now near freezing sheets of it came down, flooding the edges of the streets. Dropping my shield, I let the cold water run over me. A chill raced down my spine, but the untangled mess inside my head eased further. The vapors bounced off me as I threw back up my shield. Water hung around me. Crystal ornaments spinning for barely a second before joining the rest of the rain on the path to the ground. Rolling my shoulders, I inhaled the crisp air.

One league step had me racing through the city. Cars, people, and buildings blurred. Even the rain stilled before crashing around my shield. Out of the corner of my eyes, a white figure shifted. Unlike the rest which moved too slow to clearly be seen, this figure followed after me: a woman in a white dress and veil. The specifics escaped me, but the off-white sheet pulled over her head and pinned around the knee line of her full-length skirt caught my attention, but as quickly as she passed into my vision, she disappeared. Stopping outside my building, I spun. Nobody was there.

"Not Shiloh," I assured myself.

There were other dress-wearing demons. Some others even wore a toga or robe, but the shroud threw me for a loop. The demon bestiary hadn't described anything like what I had seen. Maybe it was just a white demon screwing with me. Lei was too lazy to prank me. Conall was likely still injured, or the Grith would've been attacked first. The Devil was pretty much entirely white. Swallowing, I raced across the street. Two yeth prowled around the corner, but I kept my eyes on the door.

Though no demons followed me inside, I only stopped when the wards glowed white around me, and the door locked behind me. Tommy's muffled snoring and droning buzz of the fridge echoed in the otherwise noiseless apartment. My headache didn't return. Guilt, however, sauntered in. Pulling a sticky note from Tyson's colorful collection, I wrote a quick apology and stuck it to the back of his laptop. It wasn't particularly well thought out. Just a simple Sorry I acted like a douche. Sliding my bag onto the floor beside my desk, I collapsed into bed.

Chapter Six

"Jon?"

A hand gently shook my shoulder. The darkness swirling behind my eyelids shifted. Calling my name, the voice reverberated, but it fractured too like light trying to pass through a thick fog. Pain radiated from my right leg up and across my chest. My left shoulder ached, yet for all the pain should have grounded me, I floated in uncertainty. Rain's drumming further disguised the murmuring. In the scant gaps of almost light, cold crept.

"Jon?" the voice called again. Blinking, I extracted myself from sleep. A fog remained around my head. Solomon leaned over me. Pressing his lips into a line, he sighed. "Perhaps it would be best if you waited upstairs. The couch unfolds into a bed."

"I'm fine," I assured him, but he set down a cup of tea like it was the answer to all life's questions. "I'm good, really."

"Black tea – well sugared. Drink it," the alchemist commanded.

If nothing else, the warmth from the mug leaked into the already disappearing aches. I wasn't injured. Nothing was wrong with my shoulder. No tweaking or anything. Yet as I rolled my head and cracked my neck, an aftershock of dull pain rippled down my spine.

Outside, rain fell. It had started a week ago in the warehouse. On and off throughout the subsequent days, rain or hail fell. Not the best way to enter into November. Joel hadn't stopped complaining about a Friday night Halloween being ruined by it. A flash of sunlight in front of the store announced Jordan's warp.

"I hate New York," he grumbled although his magic kept him dry.

I grinned. "We could spend the day somewhere else. I've got my passport. Jamaica here we come?"

"Not happening." And so my dreams of a weekend vacation to warmer climes was crushed. Cruelty, thy name was Jordan. "Good news first or bad?"

"You're not taking me to Jamaica, so keep the bad news coming I guess."

Sitting down across from me, Jordan said, "Lei had some trouble finding your connection to Hell, but he finally managed. He's now completely out of commission, and my apartment stinks like a fast food bathroom."

He paused as if waiting for pity. Glancing at Solomon, I took a gulp of tea before saying, "That sounds bad for you, but I sense the bad for me is still coming?"

"George – unsurprisingly – was right. Someone, likely Conall, has formed a link with your connection to Hell." Like a well-choreographed song and dance, Jordan immediately continued, "Good news: it seems to just be on the feed, which means some basic meditation should be able to keep him out of your head."

"But that means he's a prophet."

89

"Inherited prophet abilities, yes."

Solomon hummed. "The Daughters won't be able to ignore that he's a threat."

"They're ignoring it just fine," Jordan said.

"Guess your Lilith theory didn't work," I grumbled and slammed the mug down on the table. Liquid slipped over the sides, but the hot tea slid right off my shield and back up into the cup without much thought. "George said empath prophetic abilities, so he's able to form connections then why is his supposedly divine ability working only on the Hell end of me. Or do we have no way of knowing if he's already done an upstairs connection?"

Jordan pointed at my hand. "You've been practicing."

"Yeah, you told me to."

"Lei suggested that Conall wasn't leeching magic off you. At least, not right now. He seems to be feeding your pipeline," he directed at me. "Maybe, it's because he's out of commission and can't use it himself."

The dots connected in my head. "Or he thinks my lack of training will make the extra juice blow up in my face."

"Probably that," Jordan agreed.

With a sigh, I glared out at the rain. "Are we hunting in that?"

"Nah, I'm taking you up to Toronto. If it makes you feel better, it's not raining there," Jordan promised, and for the lake between them, there was always a chance of sun even if Toronto would likely be just as cold. Quick goodbyes had us league walking, the long way around thankfully, to the Grith. As the world flashed by, Jordan hummed. "How are your classes going?"

"They're fine."

"Wonderful – then you'll be helping Ros grade papers while I reinforce the wards," Jordan said.

I groaned. Keeping pace, I begged, "How about she trains me for the day? Like an impromptu introduction to weapons or something."

"Ros doesn't have time for that. If anyone would teach that, it'd be Kasimira, and I still don't trust her alone with you and sharp objects," the Source retorted with a smirk.

The thick, low-hanging clouds spread over Toronto, so my hopes for sun were dashed. Despite the dark, no rain fell. Looming against the dark sky, the Grith glimmered. Wards shimmered across the sky, and though mortals wouldn't be able to see the glow unless they knew to look for it, the overt shining revealed how weak they were. A swarm of baoht dive-bombed the warding. They snapped and evaporated upon contact.

"I know they're stupid, but that's just suicidal," I said.

Running a hand through his bleached locks, Jordan frowned. "The Wild Hunt might be redirecting demons to weaken the shield."

As the last of the baoht sizzled, I bit back a laugh. "Not much of an effort."

"Not yet," Jordan retorted.

We passed through the walls, and when we reached the other side, a shimmer of multicolored light rippled along the inner warding. Every hair on the back of my neck rose. The yard stood empty. All the windows had their shutters sealed. They treated changing the wards like a bomb drill. Rather than individuals on the corner walls, pairs guarded the innermost wall in military gear. An additional pair watched our entry from either side of the gateway. One of them, Abeni, pressed a hand against the shield as soon as we were through. Her soul lit. When she reinforced the wards, a domino effect unfolded. From each pair, one placed a hand and ignited their souls.

"If the wards are that weak, is once a week enough?" I asked.

Shrugging, Jordan jogged up the stairs, leaving me through the halls. They had locked every door, so I didn't see anyone on the way from the front hall to Monday's office. Kasimira and Ros waited for us there. Both sisters stared at a single monitor. Wolfram paced the few steps back and forth in his cell. Rectangular and maybe only a foot bigger than Wolfram was tall along its longer wall, the cell had no furnishings. It barely had walls. They displayed him like a piece in a museum than a prisoner. A transparent box covered in runes.

Biting the cuticle of her thumb, Kasimira shifted from what foot to the other. Her red hair rested in a high knot. Wispy curls fanned about her face. Though as fierce as ever, her nerves appeared frayed. Sitting on Monday's desk, Ros combed her long blond hair with her fingers.

"Ros, Kasimira," Jordan greeted.

Kasimira hummed. "Monday's outside."

"We found a demon digging at the far back wall this morning," Ros explained. "Between them and the yeth pack around Lake Ontario, Malcolm's concerned Conall's recovered enough to prepare an assault against the warding.

"Which is why you have three layers of wards," Jordan noted.

Nodding, Kasimira glanced at Jordan. "You and Monday will drop the outer warding, reinforce then move inward. Even if something manages to get between layers, you're burned as you go."

"I know how to reinforce haven warding." Despite his words, Jordan maintained a respectful tone.

Ros stepped back, pulling her eyes from the monitor. "Theda's on Wolfram. Jon can stay with me here." She gestured at a pile of papers stacked to the right-hand side of Monday's desk. Handing me a paper, she smiled, but tension twitched in her jaw and cheeks. "Here's the grading key. It should be straightforward. I appreciate your help."

She planned to stay with me. That didn't sit right. Picking apart the situation like a scab, my brain spat questions. Beyond the three layers of warding, the Grith had runes on the dungeon and Wolfram's cell. Two of those kept Wolfram in place, and he seemed aware of what was happening. Otherwise, he wouldn't be pacing or tracing the wards on each pass. Even with the baoht, the greatest chance of mistake laid in shifting those inner wards. Once out, Wolfram could league it out of the wards, leaving nothing but disaster and murder in his wake. While I had never tried to jump warding, every bone in my body suggested it was a bad idea if not outright impossible to do without weakening the wards. Not that Wolfram would care.

All of this, yet the most powerful of the Jaeger sisters wanted to stick with me. My eyes narrowed. Jordan blamed Ros's influence in the children's education, but he built rouses from less convincing fallacies before. Ruthlessness and sheer force of will powered Kasimira. Honestly, Theda would've been the better bet.

"No problem," I murmured. "But maybe I should stick by Jordan or reinforce the front gate with Abeni."

"We don't need you there," Kasimira snapped.

Resting a hand on her sister's shoulder, Ros sent a small smile my way. "Thank you, but Abeni and Meinhard have it handled."

Jordan shoved me into the chair nearest to the pile of papers. "Be helpful. Do what Ros asks of you?"

"Yes, sir," I drawled.

Jordan pressed his lips together. "Not every job is exciting."

Pulling the papers to me, I summoned a red pen to fly through the air into my hand. "Already knew that, Miyagi."

"Then you know better than to use your magic in here," he remind me. WIth a shake of his head, he left before I could respond.

Ros slipped from the desk into the seat across from me. Forcing a smile, she clenched her teeth. Her red pen dug into the page. If she pressed any harder, she would mark the desk. All the while, Kasimira glared at the monitor. On the screen, Wolfram pressed his hands against the walls of his cell. Sparks crackled along his fingers, but he ground his teeth and kept pushing. A vehement line of curses flew from the red-haired psychic, and Ros immediately swiveled to face. Kasimira's hand dropped to her side, and blood gathered along the bed of her nail.

"How does he know?" Kasimira grumbled.

Standing, Ros sighed. "He's been practically comatose the last three days. Maybe he's bored finally?"

"Or he's been told we're changing the wards. This is why I suggested not telling anyone until the day of!" When her elder sister handed her a tissue, Kasimira huffed but pressed it against her nail. "He knows. Look at him! He knows."

Wolfram's brows furrowed. Bearing his teeth, he clawed against the walls, but anger didn't color his gaze. Sparks danced in his nearly black eyes. With only the wards lighting the cell, the screen flashed like lightning. His sharp features stood in stark relief. They matched his demonic aspirations.

"He's got no contact outside of us. No magic, no way of communicating. We have him under watch every second of every day," Ros assured her sister.

The mage's hands dropped from the walls. His eyes darted to the camera. Rearing one hand back, he slammed his fist against the wall, but he'd need a diamond if he wanted to break out the mortal way.

"Is he trying to kill himself?" Kasimira snapped.

Crossing her arms, Ros sat on the edge of Monday's desk. "If he knows, it's on his own. None of the children got in – nobody could sneak past everything we have in place."

"How? We've staggered his meals and the lights are off at random intervals of eight, ten, and twelve hours. His internal clock never seemed that good when it came to anything before," the red-haired sister said. Shaking her head, she left, grumbling, "I knew we were being too easy on him."

This whole affair screamed trap. Jordan and Monday might've thought they could reinforce the wards without incident, but the more Wolfram pushed, the more likely they were to break down. His magic wanted in, and he wanted out. Even without the Wild Hunt, the pressure risked overloading the whole mess. One good flood of minor demons and the whole house of cards would fall apart. Struggling not to fidget, I glanced to the door, but Ros faced me before I could make an escape.

"It's best if you stay here," she reminded me. "If Conall and you have a connection, it's a safe bet there's one between Wolfram and him too."

"And what? I'm gonna get roped into murdering Wolfram because Conall wants it? The link is in Hell. My shield is strong, and I'm flaring my soul daily," I retorted.

If I flashed my soul every few hours, she didn't need to know. Exhaustion was my problem, not hers, and I was fine.

"Exactly," she agreed. "Warding can't touch Hell, but you're not warded to block off the connection completely, or your magic wouldn't work either." Collecting her hair to one side, she braided and unbraided the strands. Her eyes darted from me to the screen, but Ros never looked away long. "Conall could cause a surge."

"I'm not a bomb."

"No…you aren't." Ros tied her braid off, and walking over to the door, she closed it. Sitting beside me, she leaned forward as if to appear smaller and less intimidating, but I had seen her fight. She couldn't fool me. "I'm sure Jordan's explained warding."

"I've read a lot about it."

Nodding, she said, "Then you understand how it's a delicate balance between magic and soul. We don't want to be defenseless."

"And our magic wants to break down the wards," I acknowledged.

97

"While the Grith has extensive warding - reinforced daily by myself and Monday, it can be exhausting to uphold warding over this size of a territory while you also teach dozens of students about their magic," Ros explained, and the light bulb went off in my head as the last piece in the circuit connected.

I slouched back in my chair. "If he surges my magic, it'll be the camel's back - straw thing, right?"

"Right."

"But I'm here. Isn't that a problem even if I'm nowhere near Wolfram?" I asked.

Her brows knotted, curving further up at the inner ends, affirming without her having to say a word. Glaring at the floor, I nearly jumped when her hand rested on my shoulder. "You wouldn't be here if we thought you didn't have control."

"Still, this is a test, isn't?"

She nodded. Of course it was. Sitting in an office, locked away from the rest of the Grith with the most powerful of the triad, they wanted to know if I was going to blow. Nothing I said could assuage their concern. They had every right to treat me like the fuse on the end of Conall's dynamite. Lit or not - I was a dangerous to everyone in the blast radius, and they couldn't know what that was until I blew.

"It's more complicated than just if you're a risk. Empathic ability can be difficult to gauge. Can he tell where you are in relation to Wolfram without Wolfram's magic being able to reach him? Even if he can, will he try to use you to reach Wolfram? To kill him?" Ros explained. Her eyes remained on me even as the rogue mage raged within his cage. "It's not just about you, Jon. There's so much we don't know about this kind of connection. Empaths generally don't form connections this permanent on the Hell-end."

"What? Is it impolite?"

"More than a bit." Her hand fell away, and with one last scan of my face, she returned to her watch nearer to the screen.

"There's got to be a way to break the connection," I pleaded.

Ros chewed her bottom lip; the gears grinding in her head almost audible. "Unfortunately, the only one we know is the same reason the Daughters won't warp Wolfram."

Hope swelled in my chest like an overfilled balloon. Jumping from my seat, I exclaimed, "Jordan just needs to take a trip under and pull a shining star act? He still warped around. We could get rid of -." The guilty weird concerned look returned. "But he can't. Because warping is all cloak and dagger, and if he shines his soul, everybody south side comes running."

Of course, Jordan didn't go down there showboating. He hid, and his deal with the Devil helped keep the more intelligent demons away, but attacking demons on their own turf - even just to undo the binding - would bring too much attention.

"Even if he warped directly to the brightest point on Earth, he'd risk waking some of the less active demons, and even the weaker ones would form a rampage. The Wild Hunt is bad enough. A completely unfocused hoard would be catastrophic," Ros intoned.

Which left me trapped. As long as Conall lived, my magic and his would be connected, and he had all the power. "What if he starts draining my side?"

"Kasi or Theda would likely be more than willing to teach you hand-to-hand combat, and with Solomon teaching you hunting focused chemistry, you wouldn't have to give up hunting." She meant it as consolation, but Wolfram screamed, voicing my helpless frustration. Ros muted the sound on the security system. "If that's what you want."

"I want my magic."

"And you'll still have it. As long as the bond supplies magic your way, it allows influence to pass your way too. If he reverses it, draining you would mean risking you influencing him," Ros informed me. Tilting her head, she sighed. "Just imagine what Wolfram would be like without Conall's influence."

"Still probably a murderer."

But she had a point. For all of Wolfram's homicidal tendencies, I understood some of the madness. All Conall sent my way was dreamlessness and sleep paralysis, but messing with my recharge schedule had me lashing out in all directions. Before, with the dreams, he had turned me around and round. By the end, I hadn't known up from down. Honestly, it made my mistakes with Wolfram a little easier to swallow. Until Conall tried to do more again, I couldn't be sure how well my defenses were against him. People were games to him. A mentality Lei might have appreciated.

Wolfram roared, tearing at his hair and skin. Slamming against the warded walls, he bloodied his fists. The mage fell to the ground and flailed like a toddler throwing a tantrum. Sweat poured down his face, and as he sprawled, his movements slowed.

"It's like he's going through withdrawal," Ros noted. My brows furrowed, but before I could ask, she added, "The first few days in there, he didn't sleep. He's tough. Used to hiding - comes with the territory of illusionists. The first disguise is always your face, so we almost missed the panic attacks, and he tried to hide them the one time we caught one live. He's vomited a few times, but this is the worst I've seen."

"Withdrawal from what? Magic?"

She didn't respond, but when I realized she pointedly didn't look at me either, it hit me. If she wanted me to say it, I wasn't going to make it easier on her. Biting my tongue, I glared at the monitor. Conall wasn't a drug, and even if he had the same effects, outside of the heavy warding, my connection was, unfortunately, alive and well.

Across the surfaces of my mind, pressure built. Not a pinprick. Like a finger, something brushed against the furthest reaches of my consciousness. Ripples broke across the surface. Outside the window, the warding went dark. A rainbow shimmered as if the shield acted as a prism, and for barely a minute, the same swirling cyclones raged before being incinerated.

101

"They've started," she murmured.

Frowning, Ros kept her eyes on Wolfram. He sat up as straight as a rod. His pupils pulled to pinpricks. Shimmering across the mortal bindings of his prison, the warding shifted. Both Theda and Kasimira watched just outside the camera's view, but Wolfram made no escape attempts. Smiling, the mage stretched out his hands, brushing the tips of his fingers against the narrow length of the room.

Static tingled up my spine. My magic remained tight and contained, but the presence fluttered at the edges of my perception. The sensation faded in and out like a bad radio signal. However, my magic remained under my control. If the copper-haired wizard eyed the Grith, he wasn't watching me.

With tears streaming down his face, Wolfram arched his back, bending backward as he cackled. He flashed his canines, white and sharp, like a threat. One hand fell from the wall, pressing to the side of his head where his nails dug into his scalp. Blood gathered. Small crimson bubbled up around his fingertips, but the knuckles never shifted. When Kasimira stepped into the video frame, he rounded on her, slamming his hands against the shields and thick plastic between them.

His eyes settled on the blood then. One finger at a time, he spelled in slow letters: F-E-N-S-T-E. When he reached the E, frustration bloomed on his face, but before he could tear himself apart for more blood, Kasimira slammed a hand against the runes, lighting a section with her soul. Magic twisted inside, pinning Wolfram to the wall. His body shook, but no matter how hard he tried, he could not bring his hands up to complete whatever he intended to say.

"Fenste...?" Ros whispered. Her brows furrowed. "Window?"

"What does that mean?" I asked.

Runes made of white light shimmered. Monday and Jordan cast them like a net. With a snap of power from their souls, the shielding snapped back into place more securely than before. All strange sensations stopped.

Wolfram collapsed to the ground. His lips kept their upward curl. Sliding one hand through his hair, he lounged, stretching like a cat in a sunbeam.

"It doesn't mean anything," Ros assured me.

Sometimes, I swore magic users forgot about the internet. Speaking in tongues failed to translate written words. With one last glance, I memorized the letters. Jordan would appreciate it anyway. Grabbing a handful of papers, I set myself to grading.

***

By the time Jordan completed rewarding, we had completed the stacks, and Ros brought me into the kitchen. Half a dozen teens rushed around cooking. Ros conducted them, and I awkwardly sat on a useless chunk of counter above Monday's wine fridge.

"Taste this!" Phuong demanded.

She shoved a spoon at me. Some kind of white, steaming mush sat in it. Taking the spoon, I sniffed. Garlic and something lemony suggested edible. I risked poisoning and ate it. Not my favorite but garlic and I got along. Phuong kept stirring, but her wide eyes blinked up at me.

"Good mush?" I offered.

She beamed. "It's parsnip puree!"

"Fancy mush."

Her nose wrinkled, but she just giggled and walked away. As if waiting his turn, Harald jumped up, handing me a teacup of what appeared to be broth.

"A few of the younger kids got a cold," he explained.

Sipping the liquid, I glanced over at Meinhard and Adalheidis. The siblings bowed their heads together. While Meinhard kneaded some dough, Adalheidis poured over her notebook.

"That tastes really good," I told him.

"It's my first time making a bone marrow broth. I've made too much, so I can send some with you," he suggested.

"That'd be great. Thanks!"

Rushing off, he didn't even bother to say anything else before burying himself back into his mass production of broth. For a small time, I was left to twiddle my thumbs, but before I managed to sneak off, Ros walked by and tapped me on the arm, forcing me back into place.

"Jon!" Adalheidis called. She waved me over. "We need you!"

Meinhard rolled his eyes. "We don't need him. You just want to show off."

She smacked her brother's arm, and when I shuffled up beside them, she set her oven mitts on the counter. "Meinhard's making bread, but I'm making pasta for dinner."

"Italian is easy to make in bulk," Meinhard noted.

"But isn't Phuong making parsnip puree?" I asked. Fan of grains or not, parsnip puree and pasta seemed a bit much. "Are you all making different meals?"

"Phuong is making spinach, parsnip puree, and venison for Conrad, Roderich, and a few of the others who have had issues with gluten," Ros explained, stepping up beside us. "We have four still sick. Harald is on that, and these two are doing the grain side of the main meal."

"And you're getting none of them," Jordan joked, sauntering into the kitchen. Adalheidis crossed her arms. "We'll be ready in less than an hour. Can't you stay?"

Jordan shook his head. "Not tonight."

"But the broth isn't packed!" Harald cried from the opposite side of the room.

Holding both hands up, Jordan chuckled. "We'll be up again on Saturday."

Seven days either suggested they wanted to test Wolfram's awareness or the wards were in more danger than Monday had believed originally. My ego preened as the kids groaned, but Jordan herded me out the door. The wards shimmered overhead, and when we made it out of all three walls, not a single demon was in sight. Without a word, he stepped off, and we league walked side by side. A boring magical day prepped to end early with studying. So much for my raging college experience.

Jordan grabbed my arm, and we slammed to a stop on the wrong side of Niagara Falls. Water thundered, and the clouds churned above. In the depths of the water at the base of the falls, havfine curled, slinking through the water, but as my eyes nervously tracked their shifting forms, Jordan shook me, drawing my attention back to him.

"Are we good?"

My brows furrowed, but when I looked away, he shook me again. "Yeah, sure, we're good if you stop shaking me."

His hands dropped to his sides. "Then this isn't about me being your uncle?"

"This what?" When Jordan glared in response, I held up my hands. "Fine. There's a this, but it's got nothing to do with you being my uncle. Is it weird? Yeah. Is the fact that you played dad for a couple years weirder? Definitely. My mom totally liked you. It's some weird Hamlet Shakespearean bull, but you helped her, and it's not like you left because you hated me or anything. Sure, my bio dad's probably a selfish dick, but – apple, tree – blah, blah."

"Glad to hear such a novel perspective."

"We've got a screwed up family. What do you want me to say?" I asked.

Shrugging, Jordan said, "A clue about what's going on with you."

"You are the least of my problems right now, so – enjoy it."

"Then are you pissed about Jokul? About Ezekiel?" he volleyed each question at me; his eyes scanned my face, but when none of them stuck, he just kept sending more. "Is Lei bothering you? The bond with Conall? Wolfram?"

"God! Seriously? I say nothing's wrong, and you keep pushing. Can't you read the room," I cried, gesturing around.

Running a hand through his hair, Jordan sighed. His eyes shifted to the havfine and the falling water. "Wolfram wasn't your fault."

"Yeah, sure."

"No," Jordan pressed. "Wolfram was on me."

I snorted. He had to be kidding. I kept Wolfram from the Daughters. When Jordan wanted to help the Daughters, I betrayed him. I attacked my teacher – my uncle. Again and again, I screwed up, and everyone just kept telling it wasn't my fault. I let them down. Such a freaking joke. They pretended to be blind to reality as if telling me everything was fine would fix the ramifications of the choices I made.

"You know, Jordan, you're just not that important," I spat. "Not everything is on you."

His eyes flashed bronze. "This one was. You didn't trust the Daughters because of me." With a huff, he leaned back, staring up at the clouds. The heels of his palms pressed against his temples. "I'm not good with this shit, Jon."

"Talking?"

Jordan sighed; his shoulders lowered as he practically deflated. "I'm saying it isn't your fault."

"It's not just that," I murmured.

His eyes jumped to mine. "Then what is it?"

"I want to meet my dad."

All expression drained from his face. Jordan blinked. His lips remained in a flat line as he said, "Oh."

"I've been thinking a lot about it. We're family. You actually might be my only sane relative. We know I'm not meeting Ezekiel any time soon, but I might actually be able to meet my dad at least. Maybe he wants nothing to do with me, but he's my dad, and I want to meet him," I explained, but the longer I spoke, the more I panicked. Jordan's expression transformed from pale to simply blank. "Maybe it's a bad idea."

Everyone had a breaking point, and somehow, this was Jordan's. His eyes flicked back and forth as if he were reading a book. Swallowing, he blinked. All in all, it struck me as rather overdramatic. Whatever had happened between him and my father, they were brothers – twins. Monday suggested my father sacrificed for Jordan, yet Jokul hung like a phantom over Jordan, and there wasn't much that could be said.

He nodded slowly. Stepping back, he murmured, "Okay."

"Okay?"

"We need to be in Rochester."

"Sure, sure." My brain flubbed. "Wait, what?"

Jordan didn't bother responding. He sped off, leaving me to race after him. Scrambling wasn't my favorite. I had enough abandonment issues without dealing with Jordan running off whenever he couldn't deal with what we were doing. Guy had the emotional depth of a knife.

Throwing open the apartment door, he tossed his coat into his room and stormed to the kitchen. One of Lei's eyes slid over to us. A tendril jumped from beneath the couch. Jumping over it, I followed Jordan as the tendril slammed the door behind me.

"Should I be concerned?" he called.

Lei's eyes shifted, keeping one on the screen at all times. Waving at the demon, Jordan scowled. "Put on your headphones. Jokul talk."

"Ugh, I hate twin-me talks." Burying himself into the couch cushions, he placed his wireless headphones over his ears.

Pacing the kitchen, Jordan said, "Seven years before you were born, Jokul and I learned Ezekiel and Solveig were expecting a child."

"Jukka."

"Yes. Him." Jordan glanced at Lei, but the demon watched his screens as he always did. "We were concerned, but when we arrived back in Iceland, Solveig threatened us. She and her sisters had set up a stranglehold on the Iceland estate – our mother's family estate. They ended up running us off. Jokul wanted to leave it. If Solveig's kid ended up consumed, it wasn't our concern."

"That sounds...a bit nihilistic," I said.

"We fought on our own for so long, it wasn't shocking. Most people wanted us dead, and Solveig – she was the person who made it that way. Anyway, we left. Jokul was sure Solveig would send our half-brother to the Grith, but she didn't, so when the Elders called in Solveig's triad for a major hunt in Russia, we headed back. Long story short, Ezekiel had guardianship. I couldn't – I couldn't leave Jukka to him." Jordan rubbed his face, leaning against the counter. "Jokul wasn't on board. He left."

"And then I was conceived, and you left too." Frowning, I drummed my fingers against the table. "Why was he against helping Jukka?"

Lei snickered, rolling right off his couch. Tendrils stretched from his void. It lifted him back onto the cushions. "No one likes being replaced."

A scowl tugged down Jordan's features. Forcing his expression to neutral, he said, "Nobody replaced anybody."

"Everyone gets replaced eventually," Lei noted.

"I thought you hated Jokul talks," Jordan snapped, glaring down at the demon.

Lei shrugged with a yawn. "I like complaining."

Glancing between the two, I murmured, "There's something I'm not getting."

"There's a lot you're not getting," the eashian intoned, smirking over the arm of the couch at me before sinking back down.

"Just ignore him. I'll reach out. If you want to meet your father, I'll find a way to make it work," Jordan promised. Running a hand through his hair, Jordan sighed. "I can't promise this will work. Jokul might never respond."

"I know. I'm glad you're cool with reaching out though," I told him.

And I was, but I also remembered the letters under Jordan's bed. Reaching out hadn't worked before. Jordan wanted to meet up with Jokul, and for whatever reason, my dad didn't want to see him. Something more lurked beneath the surface. Though no one would tell me the full details of their falling out, I doubted it was as simple as Jukka being born or even Jordan wanting to take care of their younger half-brother. When – and I knew I was being pessimistic, but I had been well trained – when Jordan failed, I would find a way to hunt him down regardless of whether he wanted to meet me or not. The more I learned, the less heroic he became, so my guilt was assuaged.

Chapter Seven

Snow came and went throughout the week, but after sunset, thick piles collected on the ground amidst the flurries by Sunday. All the melted slush froze, so I walked a few centimeters off the ground. The temperature dropped, and the streets emptied. Above my head, the street light flickered. Like the idiot in the horror movie, I stopped and looked up at it.

"This is probably a bad sign."

Out went the light. So did all the lights on the street. A swarm of baoht flew up into my face. The small bugs clicked and buzzed around my face, sending me sprawling backward. Though I caught myself midair to float, the molten mouth of an amswae erupted from the baohts' shadows. Each time I took out one demon, another jumped up, and as I fumbled desperate to get the ground beneath my feet, a figure shimmered on the Genesee. My gut screamed havfine. Everything in me demanded I look away, but the white glowing form hovered above the edge.

The churning water stilled and froze. Fluttering in the wind, an off-white sheet covered the strange woman standing on the river's surface. If there had been holes for eyes, the form would have fit a cartoon ghost. Fog rolled across her feet. Ice spread, crawling forward ahead of her steps.

A flick of my lighter sent up around me. Tongues of fire licked up the darkness, growing to form swirling walls which shot up into the sky at my command. Baoht exploded like tiny fireworks. Melting back in on itself, the amswae collapsed. Sliding my left foot back, I raised my fists to shield my face for whatever came my way next, but in the vortex of my fire, the only one big enough to appear through the light was the white phantom.

"Who are you?" I demanded.

A question offered for a question if it required or an opening for an introduction if she wasn't a demon, but the figure paused in the middle of the water. Her ice crept out, and small flakes drifted down through the air around her. All folklore grew from Hell's sinister roots, so the Snow Queen must have too though I hadn't seen any lore on the Snedronningen in the demon bestiary. However, she didn't look like a queen. Neither jewels nor crown marked her as royalty. She more so reminded me of those empty rich people's homes in movies. White cloth draped over, preserving her for someone else's return.

Through the pale curling fog, the hulking shadow forms of yeth prowled. Their black claws clicked against the ice. Shadows and voids melded, spreading out beneath the pack. They flickered, but the light never changed. Any hope of her not being a rogue blew up in my face.

With a howl, the hounds of Hell charged. They leaped through my wall of fire. Their jaws snapped. Snorting once they landed, they left soot in their wake. Street fighting against wolves always would be a terrible idea. If any mixed martial artist faced a group of bears, I had never seen the video, so I was stuck facing teeth and claws with all the finesse of a wanna-be fire bender. Solomon's Tai Chi suggestion no longer seemed a joke. Screw weight lifting with Tyson. There had to be a karate dojo or martial arts club on campus. If my overpowered mentor wouldn't teach me, I was not messing around.

Snapping jaws lunged from all directions. Others reared onto their hind legs, climbing over those closest to me to leap over every move I made. My eyes darted from one opponent to the next, but their shadows shifted with the light, and every time I moved to strike at what I hoped would be their void, I managed only to singe their already ash –covered fur. Teeth sunk into my shield around my forearm. Although the beast's canines failed to puncture my skin, the pressure of the shield translated across my skin as I wrenched my arm back, lifting and throwing the hound off with fire and air. The yeth's claws skittered across the ground. Catching itself like a cat, the hound of Hell raced right back into the fray.

They knocked me down. Beneath me, the ground dropped, and I slammed it down, sending a wave like an earthquake radiating out. Some managed to keep their feet beneath them, but enough fell for me to scramble to my feet. They came at me like a tidal wave, and with every attack, my defenses failed a bit more.

Packs weren't as common as individual hunters in Hell. Even baoht, which flew in swarms, were only out for themselves. Failures at teamwork, demons on a whole could be isolated and dealt with according to their species-specific limitations. That was what made the Wild Hunt horrifying. Multiple types of demons with different weaknesses working in tandem offered a rather impossible advisory, and yeth were their natural born counter. They worked like wolves in a pack, and the larger the pack, the more powerful the group became. As long as one yeth stood back, the rest could shift their wards beneath the other, making them practically immortal. Of course, if that yeth was as self-serving as the rest of Hell's denizens, it could just run off with the void, giving just enough back to separate the voids completely from the rest of the group.

I launched like a rocket into the air. Right beside the shrouded figure, three yeth remained. A large void loomed beneath them, but to strike it, I would have to directly attack the rogue, and technically, I had no proof that she controlled the yeth. If she had indebted the pack, she had to be a wizard. Warlock versus wizard – pretty clear winner. Not like I could sneak up on her. I had no choice. I had to retreat.

Soaring higher into the air, I half-ran half-levitated, hoping the yeth and the rogue weren't on my tail. Fear kept me from checking. By the time I landed outside my apartment, there were no yeth insight; however, snow had begun to gather on the ground. Grass still poked out through the growing white. As my feet touch the ground, I skidded to a stop, but the snow wasn't alone. Black ice covered the roads and sidewalk. Only a quick spell kept me falling on my backside.

"Stupid, shitty day," I growled. Tugging my jacket around me, I stormed inside, racing up the stairs.

A few people moseyed around the lobby, but they didn't spare a glance at me. A few murmured about the snow in hopes of a day off, but the University of Rochester hardly ever took snow days. The city knew how to handle snow and ice. Lake Ontario gave the region enough snow yearly for the locals to know when to send out the salt and plows. My whole body ached. Rolling up my sleeves as I climbed the stairs, I double-checked for punctures, but the yeth managed to only mottle my arms with bruises. Their teeth overlapped, and the pressure of my shield spread the force enough to mostly disguise the cause of the marks, but there was a clear bite mark on my left forearm near the elbow. Long sleeves were the order of the next few weeks. Luckily, winter had come to Rochester, so it wouldn't be hard.

Unlocking the apartment door, I paused, praying to the universe that everyone would be asleep. The door swung open, and only darkness greeted me. Relief washed through me, and when I shut the door, a weight fell off me fast enough to make me dizzy. Bruised – in body and ego, I leaned against the door. I slid down with a groan. Body bruised. Ego smashed. A strategic retreat sounded great. It sounded like something a military mastermind would do, but the reality remained; I had run away. One or two yeth weren't a problem, but a pack of them and a rogue outmatched me without a doubt.

Pulling out my phone, I rang Jordan. Like a jerk, he let me go to voicemail. "Hey, it's Jon. We've got a slight problem. There's a rogue in town with a pack of yeth. I think she's using the Lady in White legend. If you could call me back, that'd be great." Hanging up, I dropped it beside me, resting my head in my hands.

A To-Do List flittered through my mind. First, I had to learn some type of martial art. Obviously, we had a yeth problem, so research came in at second place. Finally, my aim sucked in a pinch. I couldn't guide every spell to the target. I need to find a way to do better. Seventeen years without a teacher. I was so far behind. No matter how many books I read, there was no way I could catch up. Magic moved with me. Years mimicking every superhero movie and fantasy book didn't prepare me when my magic couldn't actually directly harm my enemy. I needed mortal fire to destroy demons. I had to have light-up toys or some other stupid secondary force. Knocking down bottles with finger guns and telekinesis didn't help with hellhounds.

Grinding my teeth, I picked up my phone and texted Solomon: *Can you teach me alchemy?*

If Solomon Morgan could take on demons with chemistry and engineering, I could learn too. I had to learn, so if I didn't want a mortal life, I couldn't waste my time chasing subjects I would never actually use. Sure, George had his business, but he was a psychic. Running a business wouldn't work for me. Accounting wasn't my future. Physics and French still made sense, but the sciences offered more help. Chemistry could teach me how to use the elements around me. Anatomy, especially first aid, meant I could fix myself. I could do math. Math made sense to me, and science was math with physical fact.

Chapter Eight

A blinding glimmer sparkled through the blinds. Snow blanketed everything. Overnight, the temperature nosedived into the single digits, and the sky decided to suffocate us. All the mostly bare trees hung stiff with ice. Their lowest branches connected to the ground, forming strange semi-translucent pillars. All in all, a horrible day for drivers, but a wonderful day for university students who rolled over in bed just to find the storm resulted in canceled classes.

Tyson, the jerk, pulled the blinds up, sending light flooding through the room. Bouncing on the bed, he threw his pillow at me. "Snow day!"

"Then let me sleep," I grumbled.

"No can do, Jonny boy! Today is your lucky day," Tyson jumped from his bed onto mine. "You've got two papers that this storm is giving you the time to write, so up and at 'em!"

"Sheesh, I did my midterms."

Pushing me toward the edge of the bed with his foot, Tyson asked, "And you submitted them? I thought you said they were shit?"

"I get a tutor one time," I groaned.

Across the hall, a thud sounded. Tyson and I both sat up in time to see Joel's door swing open, and the quarterback stumbled forward to lean against our door frame. Wrapped in his blankets like a toga, he slid down the wall. Drool crusted on the corner of his mouth, and as he sunk toward the floor, he curled further into his blankets.

"We who are stuck here with you idiots demand pancakes," Joel said.

A sharp shove sent me out of bed. Smacking Tyson, I glared. "I hate you both."

"Pancakes!" Tyson cheered.

Kicking Joel on my way by, I pulled up my sweater's hood. My bed had been cozy. The blankets warmed through the night, and the further I went into the common space, the colder the air became. Basics physics. Stupid thermodynamics. Glowering over my shoulder, I shuffled into the kitchen. As long as Joel remained in the hall, I couldn't just set my magic to the task. Pancakes – golden and delicious – but annoying to make. While I grabbed the ingredients, Tyson bounded into the shower. Everybody was up but Tommy, so I had the lovely gift of Joel worming his way into the living room.

Rolled into the tight cocoon of his blankets, he glared up at the couch. "We should invest in a shorter couch."

"Or you could stand up and use the one we actually have," I retorted.

Joel groaned. "Shut up." I did, and he remained on the floor.

Snow had a way of dulling sound. When I closed my eyes, I didn't see black. A long dirt road and snow stretched before my eyes. Sliding and thuds of hobbled footsteps vibrated up my legs, but they didn't echo. In a trance, I stirred the batter, poured and flipped the cakes. Loneliness scratched at my head. They weren't my memories. Thin and shimmering like dew caught on a spider's web, the edges between me and the strange visions shifted in and out of view.

Rubbing my eyes, I rocked back on my feet. Pain shifted up the base of my skull. Soft shushing followed. A cold finger pressed into the other's forehead, and the darkness returned. Wherever the Erlkonig hid Conall, the wizard was waking up. His wounds weren't healed. Lei, a far less powerful demon, completely voided injury from Wolfram's arm, but the Erlkonig, who obviously cared about Conall, hadn't. Perhaps pain was a lesson. More likely, it served as punishment.

Tyson popped up next to me, and grinning when I jumped, he grabbed three plates. "Coursework till noon then one-on-one video game tournament?"

"Sure."

"No," Joel protested with a groan.

"Are you protesting the coursework? Or gaming?" Tyson asked.

"Both," Joel groaned. "Bacon and sleep."

Setting the pancakes and bacon on the table, I slouched down into a chair. "Who even got the bacon? It's the fancy stuff."

"Pretty sure Tommy did, so we probably should save some," Tyson said.

"I'll grab a container." Leaning back in my chair, I stretched, and my sleeves rode up, revealing bruises all up my arms. Those had definitely not been there last night. My pulse ticked up, and I tried to play it cool. I managed to get the stripes set aside before they were noticed.

Tyson grabbed my arm. "Man, what the heck happened to you?"

Pulling down my sleeves, I slathered my pancakes in syrup. "It's icy out. I fell on the way back last night."

"Bull," Joel called from the floor. "Give me bacon!"

"If you want food, come over to the table," Tyson retorted. "And those aren't falling bruises."

"Are you planning to be a doctor now?" Joel grumbled as he stumbled over to sit down next to me and across from Tyson. "I hate you all. Give me the bacon."

Pulling the plate toward him, he treated it like her personal plate. He formed layers of stripes between pancakes. While Joel's stomach guided him, Tyson refocused on me. "What happened?"

"Fine. I'm trying to get in shape, okay? It's a little embarrassing how shit I am in a gym. Just ask Tommy when he gets back," I lied, and Joel snorted, snickering, but Tyson seemed to believe it and quickly moved on to other topics. It wasn't until he'd gone off to get a head start on an essay that Joel turned to face me.

He clapped me on the back and said, "You're getting better at lying."

I sputtered, and off he went, leaving his plate in the sink, as he retreated back into his room. He had already shut the door by the time I managed to yell, "I cooked! I'm not cleaning this mess!" None of them responded. "Jerks."

On the plus, being left alone, I pulled out my phone, leaning against the counter as my magic went through the process of scrubbing everything and putting it away. A few air triggers on the doors kept me aware even as I dove into the biology and chemistry departments' faculty. I hadn't taken a lot of science classes, but my physics professor, McClellan, had mentioned Dr. Charles Voigt. The two worked on several side projects together. Dr. Voigt's papers self-confessed love of superheroes and theoretical anatomy won me over rather quickly.

The lock of the front door clicked, and I abandoned my computer, sliding across the floor to catch the pan and sponge before Tommy strode into the apartment. Snow caked him from boots to hat. Like a living snowman, he shuffled around. Wet slush built up as he tugged off bit by bit. His dark darted up at me.

"Help?" he murmured.

I raised a brow, smirking. "You sure?"

"I'm making a mess. Please?"

Ditching the pans, I dried off my hands and slid to the side. Water jumped into the air. Hot air spun around him, and as the snow melted, the water gathered into a river, gliding through the air to drain into the sink as the pans bounced over to the towels to dry off. By the time Tom removed all his gear, there wasn't a spot of snow anywhere, and I dropped the lines keeping track of Tyson and Joel.

"Thanks." Tommy sauntered over, grabbing a plate and the remainders of the pancakes. "What're you doing?"

"I'm switching majors. Have you ever had a class with Dr. Voigt?"

Glancing around to the picture, Tommy shook his head. "Looks young."

"He's got two doctorates, and he wrote three papers on comic book characters and their theoretical biology," I said, rotating my laptop, so he could get a better view. "I think I want to be him when I grow up."

Tommy pulled out his phone to text him. "I think Demetrius has him for an advisor. He teaches some required pre-med, right?"

"Looks like it."

Major requirements weren't too bad. My electives transferred, but my college career would be extended at least one semester. Considering Jordan shelled out for my scholarship, he could pay if anything went wrong. That was what uncles were for, right? Weird, estranged, guilty for all the wrong reason uncles at least, so money wasn't a problem. Biology opened a number of new career options, and even if Jordan took my magic, I could be an alchemist like Solomon Morgan.

This just left one problem.

"I helped with the snow, so you owe me," I told him, but for all his niceness, Tommy recognized a leading statement.

"I'm not helping you tell Tyson."

With a huff, I scratched the back of my neck. "It's not like we're in all the same classes anyways. Plus, he's gotten a lot less mother hen-ish."

"You know I can hear you, right?" Tyson called.

I glanced at Tommy, but he offered me nothing than a shrug as he hunted for the remains of the bacon. Swaggering, my roommate joined us. He leaned against the back of the chair across from me with a smarmy smile.

"My ears are burning, so let's get this over with," he prompted.

Fingers drumming, I sucked it up and got on with it. "I'm switching majors."

"What? No more Dynamic Duo?" Tyson asked. His shoulders slumped. "Why?"

"I've been struggling recently, and after thinking it over, I just don't like studying business. I like the math, but..." I struggled to find the words. This whole line of questioning at thrown me. For all my flakiness, I wasn't such a shit friend that I would completely disappear on him if I changed majors. We shared an apartment. His family adopted me on holidays when I couldn't get back to Boston, so he couldn't care about that. Being the eldest, he probably thought I was changing on a whim, and I couldn't explain why that wasn't the case without outing myself. "I think chemistry is going to be a better fit."

"The Business Bros are dead," he lamented.

"It's not like we won't still be living together," I replied, and he shrugged. "Come on, Tyson. It's not that big of a deal."

"I know. It's just a bit sad. End of an era," Tyson said with a small sigh.

For a beat, guilt swelled up within me. Though I had no intention of changing my mind, Tommy sat, eating pancakes like a personification of my conscience warning me to consider my friend's feelings. Tyson supported me. The least I could do was offer an olive branch.

All those thoughts resulted in me saying, "I'm not going anywhere. You wanted to work out together, right? We can train or do something." Vague phrases like that seemed like an out at the time. Little did I realize Tyson saw it as an opportunity too.

Tilting his chin up, he beamed. Tyson pushed a pamphlet across the table. "Great! You can take the E.M.T. training course with me."

"You dick," I gasped. "You two planned this!"

"Not me," Tommy exclaimed, holding up his hands before ducking away with his plates to the sink.

Tyson kept beaming. "I told you I could hear you guys."

"Yeah, but you planned this in – what? – two minutes?" I took the pamphlet. Flipping through it, I had to admit it fit perfectly with my goals, but giving Tyson an inch risked a mile, and I wasn't that enthusiastic. "Sure. I'm in. Us two idiots saving other idiots."

"And the occasional nice old lady and panicked parent," Tyson added.

Magic couldn't heal, but I could beat an ambulance across town any day, so with a nod, I slid the pamphlet back to him. "Sure. What does it cost?"

"There's a group that helps interested students get certified, but there's an application process. Plus, it does mean that we'll be doing some volunteer work for the on-campus medical response team," Tyson warned. There was always a catch. "It's fall only."

"Does that mean I've got several months alone before I'm stuck with you again?" I joked, and Tyson shoved me.

Slinking out of his room, Joel held up his extra controllers. "Cutesy time is over. There's a sale, and I'm destroying you all."

Magical skills had no pay off in video games. Add to that fact that I never had them growing up and my lack of time to practice, and my roommates destroyed me first each round. As the three fought, I gorged on pizza bagels and chips.

"Stop fooling around and kill each other already," I said, kicking my feet over the back of the couch.

"Ever occur it's an actual competition between us?" Joel asked.

I snorted. "Tommy could kick your butts. He's just playing nice."

"Bull," Tyson scoffed.

Joel chuckled, elbowing Tyson. "Divorced kid with all the game systems and an overly competitive extrovert beat by the mama's boy eldest son? Yeah, right." Glancing over at Tommy, I smirked even as his calm expression never faltered. His thumbs flew. Joel got knocked out first. Jaw dropping, he gaped at the screen. "You..."

"Crap-crap-crap," Tyson cursed.

He leaned forward, but no matter how much effort he put into running away, Tommy popped up at every turn. Bright colors flared across the screen, announcing the winner, and Tyson groaned. Falling back against the couch, he tossed his controller uselessly at his side, glaring at me then Tommy as if uncertain who to blame for his defeat.

"Lucky shot," Tommy said, shrugging as if he could just brush off his skill.

Shaking his head, my roommate grabbed his controller, starting the game over. "We're doing a rematch."

"I'm not overly anything. This is healthy levels of competitiveness," Tyson argued. He went straight after Tommy, but his focus left him open. As I was never one to pass up a golden opportunity, I hit him twice in the back, knocking him out of the game first. "That was a cheap move! We're playing best out of five!"

"Yep. Definitely not overly competitive," Joel drawled.

Outside, the clouds hung low as flurries rushed. They blocked out the dim graying light which pierced the storm, but dark shapes raced within their dull shades. Flurries rushed by the window. Ice gathered on the window pane. At first, the fluttering of her dress and veil blended with the snow. She moved like a twirling phantom. While Saint Nicholas had his fantastical flying reindeer, the shade had a racing pack of hellhounds. Like dogs of the Iditarod, they raced in a wild formation across the skies. Their howling blended with the roaring winds.

A hand smacked my side, and Joel smirked. "Get your head in the game, Blythe."

"I think my ego's taking enough of a thrashing for today," I retorted, setting down the controller. "I'm gonna check on Jordan. Maybe steal some of Lei's snacks."

"Lame," Joel scoffed.

"Want me to come with?" Tommy offered.

Shaking my head, I pulled on my coat. "I'm good. It should be pretty quick."

"I vote not-it when you get stuck somewhere half-frozen," Joel said as he smashed the buttons on the controller in an angry frenzy which would only manage to get him killed faster.

With a quick combo, Tyson put him out of his misery. "Don't you know? Jon's all grown up. No mama henning needed."

"Oh, shut up," I grumbled.

Sliding down into his feet, Joel demanded, "Then bring us burritos, cheese puffs, and those weird wafer things."

"Anything ridiculously fancy and imported," Tyson voted.

"You'll be disappointed," I warned as I tied up my boots. "Lei's got the taste buds of a mutated, anthropomorphic turtle teen."

Joel blinked. His expression fell away, blanking as he stared up at me. "Then...he has pizza?" The three guffawed as I rolled my eyes and headed out the door.

Chapter Nine

Ice entombed every surface. Not a single branch uncovered. Every bone in my body screamed to go back inside, but unknown crept around the shadows of my mind, pushing me forward. Snow drifted down. They spiraled, melting against the edges of my shield, but the longer I kept the head close to me, the more the chill pushed across my fingertips and along my connection to Hell.

When the cold finally broke my warm bubble, a pillar of white stood ahead of me in the field. Dark shadows gathered at its feet. In the blizzard, billowing clouds of freezing vapors shrouded the hounds of Hell. The yeth trotted through the white. Ash and soot marked their passing.

"Hello?" I called.

The woman remained silent. Her hem disappeared below the snow line, but nothing melted, so water didn't travel up the discolored linens of her skirt. Lacy fabric covered her fingers like crystals across a window pane. Over her head, her shroud hid her face. From the side, her sloped brow blended down with the sunken line of her nose. Even the tether about her throat couldn't bind the fabric enough to accentuate the delicate shifts of her features.

Pulling my lighter from my pocket, I balanced my gloved thumb on the trigger. "Hello?" I called again, and the woman tilted her head back.

If she breathed, no heat misted from her breath. I, however, puffed out steam with every breath.

The closest of the yeth sat at her feet. It lifted its head, yawning as if to show off the sharp edges of its fang-filled mouth. Like a shark, lines of pointed teeth lined its mouth, and while they matched wolf canines, the quantity sent my heart racing. Dropping its head, the yeth glanced my way, tilting its head as if asking if I honestly thought getting any closer was a good idea, but whoever this was, she matched Joel's description, and if she used her powers to play a prank on my mortal friend, I had every intention of making her answer me.

"I'm Jon," I offered. "I heard you were around the University of Rochester campus, and I'm pretty sure I'm the only user that goes there, so I thought…" Gesturing back and forth between us, I shrugged. "Were you looking for me?"

Her chin dropped to her chest, and she tilted her head away from me as if leaning in to hear me better. Two more yeth sauntered over to her, but they remained standing; their eyes bore into me. Bad decision. Definitely another Wolfram level bad idea because I was a complete idiot. Smart people didn't go out of their way to seek bizarre strangers who may or may not be demonic, and if they did, they told people. Especially their teacher.

Pulling out my phone, I sent a quick text as I said, "Are you new to the area? I'm originally from Boston, so if you're expecting somebody else, I probably won't be much help, but I could know a few people who could."

"I don't need help."

Her voice was deeper than I had expected. Like wind against an old house, it creaked. When she faced me, her body lifted to float like I was above the snow and ice. She glided across the snow. Her feet skimmed the frost until she stood before me. Up close, her dark skin showed through the thin shroud. Black crept up her fingertips. Rusted red painted of the lace gloves. It gathered along her nail beds.

"Okay but a few mortals saw you," I told her.

Brushing her fingers over the stitched runes which pinned her shroud to her dress. "I apologize if my disorientation was inconvenient. This city is a bit different than I remember."

"When were you last around here?"

The air vibrated, and a warp opened behind her. Raising her hands, she jerked her hands open and forward. Like a sonic boom, the air jolted, sending me up and flying. My back slammed into the hard snow, and the buzz of a warp vibrated across the ice and right up my spine. Beneath me, the frozen water melted. It flooded my jacket and jeans, chilling me through, but I couldn't move. Every bit of me tensed before the warp shut, and feeling snapped back into place.

Slowly, I rose. A hand pressed along the back of my head, but it came away clean. No blood - just water poured down the collar of my coat and shirt. The yeth vanished too. Alone in the middle of nowhere, my stomach sunk, and my phone rang.

"Hello?" I grumbled over the line, standing and brushing snow off of me as I forced my shield back into place.

"Glad to hear you're alive," Jordan drawled.

Pulling the water from my clothes, I dropped it around me, and the liquid immediately froze into a circle of ice.

"If you were worried, you could have warped here and joined me." With a flick of my thumb, I sparked the lighter and wrapped heat around myself before starting the trek toward Jordan's apartment. "Mind if I head over your way?"

"Lei's home. I'm not."

"Great. No lecturing and all the take-out I can think of," I cheered, but my enthusiasm fell short. "Don't think she's a demon. Has some really obvious frostbite, but she didn't seem to notice it."

"Anything else of note?" Jordan asked.

"Runes on the shroud - I can probably draw them up and send them to you. A few yeth skulked about." Sighing, I glanced back, but the field remained empty. "Pretty sure this one's obvious. She's a draugr."

"No illusions? It might be cold, but illusionists could still - "

Interrupting him, I repeated, "She's a draugr. She warped - so definitely a wizard. Signs of injury and decay with a shroud."

"I get that, but we haven't had a wizard die, and draugr or not, I should've felt something."

"Maybe your radar's broken. You didn't feel Conall popping in."

Static popped over the line as Jordan stayed silent just long enough to make me check that the call hadn't dropped.

"The Hamelin kids have skewed my senses. He had to have entered at the same time in a nearby area," Jordan offered, but even he didn't sound convinced. "I need to take the time to recount."

"Count and identify everybody?" We weren't a big community, but there were enough that I couldn't imagine it would be quick. "How long would that take?"

"Longer than I have time for at the moment."

With a snort, I slowed to a mortal walk. "What exactly are you spending all your time on?" Jordan hummed. The phone crackled, and my signal dropped. As the droning tone buzzed into my ear, I paused, glaring down at the screen before clearing the screen. "Keeps up while I league walk – can't handle the Heights."

Dodging between the building and the parking lot, I crossed past the Rochester Museum and Science Center. Lights were on, but nobody was around. The museum had closed a few hours earlier. Snow swirled in spirals down, melting almost as soon as it touched the still not entirely frozen ground. My breath rose in curls of steam, and as I rubbed my hands together, my stomach growled in anticipation of whatever food I could convince Lei to order.

If I had superhuman senses or inherited any of the almost precognitive awareness my father supposedly had, I might have seen her coming. But with the slowly darkening gray clouds and white swirls, her dress and shroud blended nearly perfectly into the gloom. I did, however, see the pack at her heels. Yeth stalked around her. They kept a distance, but there was no doubting they followed her despite some being slightly ahead of her. Ice gathered along the exposed spines of their backs.

Throwing up a shield, I shifted into a defensive stance, but the surprise set me off balance, so when she league-stepped the remaining distance, I wasn't ready. Like a rag doll, she picked me up and tossed me aside. My back slammed into the glass, and it cracked behind me. Sliding down, I fell to my knees, blooding running down my head to drip onto the cement of the sidewalk under my hands. Shards littered with each breath.

None of her hounds looked at me. They trotted along the outside with their heads low to the ground. Without lungs, they snuffled, sending flares of black smoke out with each sniff. The pristine white of the newly fallen snow mottled gray.

My vision narrowed and widened. Spots danced, making my stomach churn, and when the frosty crunch of snow grew louder, I sat back on my heels. Warm liquid ran down the back of my neck. This time, I was pretty sure I wasn't as lucky.

A discolored shroud covered her head, and lace disguised the marbling blues, purples, and blacks of her fingertips. Her near black eyes stared down at me.

"Call for him," she said.

Everything around and behind blurred then sharpened back into focus as her form shifted. Squinting didn't help. Pressing my fingers into the cuts across the back of my head, I groaned as bits of glass shifted.

When I shifted to look over my shoulder, she stepped closer and repeated, "Call for him."

The window wasn't even shattered. Sure, a few bits were missing of the outer layer, but I had curled my back. My head shouldn't have hit. My back should've got the worst, yet besides a growing ache, my jacket shielded me from the glass there.

"You threw me into a window," I grumbled, glaring up at her covered face.

Fluttering in the breeze, the ends of her shroud rose, but stitches through it into her gown kept it from revealing her face. On the underside hem of the sheet, metallic thread stitched rune work into the piece. The pattern wasn't one I knew.

"Call for him," she demanded again.

"Heal me," I retorted.

One of her hounds drew nearer. Getting healed by a yeth wasn't necessarily something I wanted. I had no desire to risk anybody but Lei. Honestly, even after seeing him stitch up Wolfram, I barely trusted him.

Waving a bloody hand at the demonic dog, I sighed. "Who am I supposed to be calling for?"

"Your master."

"Don't have one."

"Do not lie to me, boy." Around us, the wind swirled, forming a vortex of chilling sleet. "Call Jordan Ostairius," she commanded. Her tone lowered like wind rattling through a hollow tree.

My lips curled into a sneer, and though pulses of sound and light interrupted every other thought I had, I managed to spat, "Call him yourself!"

Shaking her head, she walked away, and the yeth drew nearer. They didn't circle like havfine; instead, they prowled straight at me from all sides. Their eyes sparkled, but the light there was only a glint from the snow beneath their feet.

The two red disks on either end of the small garden shook. Vibrations echoed, but all eyes remained on me. Like a giant shovel, the red disk flew from its position, clearing the first line before rounding me and slamming like a giant castanet against its second.

Roaring, I leaped to my feet. Glass shot out. Each grain plucked from my body and around, rushing like a sandstorm toward her. There were many, but the cement dissolved beneath my feet, and behind me, the glass cracked and tore apart without warding to defend it from my magic.

"I'm not just some call button you can punch around until Jordan shows up," I yelled as the sharp shards cut across the swatches of fabric covering her.

Raising a hand, she deflected my attack to the side. "If he took your apprenticeship seriously, he would come." She halved the distance between us. "I have no desire to kill you, boy. You aren't corrupted, and I don't abide by killing innocents."

"Then why are you hunting Jordan? He works with the Daughters."

"Damn the Daughters," she raged, and her dress and shroud fanned out around her. She grew. Towering almost three stories tall, she contorted, her back arching as her heels dug into the frozen earth. "Damn them all to Hell!"

"Well now...that's one way to get my attention." Jordan's voice carried over the wind as he swaggered to stand between the two of us.

She withered, deflating back to human height. "Ostairius."

"You have me there. I don't know your name," he told her, but she didn't reply.

The wolves charged, and hail rained down around us, clinking against the ground in globes the size of marbles. Jordan's soul expanded, a bright shield of golden light which enveloped me, chasing away the cold which had leached the feeling out of my extremities.

His fingers ghosted over my injuries. "You keep forgetting to shield yourself from head to toe."

"I didn't expect to get charged crossing behind the Rochester Museum and Science Center," I grumbled. "I'm right though, right? She's a draugr."

Jordan nodded. "She's a draugr."

Groaning, I resisted the urge to facepalm. My head was enough of a mess without my help. "I got beaten up by a corpse?"

"A wizard's reanimated corpse," he offered as if that made it better. Sweat beaded on his brow, and my stomach lurched.

"Holy shit," I cursed. "She's going to break your shield."

I pointed beyond him to where she had stretched and slammed down against his shield like a giantess. The yeth waited at the edges. Those with ears had them pulled back. The hackles rose, but they didn't approach, waiting for her to beat the shield down instead.

"And you have a concussion, so warping really isn't in the cards," he retorted.

"I can league it away?"

"I'm going to see how tall I can get the shield before it collapses. Go up and out - over them and get to the bookshop." Jordan faced her, squaring off as his hands drummed against his thighs. "First lesson on draugr - fire harms them, but light just makes them angry."

"As long as they have skin, the remaining vestiges of their souls protect them," I paraphrased. "I've read the books."

"Good."

His shield rose around him. Like a golden, shimmering chimney, his shield stretched, and she reared back, the darkness of her eyes glared down, but the rest of her features blended together beneath the fabric.

Shooting in the air like a rocket, I raced out as she slammed her gloved hands on the top, pushing Jordan's shield, and rather than waiting for her to break through after exhausting him, he dropped the protection magic, letting her stumble forward as he flicked his lighter and sent the flames up in a swirling cyclone. I glided through the air, skating upward and out through a swirling wall of vapors, outside of which, the draugr and Jordan's pillar of fire disappeared from view.

Or at least that was the plan. Instead, I made it a block. The yeth surrounded me mid-air, but a wall of fire kept them from getting too close. Their voids melded together. Any time I attacked one, the others lent out their void, or the void bounced to meld with another opposite of where I had aimed my attack.

"You weren't this tough with Giuseppe," I grumbled.

Beneath me, the snow had already melted. Water gathered around my feet, and as the hounds breathed soot, it slipped black as ink around my feet. We faced off like an old western. Shimmering just out of view, Jordan fought, and as much as he might have wanted me to escape, our best chance remained the two of us together.

Raising my arms, I tossed the fire. While the flames spiraled and sent the yeth to scatter their voids, I shot myself into the air. They trailed after me. Each huffing breath and lunge left me racing faster. Sweat beaded on my brow. The droplets nearly froze despite the trail of fire at my feet.

From a nearby lamppost, Jordan drew electricity. Plasma bolts jumped around the pale orb at the top of the metal shaft. The glass cracked. Any minute and the energy would be too great. Shards would fly. Towering over him, the draugr rained down spears of ice, and even as they collapsed to the side underneath the heat of Jordan's still spiraling tower of fire, the ground shook. Pieces of pavement shifted beneath his feet.

Racing around them, relief and guilt wrestled in my chest as the pack broke off to charge Jordan from behind. The lights weren't built to maintain the charge he demanded, but there was something inside the building better suited. Setting my eyes on the top floor, I climbed through the air.

The draugr slammed a hand against the building. As if I were a fly, she swatted my path until Jordan spread the fire across the pavement into a wall which slammed forward, pressing her further back into the small garden where she had originally charged me. They danced back and forth. Jordan swiveled to keep his back facing me.

If I wanted to tap into the circuits, I had to break through the building, and the illegality messed with my mind, but I was out of ideas. Pressing my hands against the smooth stone, I pushed down the panic rising inside me. The wall peeled back. Stones fell to the ground, and drywall crumbled. Wires and pipes came into view, but they weren't what I wanted.

In the darkened room, the two Tesla coils stood on stage. Like sleeping giants, they waited.

Lifting them off the ground, I pulled them to me. Wires shifted and everything upended. Chairs flew. All the bits and pieces of wreckage became projectiles, slamming against the draugr, but even as she shrunk, her strength remained. A bolt of plasma twisted around her fingers before she tore the lamps out of the ground, sending them and the concrete back against Jordan and toward the museum and planetarium.

"Don't kill me," I pleaded, and with a flick of the switch, the coils came to life.

The list of songs jumped onto the computer screen, and whoever had played last had a serious love of science fiction. Bolts of plasma flew through the air, and even as I grabbed the energy to intensify and redirect at the draugr, the tune remained generally clear. Attacking with the Imperial March made my year.

Jordan twisted round. Back to back, we passed the electricity between us. The ice melted beneath us, and as flickering bolts jumped to dance across the water, only a thin shield kept us safe as we worked. We wove a net of plasma. Each lamppost became a stake in the fence, blockading the draugr and her yeth. The hounds growled. Flashing their teeth, they huddled. Beneath their feet, their voids swirled. While they shared their voids, they could only be so far apart, and with sparking electricity between them and freedom, they had to fight or fall back into Hell.

As the song ended, I tightened my grip on the plasma. Bolts danced up my arms. They bounded off us as if we were coils as well, but the stray bolts which slammed beneath the yeth's feet kept the pack at a distance. Heat built inward from the crackling electric net.

"I will be a Jedi like my father before me," I joked.

Scoffing, Jordan elbowed me. "He's not nearly as bad as Vader."

"Sure thing, Obi-Wan."

"Imagine me smacking the back of your head because that's what's happening the second we're no longer fighting for our lives," Jordan told me.

"But I have a concussion."

The draugr shifted. Her shroud billowed as she glided toward the barrier. Dim light swirled around her, crackling before fading out in snaps and fits of light. Dead and with a severely darkened soul, she could not sustain a shield, and when her fingers neared the webbing of electricity, a snap of light jumped, and the lace burned. Her fingertip blackened. Rubbing her fingers, she shifted her weight, but with each movement, she stumbled and the light of an almost shield flared and broke around her.

Pulse thundering in my chest, I bit the inside of my cheek. Jordan twisted plasma. His shield shimmered as if to emphasize the difference between us and her – between the living and the dead. A chance remained she didn't know. With each flare, hope fluttered in my chest. It could be simple. Maybe with this enemy, we could reason.

147

Mammon's summoning darkened the whole of the city. Even with Jordan's deal, damnation festered like a beacon beneath the thin veneer of normalcy, but after Shiloh, the havfine and the Wild Hunt, maybe we had time. Time for me to get my life together.

The draugr curled the burnt ends of her fingers into fists. Snow and ice melted to slush at the edges of the fence, but as she staggered toward the yeth, ice rolled in spikes and spires from beneath the rustling of her discolored hem. Wind swirled up around her. Cold slammed in cyclones against our attack, sending shards of frozen water into the air. Flakes rushed in swirls. It was like being trapped in a roughly shaken snow globe. However, Jordan and I held firm. Together, our magic buckled but did not break.

"Does she realize she's dead now?" I called over the tempest.

Jordan shimmered in and out of sight behind the raging white. "It doesn't matter," he shouted back, and the winds wailed. A sharp roar joining them before the yeth's howled. "Keep your shield up," he commanded, pulling me close so we stood with our backs almost pressed against the sizzling heat of the plasma barrier. "We need to flare like I did with Shiloh. You need to hold the barrier."

Reinforcing my shield, I manipulated the air around my words. The sound waves shifted, contained as I sent it to him in hopes she wouldn't hear. "That wiped you out. Are you sure that's a good idea with the yeth?"

Jordan never had a chance to reply. The yeth charged. Electricity buzzed across me, and I held firm as Jordan exploded into a swirling mass of fire. Tongues of flame fanned against my shield. A fine layering of magic kept some distance, but even the gaps of cold air failed to assuage the building heat. Sweat beaded on my brows, but the draugr's ice refroze with each melting. One half of me edged toward freezing while the other nearly burned, and I couldn't risk turning to shift between the two.

In the blurred white of the storm, she flashed into being like a poltergeist. One moment, nothing except ash, snow, and ice flashed before my view. In the next, her shrouded form towered over me with her heeled boats floating off the ground. Buzzing in my ears, a voice whispered, "Now." A bolt flew through the air, slamming directly into hers. She flew back. Her body collided with the netting where she sizzled, but her shroud didn't char like the lace of her gloves or her fingers. All along her hem, the runes activated. They flared a bright red, and as they flashed, she shifted back and forth between two faces: an emaciated corpse and a dark-skinned woman. Threads split. Her shroud lifted in the wind as she fell to the ground. Ice swelled up around her.

All around her, the yeth gathered. Steam rose in rolling plumes off her back. The binding holding the shroud around her neck broke, and while the majority remained whole, cuts formed gaps in the fabric. One bloody eye glared up at us. The skin of her cheek pressed in on itself. Blue and

149

purple painted her lips, but it wasn't lipstick. Sunken and shriveled, she was a mummy frozen and enraged, but as her magic pulsed, her face shifted back and forth between the corpse she was and the woman she had once been. Black wisps of hair, kinky and fine, framed her face. Her blood eyes turned dark brown, but the proud line on her jaw stayed the same.

"Ostairius," she growled as if his name were a curse.

Her fingers clawed into the muddy ground, and though ice spread around her and the yeth at her side, the heat in her eyes threatened to burn Jordan alive. I wasn't even on her periphery. The air shifted as she stood. A haunting figure in white contrasted versus the pitch black of the hellhounds' voids. Like a curtain falling over her, a warp rippled. Smoother and easier than any of Jordan's frankly.

One second, she was there. The next, the draugr vanished, and the pack of yeth ducked through voids, returning to Hell. Smoldering in the runes of their room, the Tesla coils stood tall and relatively unscathed. However, the hole remained. Along with the wreckage on the lawn and in the parking lot, the destruction opened up a number of questions I wasn't sure the Daughter's Elders would appreciate.

"I broke a museum," I whispered, grabbing hold of Jordan's shoulders. "My mom is going to kill me."

"Jon, just shut up," Jordan commanded.

I, however, couldn't keep my mouth shut. "There's a huge hole in the wall. Illusions or not – that's dangerous. What if a kid falls out of the hole, thinking they're leaning on a wall?"

"You have a concussion. I'm taking you to Lei."

"But I broke a museum. Am I going to go to jail? How would I explain this? Are we going to say it was a gas leak?" My brows furrowed, and I frowned. "I don't think anybody would believe that."

Pulling me to lean against him, Jordan pulled out his phone. "I'll handle it."

Whatever calm handling Jordan planned, a howl caused him to stiffen. He hung up, and before I could comment on the hole in the museum again, static shifted the world. Gravity twisted as Jordan opened a warp beneath our feet. Falling through the ground and then sideways onto the street, I stumbled into a failed attempt to run and end up on my face.

"Get up," Jordan demanded, grabbing my arm.

"Or I could just die here. That sounds good," I grumbled into the sidewalk.

A gust of wind lifted me off the ground. My stomach churned, but Jordan dragged me across the street, league-walking this way and that, doing nothing for the disorientation spinning my head. By the time he tossed me into a chair in his apartment, I had no idea which way was up.

Listing sideways, I groaned into the chair's arm. "I think I have a concussion."

"Then told fall asleep," Jordan suggested, tugging me to sit up straight.

Lei watched me with one eye. With his hood up and tightened around his face, his half-hearted attention failed to disguise the glaze in his expression.

"You have multiple injuries," he said.

Jordan came up behind me around the same time and pressed something against the back of my head. "Fix the head wound first."

Holding up his hand, Lei sighed. "Move him over here."

"Do you want him to bleed on your couch?" Jordan retorted.

"Wait. I'm not bleeding that much. Am I?" I reached to pat my hand, but Jordan smacked my hands away. "Am I going to be paralyzed?"

"Maybe," Lei said as Jordan hissed, "Don't be stupid." Which wasn't exactly a no.

"Jordan?" My fingers dug into the chair's arms.

The couch slid across the floor, and Lei rested a hand on my wrist. "You aren't paralyzed today. Tomorrow, I can't see the future."

"He's lost enough brain cells without you feeding the stupid," Jordan snapped, but he took the compress away, and my skin shifted on the back of my head, stitching back together as if nothing had happened.

Demonic healing itched. Lei voided the injuries, so they didn't scar, but for all its perks, the voiding wasn't nearly as pleasant as I had hoped. Like taking a hot iron to the face, searing pain burned across the back of my head and down my spine. Bruises not even fully bloomed on my arms retreated, and half the battle wasn't just not passing out, it was allowing Lei to work.

"If you fight, it hurts more," Jordan warned. "He doesn't need permission to heal surface wounds, but anything else - he needs to be let in."

"Seems like a bad idea."

Lei snorted. "Would've eaten you already if I wanted."

Jordan vanished into the bathroom, shuffling through the drawers. Ridiculous. As much as I fussed, Lei healed me regardless. When Lei's hand dropped, his couch retreated.

"If you vomit in here, aim for my void," Lei told me, sending a flood of black to the left of my feet.

"So my barf ends up in Hell?"

"I will aim at my least favorite sibling," Lei replied.

His eye slid back to focus on the screens. When I shifted in the chair, the volume increased, and the eashian scowled. Obviously, he was done talking.

"Can't I get some pills for this headache?" I called, unable to even think about leaning back to look for Jordan.

153

Depositing a water bottle at my side, Jordan clucked his tongue. "Not with a possible concussion."

"Didn't he just void it?"

"If I voided it, you wouldn't need painkillers," Lei informed me.

"It's better if he only heals exposed wounds and minor contusions. We'll keep an eye on you overnight, but you should be fine. Natural selection pushed users to be durable." Jordan patted me on the back then headed into his room, closing the door behind him.

"And I'm just supposed to sit here? Not even helping me to the guest room?" Standing sent the room spinning, so I sat back down, and it hit me. "I broke a museum."

"You didn't break a museum. Sometimes buildings get damaged. You've seen enough superhero movies to know that," Jordan yelled through his door, and after a minute or so of murmurs and silence, he returned and set his phone down on the kitchen table. "Ros will use it as a lesson for the mages."

"They're going to rebuild the wall?"

Running a hand through his hair, he huffed, "Yes."

"That's so cool!"I patted my jacket down until I could pull out my notebook. Though my head spun, I needed to sketch the strange runes on her shroud while I could still remember them. They were still Nordic runes, but the pattern was all wrong. "Those runes on her veil – shroud thingy wasn't in your runic pamphlet."

"Pamphlet?" Lei's nose wrinkled.

Jordan shrugged. "It was more like a printout."

Snorting, I shoved the notebook away. "It tri-folded. It was a pamphlet."

"Whatever. I gave you three books on top of the pamphlet, and this wasn't in any of those because this," he said, tapping the drawing, "Isn't something I've seen before either. Best guess – it was meant to subdue a draugr."

"Well, that failed miserably," I retorted.

"They're on a piece of fabric. I'm surprised the wards worked at any point," Jordan exclaimed, tossing his hands up. Lei smirked, sinking into the couch cushions like the smug jerk he was. Rolling his eyes, Jordan ran a hand through his hair. "It wouldn't have been the only warding. Somebody let her out."

This was insane. Nobody in their right minds would set a draugr free. Between demons and rogues, they were the strangest bit of magic Jordan had ever introduced. Dead wizards straddled the line. Their souls weren't collapsed abysses, so light didn't harm them like a demon, but heat did. Somehow, despite straddling the line of magic user and demon, nobody acknowledged the possibility of a draugr stepping over the line completely.

"None of this even makes sense," I complained.

Lei shrugged. "Magic users are willfully obtuse."

"Ridiculous."

"Are you surprised?" Jordan grumbled. "How many sects of Christianity are there?"

"How many religions exist?" I retorted.

Lei groaned. "We get the point. Magic users are idiots."

Glaring at the demon, Jordan waved away the entire conversation as if it were too inconvenient to deal with at the moment. "We need to consult with Monday."

"Because you actually want to? Or because you think we need to 'mend bridges' after the whole Wolfram fiasco?" I asked, and man, those were the wrong questions to ask.

Jordan glared, and Lei's eyes widened almost owlishly as he glanced between the two of us. Right when the silence stretched, and I opened my mouth with an excuse, which would undoubtedly make things worse, Lei snickered and sunk down until only his dark eyes were visible over the back of his couch.

"Look at that cockiness," the demon crooned.

"Don't encourage him," the Source scolded.

Lei cocked a brow. "Or we just eat it now and avoid going north."

Jumping in to agree, I added, "I'm with Lei. Why involve anyone else if he can just eat the draugr?"

"It might upset my stomach," the demon murmured.

Rubbing the bridge of his nose, Jordan commanded, "You two," he pointed between us. "Stay."

He glared between me and Lei as if we were a pair of dogs he feared would jump up on the furniture if he wasn't paying constant attention. Crossing my arms over my chest, I glowered. Lei, for his part, just flipped Jordan off as he fell back onto the couch. Jordan shook his head, and off he went into his room, shutting the door behind him as if I couldn't manipulate air well enough to hear whatever I wanted through the door. Sure, I was being cocky. Jordan could easily overpower me on his worst day, but his absence sort of worked in my favor. While he called ahead to Canada, I absconded to the kitchen.

"Hey, Lei, you got a bag I could borrow?" I called, digging through the cabinets for the food I had promised to bring back.

Like a vampire rising from the crypt. Lei sat up. His eyes narrowed. Shadows shifted across his face. "Why?"

"I promised snacks," I explained, holding a tub of cheese puffs under one arm as I grabbed for the wafer candies with the other.

Brows rising, the demon smiled. "Oh!" Boxes marked with online vendors jumped out of Lei's void. They folded and taped themselves before dropping on the table. "I'll transport them outside your apartment."

Holding the cheese puffs to my chest, I squinted at him. "You can connect your void to my apartment building."

"It's why you ward your apartment."

My lip curled, but I slowly back the boxes. "Does that mean you could warp me places?"

"There's a chance I'd accidentally digest you."

"Right," I muttered. "Voids – black holes and colostomy bags. A great combo."

Lei nodded sagely; his void arose like a blanket around his shoulders. "Separating your digestive tract from your respiratory system, when you don't need to breathe, seemed like overkill, but it makes more sense than a human's mixed up systems."

"Sure, sure," I agreed.

My attention remained on the task at hand, and if Lei was open to me taking his food, I would grab whatever I could, filling boxes with everything I could get my hands on. Each time I finished up a box, tape flew up and sealed it. Like some demented carnival shoot, they slid one by one down through Lei's void.

"Send a rock too," Lei instructed. His eyes jumped from screen to screen independently. "I can't actually directly touch the door."

"You don't have rocks here."

"I'll find a rock."

Writing a note on the top of the last box, I chuck it to Lei. Tilting, the couch lifted. Like a hungry maw, his void stretched back upon itself,

158

and a dark tendril slapped the box inside before snapping closed just as Jordan stepped back into the room.

With a sigh, he said, "I don't want to know what I missed."

"You need to go grocery shopping," Lei informed him.

Jordan snorted. "You're the one with money in this relationship."

"Ah, yes…unfortunate." Lei pulled out his cell phone. "Why does food taste so good?"

"Because humans have to eat, and we're generally for making anything we have to do as pleasurable as possible," I replied.

With a hum, Lei sunk down, and Jordan tugged shoved his phone into his pocket. "We're headed to the Grith."

The eashian perked up. "Bring back baked goods."

"You don't need to eat," Jordan reminded him.

"I don't need to do a lot of things. Bring me pastries," Lei commanded. He waved his hand, dismissing us before pulling a blanket down upon him. Shaking his head, Jordan headed out the door, and with a wave, I followed.

Chapter Ten

Shadows loomed over the Grith. Its halls weren't as silent as the last time we had come, but as the Daughters shifted children away from the haven, the dropping numbers quieted those who remained. Soon, the house would hold close to what it had when Shiloh attacked, but while there had been a certain fearful liveliness then, the crowds of Hamelin left their mark.

Kasimira greeted us halfway to the door. "Ros is teaching," she informed us, leading the way to Monday's office. "I'll be taking over the shift from Theda in a few minutes." Her eyes darted from Jordan to me. I could practically hear the gears in her head turning. We weren't here to redo the wards, and Jordan hadn't bothered calling ahead. Lei's healing left no sign of the fight. Outside Monday's office door, she hazarded a guess. "We haven't found a solution for the connection between Jon and Conall."

"I'll deal with it myself once," Jordan dismissed.

Kasimira crossed her arms over her chest. "You found a way to identify Conall and remove his magic?"

"While that would be ideal, he's not on Earth, and my powers don't extend to Hell," Jordan retorted.

With a nod, Kasimira opened the door without knocking. Monday sat with his legs crossed and fingers steepled. His forefingers pressed against his lips as his eyes remained on the monitor. He didn't bother looking up as we entered.

"Ostairius. Jon," the wizard offered in greeting.

"Monday," Jordan returned. "He seems as unbroken as ever."

Wolfram lay on the cement floor of his cell. All around him, the walls shimmered with runes. Anything that could be overturned had been. His bed, a minimal metal frame, had been bent where possible. Pieces of his mattress clung to its sharp edges, and the interior padding covered the floor, absorbing the splatters of blood from his rages. Where his hair had once run straight about his head, it curled and waved, covered in blood, dust, and sparse threads from what I assumed had once been a blanket. No amount of mess, however, could stop the runes beneath his feet. Layers of warding in plates and shifted layers of concrete held him fast in place. If not for those, the Daughters would have moved him. If not for the Wild Hunt's shifting patterns, they might have risked the attention to secure the mage, but with both faced against them, Wolfram would remain a prisoner within the lowest level of the Grith though his victims' friends lived in the floors above.

Drumming her fingers along her arm, Kasimira sighed. "It would be easier if we had something to motivate him, but all he ever mentions are Jon, Conall, or whatever he thinks will get a rise out of us."

"What's he saying about me?" I asked.

Jordan's perpetual frown turned to me. "Do you honestly want to know?" I shrugged, and he rolled his eyes, shaking his head.

"He often mentions your mutual connection to Conall. I believe it is safe to assume he has a similar connection though why Conall wouldn't have used that to his advantage, I don't know. He could've leached Wolfram's magic completely," she said.

Monday hummed. His hands dropped, and he spun to face us. "Unless we are incorrect. A long life does not mean mastery over his prophetic abilities. It's unlikely that he had a teacher, and it would not be unreasonable to believe the Erlkonig would discourage any human connections, in which case, Wolfram would've been his only empathetic bond until Jon and perhaps Gerhard." Dark brows furrowing, the wizard studied me. The weight of his gaze itched, and it took everything not to flinch when he said, "Has he made any contact with you? In your dreams? A voice in your head? Feelings that don't seem to originate from anywhere?"

"No." The negative flew from my mouth before I had a chance to even think. Jordan raised a brow, but the rest just kept staring. "I haven't heard anything. No dreams. It's really weird."

Kasimira clucked her tongue and deadpanned, "We're not lucky enough for him to be dead."

"No, we're not," Jordan murmured. "If he were dead, the Erlkonig would've turned his attention on killing Wolfram himself."

"Why bother?" she questioned. "He'd be up against the most heavily warded private residence in the world. The only buildings more heavily warded are two of the Daughters' main compounds and the Sons' monastery in Nairobi."

Monday sighed, drumming his fingers against the desk. "The Wild Hunt has broken through similar warding when motivated in the past. Merlin's warding in Camelot."

"They had a number of rogues on their side at the time," Kasimira reminded him.

Jordan ran a hand through his hair with a gruff exhale. "I can't sense him as long as he's in Hell, but the Erlkonig's left the hunt. He wouldn't do that if he didn't have good reason to stay in Hell."

"If he were in Hell, his ability to send influence would be greater, not less," Monday posited. "Unless he's unconscious."

Kasimira glanced at the clock. "You three can continue arguing. I need to relieve Theda." She stalked out of the office with one last glare at the monitor. Whatever comforts Wolfram had destroyed in his cell, I doubted he would have the next time I saw him.

"It's been a couple of weeks. He wasn't that injured, and the Erlkonig could have simply voided his injuries," Jordan argued, but Monday shook his head.

"A wound is a lesson to him," the wizard returned.

The dark emptiness of my dreams suggested Monday was right, but I had reinforced my shields. Wards marked my bed frame. My lack of dreams could be something else even if my gut told me otherwise. Conall wiled his way into my magic, and from there, he had a way into my dreams if I gave him any sort of breathing room, but while they had been horrifying, Conall had warned me. Every invasion forewarned Wolfram's betrayal, and if I had listened to him, there was a chance Gerhard would've been saved. The ease with which he entered my mind – and Gerhard's – didn't strike as somebody untrained. The connection seemed second nature to him like Wolfram's illusions. Deep in my chest, uncertainty tangled - dangerous and inextricable as poorly run wires. A current ebbed there.

In his cell, Wolfram picked at his arm with his blunt nails. His eyes stared blankly ahead. If possible, the hollows beneath his high cheekbones had grown deeper since his capture. He looked like one of those animals in a Sarah McLachlan commercial - abused, starved, and chained. It was his eyes which differed. No hope - no pleading shined in them. A clock ticked down the hours in them instead. Hope implied a lack of knowledge. I couldn't tell if his certainty came from arrogance or knowledge, and if the latter, I had no idea if he waited for his execution or his rescue, but who would even be coming? Conall needed to kill Wolfram. The Erlkonig refused him, and none of the Hamelin children even wanted to acknowledge his existence. There wasn't anybody else to come.

"I'm not dreaming, doesn't mean he's not," I whispered, half-hoping nobody would hear me.

Of course, Jordan always listened when I least wanted it. "No influence out; no influence in," he reminded me. The wards cut off Hell - period. No question of who dialed.

"Unless it's not done through Hell," I suggested.

Jordan snickered, rubbing the bridge of his nose. "Jon, he's connected with you through Hell. Empathetic bonds…they're complicated, but no matter how he formed the bond, those wards should keep him out. Even if it was soul to soul."

"Which is highly unlikely," Monday added. "They barely have any spark left in either of them"

"But what if that remaining bit of light is their connection? That would explain why Conall has to kill Wolfram to fully demonize, right?" I pushed. Both stared at me like I had grown a second head, but at least, they weren't looking at me like I was an ignorant idiot. They knew more about this than I did. Prophets weren't exactly priority one in Jordan's lesson plan. "If their goal was demonhood, opening their minds to each other's magical influence wouldn't be that far-fetched."

Monday's lips twisted down into a deep frown. "It should still be stopped by the warding though."

With a wave of his hand, Jordan brushed the conversation aside. "We've got a bigger problem."

166

"Than the Wild Hunt?"

"There's a draugr loose in Rochester," I informed him.

With a frown, Monday stood, rounding the desk. As he approached one of his built-in bookshelves, he pressed his hand against an electronic panel on the wooden section. A green light blipped. Sliding into the ceiling, the wood revealed metal and a keypad into which Monday quickly typed a six digit code. As the metal joined the wood, a new shelf of books came into sight along with a number of small boxes of various sizes though none bigger than my phone. Alongside them, there were small notebooks not unlike my own.

"Describe it," he commanded, pulling a number of books from his shelf.

"Female, mid-Victorian period dress, runes on a veil which was originally tethered at the throat and stitched into the skirt with some gaps to allow for arm movement, but I can't be sure that was intended," Jordan described. He held out a hand to me for my notebook. "She has a pack of yeth."

"It's not like she commanded them around or anything," I added.

Monday pulled out a text. He flipped through it, glancing up at the notebook which Jordan had opened to the sketched runes. "You couldn't take a picture?"

"Of course, why didn't I take out my cell and ask her to stand still?" Jordan drawled, but

Monday slapped the book shut and pulled out another.

"You could have taken a video."

His tone riled me. Between a back of over a dozen yeth and a draugr, we had managed to contain and limit the damage, but nothing ever seemed good enough for magic users. There was always more work to be done. With a scoff, I crossed my arms over my chest. "We were kind of working with plasma at the time, and with her and the yeth, we're lucky the worst either of us got was a concussion."

The wizard hummed dismissively. He went through two more books, placing one of the two on the desk before returning to his shelves. On the open pages, an anatomical diagram engulfed it in a series of runes. They matched the shroud. All the other text was in Spanish. Luckily, Romance languages were similar enough that I could recognize a few words. The text instructed the reader to tattoo the runes as part of the burial practice if cremation wasn't to take place. Pulling out my phone, I snapped pictures of the pages. Whoever wrote it focused a lot on post-death rituals.

"Okay, tell me I'm wrong," I said, pointing to a picture a few pages further into the notebook. "This tells how you leather human skin to preserve runic tattoos? Isn't it still someone else's skin? Doesn't their will keep the tattoos from being usable by other magic users?"

"Bodily autonomy is clear. Sentimentality and utility...not so much," Jordan replied.

Thuds echoed down the hall. Monday didn't even blink. "Ros must be finished with the younger ones."

"Jon, close the door," the Source commanded.

"You could do it," I grumbled, but before I could cross the room, Theda sauntered in with Ros following close.

"Jon!" Ros smiled. She pulled me into a tight hug. "Are you hungry? We have some pasties in the kitchen."

Jordan scoffed, "He's fine."

Rude. I could always eat. There was no free food that I would turn down. A witch in a house of sweets could pop up, and I'd still try to grab some to go.

Ros patted me on the shoulder. "We'll pack some for you to take."

"Have I ever told you that you're my favorite?" I said with a grin.

She smiled back at me as she stepped up beside Jordan to study the notebook. "A draugr? I suppose it would be too much to hope this was purely academic."

"No such luck," Jordan murmured.

Pulling down another book, Monday frowned. Ros picked up the first. She sat back on Monday's desk as Theda glanced between Jordan and Monday. The sisters' expressions matched. Brows furrowed. Eyes narrowed. Wrinkles formed

169

across their foreheads, and nearly identical frowns pulled down their features. It was a far more natural look on Theda. Ros's natural upturned lips twitched as if fighting the countenance.

"Should I even waste my time asking if you've informed the Elders?" Theda inquired.

Monday pressed his lips together with a sigh. "Until we have fully grasped the circumstances, the Elders would merely slow the process."

Humming softly in neither agreement nor disagreement, Ros pressed a bit further, "And what will the process be?"

"That depends. When I worked with the Sons, a group discussed a draugr from the mid-1920s in Indonesia. There wasn't any warding like the one here, so if the wards turn out to be dampeners, things should be easier. If not..." Jordan shrugged, letting the thought continue without the words.

"If there are no unforeseen complications, we should be able to isolate and eliminate the draugr without too much difficulty," Monday agreed; however, his brows furrowed. "However, that would be assuming no one here has any qualms about destroying her without identifying her."

"Do you?" Jordan returned.

The Grith wizard frowned, tapping the cover of the book in his hand with his forefinger. "I find it disconcerting that a draugr appeared without our knowledge, with clear markings of containment, and no idea who released her."

"And what?" Theda huffed. "We should just wait to take care of her until we discover who is responsible. With the Wild Hunt in the area, the yeth will just continue to gather. We might even get a clear idea of the full population if we're unlucky."

Monday inclined his head to the side. "Perhaps."

"But if we don't know who is responsible, we risk being unprepared for what comes next," Ros said even as her sister rolled her eyes.

"Does it matter?" I pondered. Both sisters focused on me, but Jordan continued flipping through the notebooks with Monday. "I mean, we have to get rid of the draugr either way. Not like she's going to tell us who let her out."

"It'd be dangerous to assume the draugr and the one who released her are working together," Ros warned, biting her lip as she glanced between her sister and Monday.

"Then you can search for who she is, and we'll work on killing her," Jordan offered, and she tore the page of the runes out of the book, setting them down on the desk. "After that, I'll recharge and get back on track. Once I eliminate the connection between Jon and Conall, we should have a bit more room to deal with the Wild Hunt."

Theda grimaced. Her lips pressed into a thin line. The tight angles of her face accentuated the dark circles beneath her eyes. Drumming her fingers along her arms, Theda inhaled and exhaled in slow measured breaths.

"What do you mean?" she asked, but she laid equal weight to each word. This wasn't a question. She gave Jordan a chance to reconsider his comment and plan.

Licking his lip, Jordan narrowed his eyes. Not quite a glare. Just a considering focus. "When the draugr has been dealt with, I'm going to go south and take care of the bond between Jon and Conall."

"And you'll attract the Erlkonig, the Wild Hunt, and whatever other demons are in the region," Theda drawled. The muscles of her jaw jumped as she clenched her teeth. Jordan only shrugged. Crossing her arms over her chest, she asked, "And what if you die?"

Raising a brow, Jordan frowned. "Is that a threat?"

"It's not, and trying to make it one isn't going to help you avoid the question," Ros said as she stepped between the Source and her sister. "Jon needs a teacher who can actually teach. Part of the reason we were sent here was to ensure Jon actually got the training he'd need to survive. You're bringing him on hunts. You're training him in magic, and we understand that you're doing everything you can, but what happens if you die?"

"It's safer to let Conall continue to influence him?" Jordan retorted.

Monday's brows rose, but Theda spoke first, "Honestly, it would be safer to have someone else take over."

"I get a say in this, right?" I asked. They completely ignored me.

Jordan ground his teeth. "Take over teaching my nephew?"

"Can you honestly say you're the best teacher for him?" Theda said.

My shoulders sagged. I couldn't argue with that. The most powerful wizard in the world and he couldn't seem to wrap his head around teaching. Pushing down the frustration churning in my stomach, I avoided Monday's searching gaze. If he weren't overwhelmed with over a hundred kids, I might've considered taking him up on the apprenticeship offer, but the idea of shifting my training to a stranger didn't fit for me. First, I wanted to stay in Rochester. Magic or no, I had promised my mom a degree. Second, the idea of leaving Yoda just because he talked in circles seemed like a getting-your-hand-cut-off sort of move, and I liked my limbs.

"Better than having him sent to the Daughters or Sons," Jordan grumbled.

Pinching the bridge of her nose, Theda exhaled slowly. "You aren't a fit teacher. He's already delayed due to his mortal raising. Sending him to the Academy -"

"Not happening," Jordan snapped.

"Can I just point out nobody even tried to train me before Jordan? Isn't there a triad in Boston? How come they never tried to recruit me?" I asked, but the two kept on going without even glancing my way.

Theda threw her hands in the air. Turning her back on him, she cursed in German - the words vibrating in my head - before she spun back around. "Do you want him to get killed?"

"I'm staying in Rochester," I murmured.

Both Ros and Monday watched me. Reaching out, Ros brushed her hand against Monday's forearm. He caught her hand before she could pull it away. The pair met each other's eyes. Whatever subtle communication passed between them, I couldn't read their intentions.

Theda, however, continued to rage. "And the classes you're failing?" she demanded.

"I got a few bad grades. Wasn't failing anything. My grades are already up, so…" I opened my hands, leaving the ball in her court with a shake of my head.

"You are struggling. It is Jordan's responsibility to be aware and help, but you weren't!" Theda accused. Her glower switched as she pointed at Jordan. "You don't even have a formal education. Are you even in a place to assist a college student?"

"I'm the Source of Magic. The day I have free time to focus on anything other than demons and rogues, you'll all already have been out of a job for a good while," Jordan retorted.

Before the two could pounce on each other, Ros stepped forward. "This really isn't our main concern right now. Anyway, Jon's already said he's taken care of the matter."

"Yeah, and I'm looking into switching majors, so it doesn't happen again."

"Switching majors? Does your mother know?" Jordan asked.

"What?" I scoffed. "No. Why – why would ask that?"

"Probably because she is your mother and deserves to know if you are having problems or making a huge decision like changing majors," he argued. When I went to refute, he silenced me with a dirty look. "I'm your uncle. I don't care what everyone says – I'm your uncle."

Theda's brows rose. "Wow."

"What?" Jordan grumbled.

"I'm surprised you would have the balls to call out blood privilege," she admitted.

"As his teacher, I'm his guardian. Both give me the only right to decide his training," he informed her. His tone fell dark and low as he added, "He's staying here. I will train him."

Monday tilted his head. His eyes narrowed, and he hummed softly before shaking his head. "Ezekiel said something similar, I believe, when the Daughters interviewed him before you and Jokul ran away."

"Funny," Jordan hissed. His jaw tensed, and his teeth ground together like a defective robot grinding rocks in its gears. "He completely upended the magic community with the Chebar Culling, abused his two sons, and nobody questioned him raising Jukka."

"We learned," Theda roared.

175

And that was my cue to leave. An illusion wasn't hard to stick up. Nobody cared about what I thought of any of this. As a vapor shell of me snuck out and headed off toward the kitchen, I headed toward the dungeon. If anyone asked, I was just grabbing Lei's pastries. They didn't comment on my retreat either way, but the illusion continued as far as the end of the hall before shattering. Opening a locked door wasn't difficult. Magic existed for a reason, and the second door, warded against magical openings, was easy enough to pick with my library card. Certain lessons I owed to boredom and a lack of watchful supervision which I could never fully repay.

Between the second door and the third, Kasimira leaned against the wall. Her foot jiggled. Biting on her thumbnail, she glowered at the floor. While Theda stood at ease at the door, her younger sister panicked, and it was the weirdest things to see, but it did make getting around her not that hard. She didn't even look up.

Standing slightly off-center in the rectangle cell, Wolfram tapped his fists against his thighs. His eyes were closed. As he rocked back and forth, he drummed out a strange beat. Behind his eyelids, his eyes shifted. They darted back and forth like he was dreaming. In his jaw, the muscles tightened, jumping beneath the paper pale surface of his skin. Stretched across his broad shoulders, the thin shirt accentuated the sharp angles of his bones. While I couldn't be certain of his exact age, Wolfram seemed to be close to my own, so despite his height and broadness, there was still room for further growth. He didn't need it. He outmuscled me even if he never did match my height.

Nothing about the man in front of me reminded me of the boy he had pretended to be. He was a master illusionist. As the vapor twisted the light around me, my nerves sparked like frayed wires. Hindsight itched twenty-twenty in my mind.

Tilting his head, Wolfram cracked his neck. His jaw jutted as a smirk flashed his teeth. "Might not have magic, but I know an illusion when I see one," he announced. Like scythes, his dark eyes slid over to the cameras.

Pushing the illusion out to the cameras, I dropped the vapors around myself. "Wolfram."

He blinked, glancing up at me. "Jon."

Wolfram hummed. The air churned around him, but the warding glowed along the translucent walls. Every inch of the room flared to life. Lines and runic symbols drained the force of his magic, leaving only a spark of static to run along his dark hair to show that he'd attempted anything at all. His dark eyes glared at the gray cement. As steam rose and the runes dimmed, his eyes flicked upward to meet mine.

"Don't waste your breath," Wolfram murmured. His brown eyes glazed over. All the passion - fury and self-righteousness bled out into an exhausted, crumbling acquiescence. "Tell them to bring the ax. I'm not someone willing to be saved."

"Because you don't actually want to be? Or because you think you can't be?" I asked, sitting down on the outside of the warded plastic.

His eyes slid shut. A hum blurred over the silence before the wards once again glowed, leaving him without a single illusion to toy with my mind. When the runes dulled, he opened a single eye. "I don't care," he confessed. "And there is so much I want more."

"Like what?"

Sharp white teeth flashed into a shark-like grin. "Killing you." Laughter tumbled out, and he slid down to lay on his side, watching me. "No. I don't care if you live or die. Not unless he cares. Then - whatever's the opposite."

"And if he connected his magic to mine?" I asked.

All expression fell away from his face. "What?"

"Your stupid friend is a magic leech. He's got a thieving pipeline to my well." With each word, his fists grew tighter, and the sadist in me loved it. For all his bravado, Wolfram cared immensely about Conall. "I mean, most of the time he gives me a power boost, so I can't call him a parasite really." Dark eyes narrowed. Wolfram shook like a volcano prepping to erupt.

"You are nothing," he proclaimed. "He doesn't want you. Any power he's lending is just a trick - just another illusion, and you're such a moron you think it's real. You are not important to him. Just a tool for his use. Conall doesn't want you."

"Nor you."

With a sneer, Wolfram flashed his canines. "Why would I want him to want me? I want him dead. He wants me dead. There's nothing more to it."

Lies got easier with practice. The ones we wanted to believe, however, came out differently than those meant to deceive. Every tell I calmed from my face taught me where to look for the gap in other's masks. Wolfram's nostrils flared. His left eyelid twitched, but the muscles along the side of the face tensed as if resisting the urge to blink. Fighting to uncurl his fingers from fists, he made his words into the illusions the wards denied him, but these ones failed to fool me.

"You're probably right. He just wants to kill you. You're just another stepping stone between him and eternity with the Erlkonig, right?" I returned, and his eyes blazed at the demon's name.

"Correct."

"Makes sense. You can't compete with the only demon that could give the Devil a run for his money," I contemplated. Fighting back a smirk, I preened as his rage grew. "Conall didn't feel that powerful, but he's got to have something if the Erlkonig cares about him. I mean, did you see how the demon practically threw himself on him?" I waited for a beat, but Wolfram only rolled his eyes. "Maybe it's the face. He's kind of pretty. Maybe the Erlkonig just wanted something nice to look at.

Most demons look like they've been through the grinder, so - pretty face, eager to please; I guess I can see it."

Wolfram scoffed. His chin jutted forward as he tilted his head back. Wolfram rolled his jaw, and with a loud clack, he snapped his teeth into a murderous smile. Running a hand through his hair, he leaned against the wall.

"Yes, that does sound like Conall. Just a pretty face."

I smirked, stepping closer to his cell. "But he's just pretty, right? I've seen some eashians, and those guys - they're almost angelic. Perfectly symmetrical."

"I'm hundreds of years old, Jon. Do you honestly think you can trick me? Conall means nothing to me. Call him pretty. Demean him. Insinuate all the damnables you want," Wolfram said.

"I'm just saying. Conall hitched his wagon to the Erlkonig, but he also pulled me into this, so...maybe I'm his pretty face." I grinned. Posing with my hands on my hips like Superman, I added, "I'm definitely his type. Tall, dark, and better than him in every conceivable way."

"You're joking."

"I'm not." Waving a hand at myself, I flexed and shifted to show off my guns. Buff wasn't my thing, but I had more muscles than flab. "Runner fit, man. You're all scowl and wrestler fit, but I've got hunter-chic."

"I don't even understand what you just said."

"Then you don't disagree!"

Slamming his fist against the wall, he growled, "You think this is funny? Come down here to pretend you're better than me? Conall would never want you. You're human - magic or no. He's fickle and arrogant and the most narcissistic bastard you'll ever meet. No matter how much you kill for him - no sacrifice will ever be enough. He'll never love you!"

With each sentence, he grew progressively louder until he screamed the last. He bawled. Tears streamed down his face, and the fire in his eyes redirected inward. After the words escaped him, Wolfram dropped his gaze, breathing harshly as if coming down from a berserker high.

"Do you -," as I spoke, his head whipped up, and his glare had me correcting, "Did you love him?"

Wiping his face with the back of his hand, he spat, "No. Of course not. Are you insane?"

Shoving my hands in my pockets, I backed away. "Good." When he straightened himself back up, I aimed one last blow. "Cause he's mine now." Spinning around, I sauntered away.

And Wolfram exploded. "Yours? Covenant be damned! He's mine! Not the Erlkonig's. Definitely not yours. Mine! Do you hear me, Blythe?" He slammed against the walls. "You're a pathetic, barely trained warlock. He could never want you! I killed for him! Do you know how many bodies I got him back in the day? I murdered villages of mortals for him. You're nothing! You hear me? Nothing! Turn around, you son of a bitch! I'm going to burn you alive, you hear me? Blythe!"

Smiling, I kept my eyes ahead. Not acknowledging him fed the flame. Chaos sowed. Vindictive needs temporarily sated. Whatever Wolfram might have felt during the ward renewal, it wasn't Conall. Nobody who had just been reassured by their crush would have acted like Wolfram. Whether the wizard was awake and biding his time or healing the slow way and completely unaware, Wolfram needed to believe he had been abandoned. We had barely handled them apart, and if they reconnected, I doubted even the Erlkonig could have stood in their way.

Pulling the vapors taunt around me, I trudge back out, listening to Wolfram's senseless screams. It wasn't much different from where he had been the last time, and if the sudden exclamations from his cell startled Kasimira once I stopped blocking the sound waves, she didn't acknowledge it. Her nails dug into her palms, but that was probably the futility of guarding a solidly trapped teenager likely inspired more frustration than his echoing cries. Quiet contemplation better suited Monday than any of the Daughters except perhaps Ros, but she was a teacher, so it could have very well been a learned suppression of her hunter's instincts rather than a natural state. Not that Jordan was much better. I wasn't. Impulse control would have kept me from the dungeon, pushed me to avoid Wolfram and all the self-loathing just the sight of him brought to me.

Hovering above the ground, I glided up the stairs, only dropping the illusion when I stepped into the empty kitchen. Heat still permeated from the cooling ovens. A slow cooker hummed in the corner with some type of savory stew, but my eyes focused on the plastic containers of pastries. Lei wanted payment, and I wasn't stupid enough to leave an easy deal with a demon opened.

"Hi." Leta stood by the doorway. With her arms crossed, she leaned against the counter with a smile across her face. "Jordan does feed you, right?"

"I feed me, but Lei asked so…" I said with a shrug.

Her nose wrinkled as she scoffed. "And how's that? Staying with a demon?" "I have my own apartment, you know that, right?" I told her as I dug through the cabinets. "Where does Ros keep the containers? Bags? Should I put pastries in a bag?"

"Reusable bags are in the drawer over there. Glass containers in the cabinet below," she said, pointing to the far side of the kitchen.

"Thanks."

Her eyes followed me around her room. "So…what do you think of them keeping Wolfram here?" When I paused just to glance up at her, she crossed the room to lean against the middle island closer to me. "They aren't telling us anything. Just filing the young kids out – telling us to find apprenticeships or other placements. Nobody here knows what's going on."

Now I knew she was full of crap. Daughters kept secrets well, so I had no doubt they would hold their plans tight to their chests with this one. However, none of the Grith kids were stupid. Also, the lack of a plan was pretty straightforward, or everyone failed to share their conclusions with me too. We stalled, faced with too many possibilities, and as long as the Elders of the Daughters feared confrontation with the Wild Hunt, the Grith would be a gigantic target, leaving its very purpose null. None of that was something she couldn't have guessed, and after Ilea, I wasn't about to be swept away because she had magic. Honestly, genetic bottlenecking suggested I should even avoid her because of that.

"If you have a question, ask it."

Leta pushed herself up to sit on the countertop. "What's going on?"

"Wolfram's here. Wild Hunt's preventing him from being moved, and the Elders don't want him dead. That's pretty much it, but you already knew that," I replied, snapping the lid of Lei's pastry container into place. "I also probably have a concussion, but nobody seems to care."

"But they let you into the meetings," she pointed out.

"If you think anything productive is happening when Jordan comes up here with me, I can promise you you're wrong. They argue. Ros flirts with Monday – are they a thing? They are,

184

right?" I shook my head and waved a hand. "Not important – though I wouldn't mind an answer, and there we are."

With an exaggerated blink, she sighed. "There's got to be more to it than that."

"Not really. Jordan keeps me close cause of the whole Wolfram and Gerhard situation. Easily manipulated I guess," I admitted with a shrug, drumming my fingers against the plastic top.

Sliding off the counter, she brushed off her jeans. "Gerhard wasn't your fault. You weren't the only one he warned. He told Meinhard and Helena about the dreams too."

"He told your sister?" I frowned. "Was she like his big sister buddy or something?"

"Helena's always been good with the quiet ones. She was here every day with him, so just imagine how she feels," Leta stated, tousling her short brown hair. "But we're human. We can't save everyone."

"We also apparently don't know how to do the one job we were really given," I muttered. Tilting her chin up, she hummed softly, prompting me to elaborate. "The Covenant is all about diluting the blood, right? The Witch and her sons weren't the only users at the time, and I get bringing those guys into the fold increased the population, but to still be around now? That's got to have been on purpose. The Daughters, the Sons – they're all about keeping track, and if the Daughters are anything to go by, everyone is keeping it in the family, and that's just weird."

"Well, the original population was entirely wizard level, so…kind of not as bad but still not great," she offered.

Ultimately, my point remained, but I wasn't in the mood to argue. "If I knew anything else, I'd tell you, but the Elders don't even know what they're doing."

"I hate feeling like we're sitting around twiddling our thumbs," Leta complained. "It's why Helena and I aren't joining the Daughters. You just wait for orders. How boring is that?"

"Is somebody apprenticing you both then?"

She shook her head. "No. We're going to figure it out on our own. Monday's taught us more than most families would, and we're on the older end, so an apprenticeship would only be necessary…" she trailed off, gesturing at me. "If – well, you know."

"You had no familial connection to the community and were completely in the dark like some kid left on Tatooine because the Jedi didn't make it to Hut territory?" I suggested when she struggled for a way to politely describe my situation.

A laugh jumped out of her, and her nose wrinkled. "Something like that."

"Yeah, I get it, but that's probably not the safest bet."

"Jordan and your dad did it," she retorted.

I snorted, chuckling as her jaw tensed and lips pursed. "He's kind of the Source of All Magic, and that definitely still didn't go great for them."

186

"And we're seventeen and trained. They were barely pre-teen."

Before I could respond, Jordan popped into the room. His eyes slid from me to Leta, and raising a brow, he leaned between us to grab one of the cheese danishes. "I don't mean to interrupt."

"It's nothing. I was just giving Leta my number for when she heads out of here," I offered, holding out my hand for her phone which she slid over to me. I added myself as a contact and passed it back.

"If Monday keeps up his cell phone policy, he's going to go broke," Jordan noted.

Leta shrugged, sticking her cell phone back in her back pocket. "Only the ones over fifteen. Nobody else is supposed to leave unaccompanied, so…"

"Right," Jordan hummed. Turning to me, he announced, "We're off."

"Oh, uh, thanks then," Leta called after us, waving goodbye as Jordan half-dragged me out of the room toward the front door.

"Text whenever," I yelled back.

A few kids hung out on the front porch. They stopped talking the moment Jordan walked out, and they watched us head out across the yard, whispering when we reached the first gateway. Abeni's dark eyes stared at us. Her expression stayed carefully blank as she knocked twice against the door, and the pair between the inner and middle walls opened the pathway.

"Take care," she intoned. Her fingers drummed against her sides. "I'll probably be gone next time you're here."

"Found a triad?" Jordan asked.

Nodding, she explained, "My cousin got injured in her last hunt. They're pretty sure she's paralyzed so…"

"Ah, so hopefully temporary," I said, and she nodded once more as Jordan headed off without another word. "Either way, good luck!"

"You too."

With that, the gate closed tight behind us. I didn't recognize the pair between, and they made no motion to speak with us. As the middle ward opened to the outer, a light flashed, signally demons attacking the outer ward. Right flared, dimming to black before vibrant light flared in return.

"You get used to it," Phuong said with a shrug.

Jordan's eyes traced the pressure as another demon collided with the wards. "We'll be doing a full replacement weekly. You reinforce it each shift, right?"

"Every time we switch guards one person reinforces it straight off and the other half way through." Her lips pursed, stretching the scars on her face. "It's getting harder though as we don't have as much time between shifts with so many people leaving."

Pressing his hand against the wall, his eyes slid closed, and his soul illuminated, passing into the wall. "Tell whoever has the early shift Saturday not to reinforce it halfway through. Jon will reinforce it then, and I'll do it at least once whenever I'm up."

Phuong bit her lip, and when she glanced at me, our eyes met. Jordan leaped between extremes. He either spread himself too thin or hoarded his power like a secret, and the unpredictability of it was exhausting. Relying on him felt dangerous. If the time came when he tired of being helpful, his absence unbalanced the whole scheme. Running a hand through his hair, Jordan scoffed, but he didn't say anything. Not like he could read our minds. Even if he could, disappointment and distrust weren't emotions he was unfamiliar with inspiring in people.

"Stay safe," I offered instead, and with a wave, she closed the door behind us, leaving us in the busy streets of Toronto.

Once more we fell into step, but when the water of Lake Ontario came into view, Jordan grabbed my wrist, tugging me to a halt. On the edge of Lake Ontario, Jordan slid his hands into his jacket pockets. His eyes traced the waves. Beneath the churning waters, scales glimmered in the dark. Havfine had returned. As long as the Wild Hunt trampled across the northeast, any lights Jordan laid would be futile. Just watching the waves suggested a lecture. I cringed. Biting my tongue, I waited silently in hopes to minimize the duration of whatever storm headed my way.

"What did you think?" he asked.

I shrugged. "Ros and Monday are doing it."

"Of Wolfram."

Odds on somebody seeing through the illusion weren't bad, so I wasn't exactly surprised, but it brought up some interesting questions about if anyone else noticed. If only Jordan noticed, I understood why he wouldn't say anything. However, any of the others in the office could've noticed – especially Monday – and he had no reason to pretend that he didn't care. Either way, Jordan caught me. I had to deal with that first.

"He's a psycho. No empathy and definitely doesn't care how he's tortured – and I think being in that room is kind of torture, but not the magic cut off. I think he can feel that he's cut off from Conall," I told him, rocking back on my heels. Dark clouds rolled above our heads. "I think he's going through withdrawal."

Jordan hummed. Rolling his shoulders, he pulled his jacket tighter around him even though his shield should've kept the air around him hot enough. With a shake of his head, he stepped forward, and the leagues blew by us as the sharp teeth and shimmering scales of the havfine slithered beneath the dark waters of Lake Ontario. Winter had come early to Rochester. Frost gathered along the water's edge. Perhaps the havfine pulled the heat from the water quicker than nature might otherwise have done. We hit the coast. Managing to keep my feet under me, I followed Jordan back to his apartment, but in the doorway to the building, Jordan stopped short.

"Until I've got an answer on the draugr -," he said, and I groaned.

"No," I interrupted. "You aren't doing it this to me again. Danger happens. I'm here. I'm the apprentice. This is what this whole thing is about!"

Crossing his arms, Jordan glared. "And when you tell your mother you're switching majors, who do you think she'll blame?"

"Me! Because she knows I'm a moron!"

"Great. Then you can tell her, finalize the switch, and double your practice at the bookshop," Jordan retorted. His face completely shut down. Lips pressed into a thin line – neither smiling nor frowning, he didn't even glare at me. "The Daughters are clearing out the Grith, so consider yourself lucky I'm not making you transfer somewhere safer permanently."

"And where would I go? Can't send me to Boston. Wild Hunt's been there. If you want to pay for me to spend winter break in Florida or California with my friends, I'm not going to stop you, but I'm not leaving people behind to get completely rolled over," I spat, and Jordan growled, but before he could speak, I aimed my only real attack and pointed out, "You wouldn't leave George here alone, would you?"

He ground his teeth, glaring further up the sidewalk, but with a harsh swallow, he pushed the emotion from his face again. "No going out alone. You hunt with me or not at all."

"What do you think I've been doing?"

His bleached brow rose, and my mouth went dry. He knew. My fingers curled, pressing my nails into my palms as he sighed, rubbing the bridge of his nose. "You're going to have to learn to trust me, Jon."

Like a brat unable to hold my tongue, I raged, "I'm not a toy you can put away when you're bored of me!" Before he could reply, I retreated, racing back to my apartment, hoping he didn't see the way my magic crackled around my fingers.

Chapter Eleven

I had never been the sort of child who self-punished. Guilt never ate away at me. Pouting in a corner in self-loathing wasn't my natural state, so the weight of Jordan's disapproval irked me more than anything else. Snow hadn't thawed, but Rochester dealt with winter like a well-oiled machine. Salt and plows cleared the roads. University went back into session by the third day, and back in the lecture hall, I glared at the presentation, debating if next week was soon enough to meet with my potential new advisor.

"Hey," Tyson hissed, elbowing me. "If you keep glaring that hard, you're gonna burn a hole in the wall."

"Sorry, man, I didn't sleep."

I had, but my other ready to go excuse would risk another lecture about familial obligations or why I shouldn't hang out with Jordan anymore. Because Tyson was a good friend, he let me get away with the probably obvious lie. If anyone knew my sleeping habits, my roommate would be one, and despite my late night hunting habits, he stayed up just as late most nights. We both focused on the droning professor, but as the seconds ticked by, a buzzing itched in the back of my head.

Going online, I tugged up my previous night's reading. The Lady in White may have been an urban legend, but there was barely anything written on her. A woman, a daughter, and a search remained the same, but the details shifted. At times, the daughter had run away while in other stories, she had been kidnapped. However, the stranger part came when I looked into the runes on her shroud. Though covered in bright graffiti, they matched similar patterns found in the abandoned subway tunnels that lay beneath the city in ruins.

"This can't be right," I grumbled, and Tyson leaned over to glare down at my screen. "Hey – personal space," I hissed.

"If you're planning a prank on Joel, our roommate agreement clearly states you must include me," he replied, reaching over to scroll down the page. "I thought we went to the subway tunnels last Halloween."

"We did."

Smirking, Tyson drawled, "And?"

"White Lady predates the tunnels –"

"Lady in White," he corrected.

"Fine, the Lady in White legend existed before the subway, but these symbols…" My brain caught up with tongue, and I cut myself off, switching back to notes. "Nothing. Sorry."

"Come on," he pushed.

"It's probably just graffiti," Tyson informed me. His gaze shifted to the professor. "Okay, I know Novak isn't the most observant professor, but even he has to hear me at this point. It's not like we're being subtle."

The tight bubble of air I had wound around us to keep our conversation and my mumbling from leaking out to other students shifted as if to remind me I had done it. All the more terrifying for the fact that up until Tyson's comment, I hadn't remembered I had done it at all. Drumming my fingers over my keys, I glanced around, hoping some more ice would pop up and let me make a hasty escape, but nothing happened.

"Yeah…maybe he's doing some reverse psych thing," I whispered as I sank down in my seat as if to avoid being spotted.

Tyson snorted, rolling his eyes, but while it wasn't the most creative lie, practice always made perfect. He didn't know I had magic. There was no reason to believe I knew better than him why nobody seemed to notice our conversation.

"Think it's the room's acoustics?"

I shrugged. "Maybe you should just pay attention."

"Says the guy reading up on urban legends during a pre-test review class. I know you're thinking of switching -"

"Going to switch!" I corrected.

With a scoff, he juggled. His pencil between his fingers. "Sure, fine - you're going to switch majors soon, but this class will still be on your record."

"I've got it handled."

His stupid smirking face irked me even as he went back to taking notes. Undead wizard kind of took priority over grades. Not that I could tell him that. How was Spider-Man the only super struggling day to day financially? All the other Avengers seemed fine. Superman balanced two jobs and everyone else had some sort of fortune - Green

Arrow, Batman, Iron Man - across comic book universes, heroes had a kind of guaranteed stability or a power - like the Flash - where they could balance the two. I had magic. Why couldn't I be more Dr. Strange and less Constantine? Were their churches that would pay for exorcisms? That counted as hunting and involved a paycheck, right? Jon Blythe - Freelance Exorcist. I could do it. Freelancers got decent pay. Believers probably paid ridiculous amounts to get rid of the smallest demonic irritant. Plus, warding more houses in Rochester wouldn't be a bad idea.

Overhead, the lights flickered. The slide moved forward, and for all that the professor shifted the tone of his voice in hopes of keeping us awake, the tone droned in the back of my head, accented with each buzz and jump of the lights. White lines waved across the screens.

"It's like the world wants me to get a migraine," I grumbled.

My eyes fell to the floor, desperate to find a reprieve from the onslaught. Ice gathered along the laminate. Tracing its path back to the door, I tensed. Steamrolled into the room from beneath the door. Frost gathered along the doorway, and inch by inch, it climbed up the frame. The lights flickered once again, and the ice and mist were gone.

A shadow loomed, and I jumped when my laptop slammed shut. "Hey, J.B., shake a leg." All around, the lights increased to normal levels as the screens at the front shut off. "You know, if you don't want me to treat you like a kid, maybe you should start getting your shit together," Tyson complained as I scrambled to shove everything into my backpack.

The aisles flooded. Elbows shoving as the mob moved out the door, so it wasn't like my not paying attention cost us much time. We would've been stuck. Reminding him of this, however, wasn't worth it. These moments were like pressure valves for the overbearing, smothering parent who lived in the core of Tyson's soul. With practice, he would master the urges. His future children owed me big.

"Think there are any pizza pockets left?" I asked, slinging my bag over my shoulder.

Tyson shrugged. "Tommy's not big on them, and Joel was holed up in his room, so...probably?"

From the room to the hall, the temperature dropped, and I zipped up the last small gap of my jacket, wriggling my sweater hood out to pull up around my head. Tyson tugged on his knit cap, and as we neared the doorway, he shivered.

"I get it is November, but this is ridiculous."

My thin barrier of hot air had me cozy, but I nodded, pretending to shiver along beside him, rubbing my arms in supposed solidarity. Side by side, we headed home. Tyson watched me out of the corner of his eyes. I couldn't be sure. The weight of someone's attention was there, but it left me lopsided. Listing and floating half-outside my head, I drifted along, barely registering the people around us until a gray cap caught my eye. Everything else held the slushy dulled colors of winter; instead of being a bright spot, the figure who caught my eye was grayscale. From the white of his shirt to his slate gray shoes, every inch of the old man seemed colorless. Curling white hair and gray peeked out from his hat and high neckline. From behind, nothing of color showed. Even his dog was black. Then he turned.

"Giuseppe." Grabbing Tyson's arm, I tugged him back.

Tyson's brows furrowed. "Whoa, what?"

"Dog?" I offered when my brain blanked on how to explain my sudden panic.

We both glanced back over at the dog. Its haunches came up to Giuseppe's waist, and though the man was short, that still made for a huge dog. Dark, shaggy fur sprouted in all directions. A narrow snout snorted. Its maw gaped, displaying sharp purely whites. While they weren't all fangs, I recognized the demon beneath the fuzzy exterior. Regardless, it wasn't necessary the cutest pup.

Shaking his head, Tyson snorted. "You're such a dork."

"I like dogs."

"It looks like Church Grim or whatever," Tyson retorted with a smirk.

"And I'm the dork?"

With a shrug, Tyson continued forward, right toward Giuseppe and his hellhound. "I know my supernatural dogs."

Giuseppe moseyed down the sidewalk. Every few steps, he stopped, letting the yeth sniff around. Big, black eyes focused on me. Out the side of its mouth, a blue tongue lolled. Saliva dripped down, and in the almost gray liquid, flecks of red caught my eye. I didn't want to know what the thing ate, but my stomach rolled.

"You've got a lovely dog," Tyson offered when we got closer.

Giuseppe smirked. His bright eyes met mine before sliding over to my best friend. "Why thank you. She's a bit of a rascal, but she's a good girl at heart." He patted its head, and the yeth sat, wagging its tail which shifted back and forth from a regular dog's tail to a mess of bones and sinew. "You can pet her if you would like."

Tyson reached forward, and the yeth bowed its head, leaning forward into the contact. "What's her name?"

"Tisiphone."

"That's an interesting name," I grumbled.

Nudging me with his elbow, Tyson dropped his hand. "It's a cool name."

"It's Greek," I told him. "One of the Furies."

The corner of Giuseppe's lips twitched up. "Are you a student of history?"

"Well, those who aren't are doomed to repeat it, right?" Sliding my hands into my jacket pockets, I slid my fingers around my lighter. Giuseppe didn't have magic anymore, but he'd never be a defenseless old man. Magic users rarely made it to old age if they weren't also horrifyingly dangerous. "Hey, Tyson, we should get going."

"But she's so cute!" he cooed, reading out to scratch under the yeth's chin.

People passed us, shuffling around the three of us. A few cooed at the yeth, and the manipulative beast tilted its head into Tyson's affection. Dark eyes glimmered. If anyone doubted animals had souls, one look into the smirk of the yeth's expression suggested otherwise. However, the demon played dog well.

"She won't bite," Giuseppe reassured me. The spark of sadistic glee in his smirk added an unspoken yet.

Shifting my weight, I glanced between the ex-mage and the demon. "What are you still doing in town?"

"I rather enjoy this city. Despite the tussle with Jordan in the spring, I thought I stayed out the year," Giuseppe stated. Tyson's head snapped up from the dog to look at me, but the hound whined, nuzzling into his hands until he started petting once more. "I'm not going to be around much longer regardless. At my age, I ought to settle my debts."

Giuseppe tilted his chin up. The gray stubble somehow softened the harsh smirk of his lips into an almost friendly expression. Though styled, his vaguely disheveled form failed to mesh with the slick-suited mage who sent his demon into my room in the spring. Red circled his eyes. Dark shadows painted the hollows beneath them.

"If you want to speak with Jordan, I can give you his number, but going to Monday might be easier," I suggested, and a second suspicious glower from Tyson, but when he stood up this time, the hound just wagged its tail almost grinning up at me.

Luckily, he didn't say anything as Giuseppe shook his head. "No, no - Jordan and I settled the matter rather thoroughly last time we spoke, don't you agree? I have nothing further to say on the matter to him, and inform me if I am wrong, but he feels the same."

I shrugged and stepped diagonally to put myself between Giuseppe and Tyson. This time, my roommate stayed silent. However, his eyes narrowed. His gaze shifted between the two of us as if a light bulb had flicked on over his head. When Tyson moved to go around Giuseppe and continue toward our apartment, the yeth lunged forward. Bearing its teeth, the demon snarled.

"What the Hell!" Tyson cried.

Dodging out of the way, he threw his hands in the air and nearly tumbled out into the busy street. A gust of wind pushed him back to the sidewalk as a car whizzed by, and I grabbed the back of his jacket, shoving him forward as I kept myself between the demon and Tyson.

"Looks like your dog might be overheating," I drawled.

"Overheating! That thing just tried to eat me!" Tyson shouted, gesturing wildly at the demon even as I pushed him forward.

"Strange," Giuseppe hummed. "She was fine while you petted her. My poor little girl," the ex-mage cooed, scratching the yeth's chin. "Did the young man scare you?"

Sputtering in indignation, Tyson put up no fight as I guided him further down the street. My shield shimmered across the cement, testing the darkness of the shadows around Giuseppe, but there was no void to be found as the old man walked out of view.

"Are all of Jordan's friends that weird?" Tyson asked.

"I wouldn't call Giuseppe a friend."

Humming, he adjusted his hat. "Giuseppe? Is he British?"

"From the accent? Maybe? I actually have no idea where he's from," I admitted.

"So, if he isn't a friend, what the heck is he? Don't tell me Jordan's such a drama queen he only has archenemies or something," Tyson joked, bumping his shoulder into mine as we headed down the street. "Actually, yeah – no – don't tell me. I want to keep the illusion he's not that bad."

Offering only a shrug in response, I quickly changed the subject. Explaining the summoning and Giuseppe's part wasn't one I had reconciled myself. A murderer walking around Rochester made me sick. With a demon on a leash, Giuseppe wasn't going anywhere.

***

The moment I could leave without anyone noticing, I rushed to the bookstore. Overhead, the sun fell beyond the horizon. As the last glimmering rays fell and the city's lights went up, the fuchsia paint practically glowed, and the lemniscates

203

glimmered in the window. But the ram's head glinted at me mockingly.

Buzzing itched at the back of my head. A migraine brewed. Standing in front of the window, I shifted my weight from one foot to the other, watching the shimmering sideways eights make their way across the window panes. Going to Jordan's apartment would be the safest bet. Giuseppe had to be draugr level news, but I could just text him and go on a hunt. The draugr wasn't that big of an issue.

My whole body clenched. Sweat gathered on my skin. Every inch of me tugged too tight, and a mist clung, leaving my fingers slick against my palms when I pressed the back of my hand against my mouth. Stumbling out of the light, I ducked into the alley and emptied my stomach on the asphalt. Eyes watering, I locked my knees. Spots jumped across my vision, and the ache in my head just kept getting worse. A shiver ran down my spine.

"Crap," I murmured, pressing my forehead against the cool siding. "Solomon's not going to be happy about that." A wave of my hand and the snow gathered melted, sliding a path straight to the gutters and the drain. "No hunting alone," I grumbled, the buzzing settled into a headache as if content with my decision. Rubbing the bridge of my nose, I sighed.

Racing across the city, I landed on Jordan's doorstep once more. However, before I could knock, the door opened and out walked Lei dressed to the nines. Black slacks and dress shirt with a matching black jacket with gold plated in the shoulders completed his armor. The lazy sprawl of his hair had been slicked back like Jordan's usual style, but the spiky coif looked classier on the eashian. Gold rings decorated his fingers. The metallic hue carried down to his shoes.

"You look ridiculous," I grumbled, adjusting my hooded sweater. "Got a date?"

Lei rolled his eyes. "Romance?" He groaned. "Too much work."

"Then why are you dressed like that?"

The demon stepped across the threshold, closing the door behind him with his tendril. "Convention tickets are up next week. Funds are running low."

Shaking my head, I asked, "Okay, whatever. Is Jordan in?"

Adjusting the collar of his shirt, he clucked his tongue, tilting his head back to glower down his nose at me. "No."

"Well…" I leaned back against the wall opposite. "That was helpful."

Though the eashian was almost a full foot shorter than me, the spread of his void against the wall nearly blacked out the door and spread down the hall, making his presence tower over me even if his more corporeal form would be kept at bay with a well-placed hand onto his face and locked elbows. Shoving his hands into his pockets, Lei snorted. His void oozed off the wall like sludge. Swaggering down the hall, he tossed his hair to glance at me.

"You coming?" he asked.

I shrugged. "Kind of need to speak with Jordan. Giuseppe's back."

"Huh, bad timing," the demon lamented. "He's gone for a while."

Groaning, I tugged out my phone, sending a text out to Jordan. "Why didn't he tell me? I swear, he thinks I'm just going to do whatever he tells me."

"Most authority figures assume that." He meandered down the stairs, waiting for me to follow as he leaned against the outer door, letting the freezing air drift into the building.

Safe practice would have me going straight home. Despite a burning migraine stopping me from going on a solo hunt – which admittedly would've been a bad idea, homework failed to tempt me from heading out into the night with a demon at my side. If Jordan trusted him enough to spend nights in the same apartment, he couldn't be that bad.

"Where even is he? Chasing after the Wild Hunt? Up at the Grith?" I pressed, but Lei rolled his head, stretching his neck. His great input was followed by a shrug. "Great. Just stupendous. It's not like I need my teacher – my stupid uncle – around. No, he can be a total flake."

Lei's arm shot out. A wall of black expanded in front of me, and I froze. Cocking a single brow at me, he released his void, and it slithered back into his shadow about his feet. "No complaining. He's off after your father. Got a lead. Stupid jerk left me alone."

"Fine. Whatever."

206

Snorting, he continued down the road. "Eloquent."

"Like you're one to talk. I'm surprised we got a full sentence out of you, and what's with the pronouns? Am I crazy? Or are you actually getting better?" I retorted, and the demon's lips spread into a sly smile, but he didn't say a word.

Walking side by side with a demon, I should have kept an eye on my surroundings, but while traveling anywhere with Jordan had my adrenaline spiking and senses on high alert, Lei did the opposite. There was no rush to his steps, so we didn't walk by leagues; instead, we wove through the city like two normal people despite the void of freezing air emanating from him or the shield which kept me warm.

All around us, the bitter air blew, but as outward calm turned my thoughts inward, everything jumbled. Jokul had to know I existed. Even if he never received those letters, Jordan's search or even the delay while in Boston had to have clued him into what had happened. Did he not want me? It wasn't like he knew me. Not everyone wanted kids. Still, I wasn't a kid anymore. Nobody expected him to raise me. Even if Jordan wanted to pass me off onto him, there were others on whom he could ditch me. Mom didn't want him back. There weren't any expectations to live up or down to, so why was he running? And why were we looking?

I wanted to meet him. I wanted to stand across from the guy who helped make me, and I wanted to see what sort of person he was. That wasn't too much to ask. Meet up with your son. Maybe a handshake and a reason for why he avoided meeting me. If he had thought I was better without him, I would have agreed. Jordan staying around hadn't exactly been smooth sailing, and we got along fine once he too was gone. All these questions ran ragged around my head; however, setting them into a phrase proved difficult. Explaining what results I assumed they would produce proved even harder.

"Hey, Lei," I murmured after a bit. "You don't like my dad, do you?"

"I don't."

"Why?"

"There are characters…" He sighed, waving his hand as if to erase what he had just said. "In stories, a plotline which leads the protagonist astray is frustrating, especially if I know more than the protagonist."

"Like a Red Herring?" I asked, and he shook his head.

Pursing his lips, he said, "Different but similar."

"Something that is a name?" I guessed, and he nodded. "And if I figure out what you mean, will it have any impact on how I feel about meeting my dad?" Pausing in his walk, he glared at the ground for a moment before shrugging. "No."

"Well – that was exceedingly pointless then."

Scratching the back of his head, Lei tilted his head, studying me carefully before shaking his head. "I do what I want."

Through the city, he led me to a tall building in the middle of the financial district; however, we didn't enter through the front door. He ducked into a side street, knocking three times against a large metal door. After a pause, he knocked twice more, and the door opened. The man on the opposite side stood a few inches shorter than me. Slicked back brown hair and thick brows stared blankly at me behind square spectacles.

"Broker," Lei said, gesturing at the man. He then pointed to me. "Stupid-me."

"Hi, I'm Jon," I offered with a small wave.

Lei slapped the back of my head. "Don't speak to the broker."

The man merely shook his head and stepped aside, letting us enter the building. Sleek glass and black stone shrouded the interior in a science fiction noir mystique. Rectangular glass plates floated as stairs. Diffused light cascading throughout the cathedral ceiling as the broker led us up the stairs. His black suit and shoes blended into walls and dark floor like he was a part of the décor. Not that Lei was much better. Aside from his golden accessories, Lei's outfit matched the broker in shade. In jeans and a hooded sweater from my high school days, I stood out. Even my leather jacket failed to lend any semblance of class.

The whole place reeked of expense. Not a speck of dust settled along the smooth walls or the long plush couches which formed a lounge on the balcony of the second floor. Inlaid into one wall, a beverage counter held five ridiculous metallic monstrosities. I wouldn't have even recognized it as anything but some modern art piece if it weren't for the milk steamer. Two dark doors stood on the opposite side of the lounge. Opening one of the doors, the broker stepped aside. A large dark wood desk rested within, breaking the futuristic décor with built-in bookcases and an area rug fit for the Godfather's study.

Lei held up one finger. "Wait," he commanded, pointing to the lounge.

With a flare of his black eyes, he spun around and headed into the office. His void stretched out. Tendrils moved one of the two large chairs so he could fall into it with a sigh of relief. Overstuffed and soft enough to sink into without being as soft as a marshmallow, it cradled Lei as well as his couch, and like a cat, he sprawled as the chair wobbled back around.

The broker adjusted his glasses. "There is a fridge with cold drinks on the far right if you're thirsty. Coffee, teas, and hot chocolate are in the drawers. Please, help yourself."

The door closed behind them, and stuck in the strange lounge, I stood awkwardly, glancing around the room. Energy buzzed around the room. It wasn't magic. The wall hummed with tech, but beyond feeling the electricity, there wasn't much else. Walking the perimeter, I ran a hand along the wall, stopping at the counter just long enough to remind myself why drinking anything in a strange place would be a bad idea. As I made my way back to a chair closest to the broker's office, the strange buzz thrummed, drawing my eyes to the first floor.

A blond man sauntered through the door. In a slick all black suit with a black button-up and no tie, the man skipped up the stairs two at a time at a jog only to come to a sudden stop when his eyes caught sight of the closed door and then me. Styled in a shaggy coif with short sides and an impressive beard, his hair left me feeling disheveled and oddly intimidated. He flicked his wrist, turning it to check his golden watch. Whatever he saw displeased him.

"What the hell is this?" he demanded, gesturing at the door.

I shrugged. "They're in a meeting."

"What shit," he grumbled. His eyes scanned the room. Landing back on me, he crossed his arms over his broad chest. "You got an account here."

"Nope. Here with a friend."

Lying didn't seem like a good idea, but the second the words left my mouth, I broke out in a cold sweat. Everything in the lounge screamed sketchily acquired wealth. Lei having an account did too. However, the guy nodded and crossed the bar.

"Everyone with anything in our line of work ends up here eventually," the man explained, digging through the drawers and cabinets for everything he needed for a cup of coffee. "If you've got a friend with an in, you'll have an account here eventually." I nodded when he glanced my way as the machine thrummed to life. "No offense, but you're a bit old to be apprenticed. That's not your master, right?"

"Not my teacher."

His brows furrowed, but a ding drew his attention back to his coffee. "Everybody's probably checking in with the Wild Hunt causing a mess."

One question answered – definitely a hunter. "Didn't know there was anyone else in Rochester."

One of his brows rose, and his lips curled into a smirk. "Rochester? Nah, I'm entering from the Boston warp." With a steaming cup in hand, he faced me. "First timer, right? Not a bad spell, right? The Daughters would be put out if they found out we've got a warp up and about in risky territory, but…" He pressed a finger to his lips with a wink. "That's our little secret."

There was no way I had stepped through a warp. My stomach turned every time I went through one, and I hadn't felt a thing. Not wanting to mess with the guy, I nodded along, wondering why I had followed Lei.

Checking his watch again, the man grumbled, "My meeting was meant to start five minutes ago."

"Don't know what to tell you," I replied with a shrug.

The man smiled. His dark eyes danced as he brushed off the front of his suit jacket as he stood. "Tell the Broker I'll see him at this time tomorrow."

Before he sauntered away, I called out, "He'll probably want a name."

"Maclyn," he said, offering his hand. When I took it, he gave it one solid up and down shake. "Maclyn Hepburn."

"Like Audrey?"

With a chuckle, Maclyn grinned. "No relation, unfortunately."

"I'll let him know you'll be here tomorrow," I promised, and he swaggered down the stairs and out the door.

When the door swung closed behind him, the door to the Broker's office opened. Exiting the broker's office, Lei rolled his shoulders. "Time to go, stupid-me."

"You know you didn't have to say anything. Just 'time to go' would've been fine," I grumbled. Turning to the broker, I said, "Some guy named Maclyn Hepburn said he had a meeting with you."

Brows rising, the broker nodded but said nothing. Through the open door, I could see piles of boxes resting where there had been none. Leaning against his desk, the broker held his glasses in one hand. He didn't seem tired. No circles were beneath his eyes, and his face wasn't gaunt, but what kind of broker was open nearer to midnight than to normal work hours? He had to be some kind of gang financier. Eyes almost as black as Lei's glanced up at me, and I ducked my head, following Lei.

"Is your broker…"I trailed off uncertain if we were a safe distance even as the thick metal door closed, locking automatically behind us.

The demon merely shrugged. "Broker is what the broker is."

"Guy gets you cash when you need it from stuff you hoard, so no questions, right?"

Pointing across the street, Lei sighed. "Bigger problems."

All along the opposite side of the street, yeth sat. Ice gathered around them. It covered the buildings on both sides and spread out like waves across the street. All of the street lamps on that side were busted. Above us, the electricity snapped, and the casing creaked. Any moment, they could blow.

"Why would they attack now? You're more powerful, aren't you?" I asked even as I dug my lighter from my pocket.

Lei's tongue darted out to wet his top lip. Dark, pointed, and black, it moved in tandem with his void which spread out, crawling up the wall behind us as his chin tucked into his chest. The glinting gold of his rings sparkled before spreading to encase his fingers like a gauntlet.

"I am hungry," he confessed.

I stepped back, inching toward the nearest working street lamp. "Should I run and leave you to it?"

"I might get a bit too rowdy if you try to run right now," he admitted, and the lights snapped from where we stood down either side of from us, blanketing the street in darkness.

His void twisted. Tendrils shot out, bending the lamps into curled pretzels as his eyes trained on the yeth. Black flooded his eyes. They filled with it like ink until there was nothing but hollow black holes. Large black wings lifted. They dripped, shimmering like an oil slick. From the top of Lei's head to the swirling void at his feet, they curled before snapping out, sending sludge flying.

The yeth did not charge. Prowling, the hounds watched, rounding and looping each other. Even though I reinforced my shield, the cold pressed against it, eating away at the warm like acid eroding flesh. My thumb flicked the lighter, and as a stripe of fire encircled me, Lei's hand shoved the air in my direction, sending me flying back as he flew forward. The shadows of his void, all along the building, writhed and stretched. They curved around my shield, holding me in place even as they sizzled against the light and heat.

I could do nothing but watch as Lei devoured them. He dug his teeth into their flesh, rending it from the bone as his void pulled them in and swallowed them whole. The more he feasted, the more color drained from him until he was entirely black and white. His pale skin glared like paper against the black ink of his features. Cracking like whips, the tendrils of his void slammed the hounds of Hell, shredding and piercing and tearing until their corpses shattered to dust, and even that, Lei's void consumed. All in the span of a minute.

When the feast ended, Lei's void dropped, slinking back into his shadow, and like a drunk, he stumbled down the street toward the apartment, calling, "Come along, stupid-me" over his shoulder. While slow and steady had gotten us to the broker fine, he flashed here and there, bouncing ahead and back, leaping miles only to stumble back half as many.

When we made it back to the apartment, Lei fell over the back of his coach. His void slithered back beneath, and the suit slid right off – just another extension of his connection to Hell. Left in his ordinary tracksuit, he pressed his face into a pillow. One eye stared at the screens, but nothing played across them. The other eye remained closed, or at least, out of sight and pressed up against the pillow.

Shutting the door, I sighed, shedding my shoes and jacket. Staying for the night hadn't been my plan, but as the adrenaline waned, exhaustion weighed me down. Glaring down at the demon, I inched around the couch, nearly jumping out of my skin when the bathroom door opened. Steam billowed out, and Jordan stemmed out in pajama pants.

"Shit!" I exclaimed. Lei remained where he had been. "Lei said you were gone."

"I was. Now I'm back," he replied. His eyes traced over me then Lei.

"We went to the broker." Up went an eyebrow, and words tumbled out of me. "There was a pack of yeth. He ate them."

With a hum, he slung his towel around his shoulders, flicking his wrist at Lei to send a blanket down on top of him. "He'll be digesting for a while then."

Retreating into his room, he tossed the towel over the door and pulled out a drawer, tossing on a plain white shirt. I, however, stood frozen. Giuseppe being in town seemed a more pressing issue, but if Jordan was back, did that mean the lead was just a dead end? Or was my dad here? Nothing in the apartment stood out. As Lei zoned out on the couch, the remaining mess around the coffee table and kitchen stood about at normal levels. The guest room's door remained closed, but that didn't mean my dad was inside.

"Think Giuseppe had something to do with the draugr?" I asked, forcing my eyes back on Jordan who shrugged.

"If Giuseppe's around, that'd be a safe bet."

I drummed my fingers against my side. "And Jokul?"

Bowing his head, Jordan sighed. With a wave of his hand, he beckoned me inside as he sat down on the bed. Leaning against his bureau, I tried to keep my cool. It didn't matter what my dad said. Plenty of people never knew their dads. They were fine. I didn't need his approval.

"It was a dead end."

And the floor seemed to fall out from underneath my feet. "What?"

"Chasing Jokul is complicated. We grew up together. He knows where I'm weak, and Source or not, there are certain things I'm just not good at. I had hoped Lei could keep his mouth shut if you came around, but I see I'll have to keep him out of the loop. I don't want to keep getting your hopes up," Jordan explained.

My eyes narrowed. "You can tell me," I pushed. His brows furrowed, so I added, "If he doesn't want me, I mean – you can tell me. I can take it."

"That's…that's not what I meant."

"You can sense all the magic users, and the only reason you said you were having problems honing in on Conall was that he was in Hell, so…" I held out my hands. "What am I supposed to believe?"

"That my brother knows how to hide from me better than a random corrupted wizard," he said, running a hand over his face. "George wasn't lying. Your father had some prophetic abilities, but they weren't – they weren't clairvoyance or anything. He was an empath. I don't have any sort of blessing. I didn't inherit any prophet shit. I'm just an overpowered wizard with radar that some people can feel. Jokul trained with me. He knows when I'm looking. He can warp in and out of Hell whenever it's convenient, or he can bounce away when I get a lock. He can't leech off me. My well is kind of untappable, but he's not connected with my magic." Jordan met my eyes, and the panicked desperation to not say exactly the full truth struck me cold.

They weren't connected by their magic. Jordan had let my father into his head, and for all I could try to push Conall's influence aside, I had never given him permission to set up shop. Not the way Wolfram had.

"Why would you let anyone in your head?"

"He's my brother. We were born together, and until Jukka, he was my moral compass. I could muscle through the abuse, but Jokul learned how to read people. Everyone said he was the one who was good. Why wouldn't I let him in?" Jordan retorted gritting out the words as if they had been repeated over and over in his head, but he still hadn't found a way to finish the thought and rationalize what he now realized had been a mistake.

"And the Daughters?" I pressed. "Couldn't they help?"

His lips pulled into a thin smile. The expression failed to reach his eyes which remained flooded with exhaustion. "Empaths are rare, and Jokul hasn't done anything to warrant being found. Avoiding me isn't exactly a problem as far as they are concerned."

"So what you're telling me is that you have a worse bond inside of you, and you can't even help me deal with the one I've been stuck with?" Sucking on my teeth, I pushed the rage down, but it bubbled up nonetheless. "If you can't kick an empath off you, how am I supposed to keep Conall out?"

Jordan shook his head. His gaze dropped to the floor, and rubbing the back of his head, he let out a long exhale. "He can send influence up through Hell, but he doesn't have you on tap like Jokul has with me. Jokul knew what I felt before I felt it. Some days, Ezekiel tortured me over and over, locking Jokul in the basement or in our room, and sharing thoughts with him was all I had to not go absolutely insane."

"Then why didn't you fight back?"

"I was a child, Jon!" Jordan yelled, standing with his fists clenched at his side. "He was my father, and we didn't have anywhere else to go." Closing his eyes, he shook his head and bit his lip. In a softer tone, he continued, "You don't trust Conall. You never trusted Conall, so keeping him out shouldn't be a problem because the only emotions you should associate with him are negative." He ran a hand through his damp, bleached white hair. Sagging back onto the bed, he released a shuddering breath. In a brittle voice, he said, "Just go home, Jon."

A chill rolled down my spine. Sharp pricks itched at the corners of my eyes, leaving me to sniff to drain the thick dread gathering in my throat. Pushing off the bureau, I shoved my hands into my pockets. Jordan remained silent. He didn't look up. Instead, he rubbed his eyes with the knuckle of his thumb. His lips pressed tightly together. Each exhale followed a measured inhale. Ducking my head, I skulked toward the door.

"You don't have to stay," I murmured, standing just outside his room. "If you don't want to teach me, I can figure things out. The Daughters would be happier too, right?" Glaring down at Lei's catatonic form, I resisted the urge to kick the couch. He probably wouldn't wake, and even with Jordan's live-in demonic translator up, the demon could just as readily make things worse. "I don't know who you promised that you were going to teach me or whatever. My dad doesn't care, so you can go if it's easier, or you know, we could just not meet up."

Jordan bowed his head. "If I'm not training you, you'll have to go back to Boston."

"Yeah, that's not happening. But this?" I gestured between us. "It's not really working either."

A beat passed in silence then another. Buzzing drilled along the back of my skull, and this time, I couldn't begin to guess what Conall wanted of me. Pushing the pain down, I glared at my feet, gritting through my frustration before I grabbed my jacket and shoes. Jordan didn't even offer to warp me back. I could barely stand, but my teacher – my uncle sent me back into the cold. Wild Hunt be damned. If he was willing to warp himself, he should've been willing to do it for me too. As I raced across the city, doubt crept into my heart. If the wind grew colder over the Genesee, the havfine stayed under the river's surface, and any others kept their distance, so by the time, I collapsed into my bed, tears froze to my face, and my headache quickly pulled me under.

Chapter Twelve

Realistic dreams were the worst. Sitting in the rickety sun porch where I had first seen the Devil's face, I leaned back, watching the silver wind swirl around the house and waited to wake up. The wind didn't howl. Instead, the phone rang. Plastic covered in lime green, the phone rattled. The long, curling tail of its wire vibrated with each intonation, but no matter how many rings passed, the call never ended.

"This might be worse than no dreams," I grumbled, wrapping my arms around me as I let my head roll back and eyes slide shut. The window panes shook. Glass shivered against wood, and the Devil stood, staring inward when I opened my eyes. "He's not here," I informed him. "Not that you are either, but the Devil wouldn't be here for me, right?"

Tilting his head, Lucifer watched me. His pale face flickered between round childhood and harsh angles of adulthood. Silver hair and violet eyes – if he was once the favorite, whoever judged that must have had as shit taste in looks as they did in character. He was pretty in the way mercury was.

When the door slammed and woke me, I groaned and curled up further beneath the blankets. Wednesdays were the best. No classes on Wednesdays. I fought with Jordan, so no going to the bookshop hoping for a lesson when Jordan wouldn't show up anyway. Shuffling steps trudged into the room, and Tyson chucked his bag down on his desk before collapsing onto my bed, sprawling like he owned the place.

"You awake?" he asked.

Kicking at him, I griped, "Today is Wednesday. Let me enjoy mini-weekend."

"Did you meet with Voigt early or something? I can't believe you went back to bed and ditched me. If you were meeting early, you should've texted. Mike and I waited for you. You never answered your phone," Tyson accused elbowing me in the back.

"What? I didn't change my meeting. Wait – what time is it?" Grabbing my phone, I checked the time. "Shit!"

I threw off my covers, sending Tyson flying across the room half with the force of my foot in his side and half from the crack of my magic which wriggled like a parasite beneath my skin, clawing its way to the surface. Dressing as quickly as possible, I raced out the door, slipping on my shoes and completely forgetting my jacket until I was already racing out of the apartment complex and into the frigid cold. Although the snow had melted some the day before, it froze against over the previous night, leaving the sidewalks and streets still covered in slick black ice.

Wrapping hot air around me, I melted the ice with each step as I league-walked my way to campus. Students rushed from building to building huddled together like penguins as they walked across the faux tundra of the river-side campus. Their gaunt faces flushed. Skittering from one harsh

224

stop to the next, I curved around the labyrinth of mortals. When I threw open the door, wind rippled back, and a girl stumbled. Her arms flew out to balance, but she only managed to slap her friends down around her like dominos. Slowing to a mortal run, I ignored the exclamations as water poured off the restrooms followed by students jumping around the water. Pins leaped from bulletin boards as I passed. Power surged; students cursed as computers rebooted, and the lights buzzed.

Professor Voigt's door stood closed. As the light overhead dimmed then flashed twice before dimming again, I took a deep breath and exhaled slowly, urging my pulse to slow until the flickering lights snapped back to normal. Then, I knocked. "Professor Voigt?" I called, opening the door. "I'm Jon Blythe. Sorry, I'm running a bit late."

Sitting behind his desk, Professor Voigt was a younger middle-aged man with somewhat static-ridden brown hair and bright blue eyes. Though he was wearing a collared shirt and an expensive watch, the fitted knit jumper mitigated the intimidation factor somewhat. With a bright smile, he waved at the chair across from him.

"I'm a fan of the ten-minute leeway as I, myself, have a habit of causing my meetings to run longer than intended," he informed me. His eyes twinkled conspiratorially. "Now, Jon, you emailed about switching majors?"

"Yes," I told him, sitting down in the chair across from him. "I'm not sure if I want to switch to chemistry or biology, but I do know I want to switch into science. I thought business would be a good choice. There are a lot of options," and accountants made good money, but I wasn't sure I should say that. "But I think I'll just make myself miserable if I don't switch to a major I actually like."

Professor Voigt pressed his palms together, leaning his elbows on the desk. "Are you sure this is the best time to make this decision?"

The carefully measured tone he used to set off sirens in my head. This had to be a trick question. Sighing, I bowed my head. This was the time. I couldn't keep running in two directions. I needed something to ground me. A way out if things went south with Jordan. Something I could do on my own, and business required teamwork. They demanded sleepless nights and careful words. Scientists could be apathetic. Nobody would care in chemistry if I didn't go to the parties or socialize. My circle could tighten. All duties owed would be just to those worth keeping, and Tyson wouldn't breathe over my shoulder with his connections, knowing every time I screwed up.

"I picked business first semester because I wanted to walk out with a job," I told him. "But it's making me miserable. I only stuck with it this long because I've got friends in the course. Physics is honestly the only enjoyable class I'm taking."

"What about French? Would you keep it as a minor?"

Shrugging, I scanned his face for judgment but only found concern. "Maybe after I get a handle on the new major."

"And why not go straight for mathematics?" Voigt pressed.

"That's not useful," I grumbled; the words tumbled out before I could stop them. "Math kind of limits my job options. I don't know where I'm going to end up, but I'd like math to be a part and maybe expand and see whether chemistry or biology is a better fit. Maybe even go the physical therapy route eventually."

A total lie – physical therapy would take extra courses, another degree, and more time than I had, but going straight for chemistry would be hard to explain. Yes, sir, I want to know how to blow up demons in case my uncle decides I shouldn't have magic. Plus, Rochester was a city of engineers. Engineers had to need chemists, right? Considering I wasn't sure I would ever be going home to Boston, and I really didn't want to deal with the magical community I hadn't realized was there in the first place, Rochester was it for me.

"But not physics?" he asked then hummed. "Similar issue, I suppose." When I nodded, he leaned back in his chair and continued, "I'll admit – I spoke with your advisor, Dr. Lyon, and Dr. McClellan. Dr. McClellan is rather fond of you."

That was news. Physics wasn't my weakest subject, and I hadn't screwed up the coursework nearly as badly as my main classes, but it was the only physics course I had, and I blended pretty well with the rest of the students dedicated to just getting through the whole mess. However, the statement suggested an unspoken problem – a first-time professor had more to say about me than my advisor.

"I haven't met with Dr. Lyon since the first semester. He approved my four-year plan, so I've just been sending him stuff to approve as needed," I admitted.

"He didn't seem to understand why you were switching, but said you seemed convinced it was the right move in your email, so he wasn't going to push back as your scholarship isn't course-specific," Voigt informed me. Not like Dr. Lyon had the energy to chase me down. He was overloaded with students. "Dr. Lyon might have been fine with emails, but I meet monthly with my advisees, and I expect to know what is going on in your life from you." His lips pressed into a thin line. "If that isn't something you can live with, you'll need to consider a different advisor." Frowning, he narrowed his eyes as if to read my mind, but before I could respond, he barreled on, "You look exhausted. Are you sleeping enough?"

"Just an unexpected late night."

"Late couple of weeks from what I've heard. Your grades dipped earlier this semester, and while they've gone back up, I'd like to hear what you believe is the cause and how you plan to prevent it going forward," he said, picking up his pen and posing it over his notebook.

Lying would've been easy. I could hit him with Henrietta Scott's death and roll from there. Half-truths would color the relationship between us, but my head hurt, and my eyes ached. I just wanted to sleep.

Taking a deep breath, I let it all out: "Last semester, I met my estranged dad's twin brother – Jordan. He's been trying to find my dad, who may or may not know I exist, for me. Turns out, he probably knows and doesn't want to have anything to do with me. Real great for my ego. My grandparents on my mom's side hate me 'cause I'm a bastard. Like literal – my parents weren't married – hence, my dad might not know I exist."

"Oh," he whispered.

If he planned to say more, he didn't get the chance. I plowed straight on. "Turns out my dad's family is way worse. Mom committed suicide. Father abused them. My best friend's grandmother, who kind of adopted me since moving here, died last month. I was there. Learned some stuff my friend doesn't know. Stuff she definitely didn't want me to know." I paused, debating whether I should include Wolfram, but Dr. Voigt didn't speak, so I fumbled on. "Kid I was trying to help pretended to be his own brother, but he had killed his brother – and some other people."

If his eyebrows rose higher, he would lose them in his hairline. "Killed? Jon, are you in danger?"

Taking another deep breath, I deflated back into the chair, the rest tumbling out. "Probably. A little bit. It's complicated."

"How complicated?"

"Well, most of it is being investigated, so...very?" Before he could say anything, I diverted, "My uncle has a whole laundry list of issues, so dealing with him is complicated, and I'm pretty sure he wants nothing to do with me, but he feels obligated. I have no idea how to deal with any of this."

Professor Voigt blinked. His bright blue eyes stared owlishly at me. Swallowing, he bit his lip and set down his pen. "That is an awful lot to be dealing with while changing majors."

"It's why I have to change majors. It probably doesn't make sense to you, but chemistry or biology makes more sense for where all that is taking me than accounting." Especially as the one businessman in my life hadn't been at my lessons in a bit.

Where was George? He had been in and out lately, so I hadn't considered calling or texting him with how crazy everything had gotten, but maybe I should have talked to him first. George worked from home. Give him a laptop, and he could work from anywhere, so if that was my argument, then there was a huge flaw in my plans, but he was a psychic. The Daughters let them get away without hunting. Hunting pretty much screwed up my chances of a regular nine to five.

"Should I be concerned that your uncle works for the C.I.A. or S.H.I.E.L.D.?" he asked, leaning forward conspiratorially.

"He's Icelandic, so I'm not sure what their version of the C.I.A. is, but why would you be concerned about S.H.I.E.L.D.?" Wrinkling my nose, I scoffed. "If it helps, he's too erratic for Hydra."

Jokingly wiping his brow, Professor Voigt chuckled. "Phew, then I say we set up weekly meetings and attend to this firmly in December when you sign up for spring courses."

"Weekly?" I nearly squeaked, barely able to contain my groan.

He nodded. "Every Wednesday, same time, you and me. We'll figure out if you're more interested in chem or bio. Feel out career goals. Talk about what's going on in your life. If you still want to switch come course sign-ups, we'll be ready. If not, my door is always open."

As if to emphasize this fact, the door opened. Professor McClellan ducked through the small gap in the door. "Apologies, I did not realize you were busy."

"Ah!" Professor Voigt smiled. The twinkle returned to his bright blue eyes. "You have perfect timing. Jon and I have just concluded." His brows then furrowed as he glanced back at me. "Unless you had anything else you needed."

"No – I'm good," I said. Thankfully, my lateness meant I had nothing to gather as I stood and headed toward the door.

McClellan remained in the doorway, blocking my way with a tight smile. "Though I'm happy to see you in the sciences at all, I still believe physics would be a better fit." His steel-like gaze glanced over my shoulder at Voigt. "Did Jon tell you he slept through all but the last ten minutes of his midterm and still got an A?"

"Wait – I got an A?"

A single blond brow rose, and the physics professor smirked. "Just think what you could do if you weren't stumbling around half-dead from exhaustion." Before I could even think up an excuse, McClellan shrugged. "Jordan explained the situation. Next time, however, I would prefer to hear it directly from you. Your grades don't have to be slipping for your teachers to be concerned about you."

I blinked, glancing back at Voigt who cleared his desk and slipped on his coat following me out into the hall as McClellan stepped back to let me through. Like rusty gears, my brain churned to phrase the mix of indignation, shock, and embarrassment running through me.

"Jordan contacted you?" I asked when my mind failed.

McClellan nodded. "Came to my office hours. Your uncle really cares about you."

Gaping, I stood awkwardly as Voigt hummed. "I'll see you next week, Jon, but feel free to call or email me if you need anything."

"Sure. Thanks." I muttered as the two headed off, and even though I should've headed out the same way. I stepped around the corner, tugging my cell phone out as I threw up an illusion to blend me into the wall. It wasn't the best I'd ever done, but with a sound barrier, nobody would hopefully see me before I saw them. The phone rang only once before Jordan picked up, but the second he started on a hello, I talked right on, "You aren't my father. You have no right to contact my professor or show up on campus. I'm in college. Seriously Jordan? I'm eighteen years old. I'm not some little kid who needs you to step up for parent-teacher conferences."

Hanging up, I screamed and kicked the wall. Cracks shot out from the point of impact. Overhead, the lights flickered. Collapsing into a crouch, I wrapped my arms around my knees, breathing slowly even as the buzzing returned to the back of my skull. Darkness bled along the edges of my vision. In the black, a figure stood. Thin and tall – even without the copper of his hair, I recognized Conall. Swiping a handout, I shoved up onto my feet, storming out of the hall.

The ground slipped, tilting beneath my feet. My hands trembled. On the edge of my mind, his lilting voice whispered, "Nobody could stop you if you ran."

Biting back the bitter retorts uselessly finding their way to my tongue, I slammed against the wall, bursting forward with a step that shattered the door from its hinges as I league-walked. Students screamed. Their voices traveled like a tidal wave, but the noise couldn't drown Conall's footsteps though he didn't have to walk to follow me. His influence itched against my consciousness. A cord tied us together. Phones rang in my mind when my ears couldn't hear a thing.

"Jon?" a hand landed on my shoulder, and I spun, dragging my finger down the lighter, but before I could swing out, Mike's face came into view. "Man, you look like shit."

I dropped the lighter back in my pocket. "I'm fine. Just…"

"Did you hear an explosion?" Pulling me aside, he searched behind me. "We should get into a room or something. It could be a –"

Pushing him away, I shook my head. "It wasn't anything. I think pipes burst or something – poor construction or something."

"People were screaming."

Rubbing my eyes, I groaned. "Why are you even on campus? You only have one morning class."

"An endearing as it is that you know my schedule, I do study at the library sometimes. Unlike you, I don't have an apartment, so I still get sexiled," Mike complained, crossing his arms over his chest.

"And you ran out here after hearing an explosion?" Of course, he did. Because nobody can trust me to take care of myself. "You should've stayed put."

Mike shrugged. "Well, I'm here now."

Sirens echoed in the distance. Grabbing Mike's arm, I guided him further away from the building. "If your roommate kicked you out, you can always come over the apartment."

"Well, that was the plan for later. I've got dibs on your couch," he replied, twisting out of my grip, but he kept walking right alongside me. "You sure you're okay. I can't afford to get sick right now."

"I'm fine."

Forcing my feet to stay under me, I focused on keeping my pace steady. Mike filled the silence, jabbering on about courses and clubs. If he found my silence strange, he didn't comment. My eyes traced the Genesee as we crossed. Gold shimmered beneath the waves. Unless some idiot had gone and gold-plated a fish, the havfine stuck close to the surface even as the sun broke the clouds. All the way home, the phone in my head rang. Conall's phantom followed.

Chapter Thirteen

Saturday meant Jordan would be at the Grith, so I couldn't wait until the weekend. From my last Thursday class, I raced northward, lifting my steps gradually until I soared above the city. Rochester's sprawl thinned until Lake Ontario churned beneath me. Snow and ice gathered on the shores. Howling carried, but whether yeth or wind or dogs, I couldn't tell.

When I landed in Toronto, Leta stood, waiting on the pier. "This is a bad idea."

"Then you should have told Monday," I retorted as we fell into step.

"If I told him, he'd have to tell Ros who would tell the Daughters. They'd think you were going rogue," she warned, shoving her gloved hands into her jacket pockets. The bobble on the top of her knit had bounced as we bounced between leagues and feet, before falling completely to a mortal pace. "You could join us, you know. Helena and I – there's a reason the Daughters do things in groups of three. You could be our third."

"Thanks. I'll think about it." Throwing up an illusion, I watched her expression for approval, but she threw up her hands with a huff and kept walking. "Can you still see me? Where did I mess up?"

She pointed out a few spots, patiently waiting for me to adjust until she moved from one to the next. When satisfied with my illusion, she waved at the gate as we strode up to the Grith. The outer wall opened, and Helena ushered us inside. The illusion held through the walls. Whoever watched either ignored me or couldn't see me enter beside Leta. Benny skipped back and forth on the porch, rushing across the yard when Leta and Helena came into view. The kid launched himself at Helena's legs, and she smoothly lifted him off the ground.

"Theda's on guard," the little wizard whispered.

Leta's brows pulled together. "Again? Do they want him to escape? This is her third straight shift."

"Ros has to report to the Daughters on the progress of the teaching plan. Kasimira is dropping off another group with the Sons, and as long as warps are a no go that means mortal methods, and she got stuck in traffic getting to the airport," Helena explained.

"And Monday needs to focus on maintaining the outer wards," Leta filled in for her sister with a growl. "We're surrounded by idiots."
"Papa Monday isn't an idiot," Benny argued.

Once the door closed behind us, I whispered, "Why haven't they found a placement for Benny yet? He's the youngest."

"This isn't an orphanage," Leta hissed. "The cute ones aren't adopted first."

"Older and extended family options go first. Older can fight – less training needed. Not to mention, this one refuses to leave Monday," Helena said, fake dropping Benny only to catch him and send the boy into a fit of giggles.

"And you're sure this is going to work? I get she's tired, but if Monday's around, won't she just call for him? Or anyone? Seriously, there's still a ridiculous amount of other people here," I reminded her.

Leta and Helena glanced at each other, rolling their eyes in unison. Putting Benny back on the ground, Helena patted his head, and he went off like a lightning bolt. Up and around the stairs until he jogged down on the ceiling to land outside the hall to Wolfram's cell.

"Theda!" he cried out. "I can't find Papa Monday or Ros anywhere!"

Dread pooled in my stomach. "Tell me my mind is in the gutter, and this isn't your actual plan."

"Well – we couldn't find Monday to get him out of the house, so…" Leta trailed off.

Theda stormed over to Benny. "Benjamin, go back upstairs. Play quietly."

"But all the big kids are in their rooms, and nobody will play with me," he retorted, sticking out his bottom lip and wobbling his chin. When Theda just cocked a brow and stood her ground, he crossed his arms and stomped his foot. "I'm going to go see Jordan!"

"You aren't going to see Jordan. If you're bored, read a book," Theda commanded.

She obviously wasn't leaving, and I had managed to get by Kasimira last time, so I went for it. Benny continued to loudly complain about the lack of attention, sending sparks out his fingers and literally bouncing off the walls. As I walked right by, Theda's head snapped in my direction. Her eyes flicked over the wall, but she didn't acknowledge me and refocused back on Benny.

Wolfram was worse than before. Blood smeared across the walls of his cell, shimmering as the wounds activated as he smashed his fists against them. Each hit had another splatter being added. White showed through the red. When I crossed into the room, he roared and slammed his forehead against the runes.

Out went the illusion, blocking the camera and replicating the repetitive slamming of Wolfram's fists. The second I came into view, Wolfram slid down the wall with a groan, "It's like putting a steak outside a starving dog's cage."

"Am I the steak? Or just the plate?" I retorted.

He rolled his head around, landing at an odd angle against the floor as he glared. "What do you want, Blythe?"

"Did you release a draugr?"

"I didn't," he replied, flashing a bloody grin.

"Who did?"

He ran a hand through his dark hair. "What will you give me if I help you?"

"What do you want?"

On the floor, Wolfram tilted back his head against the wall. "You're so stupid. Haven't you learned open ended questions like that never end well?"

"Works well on an iggit," I retorted.

"But not on magic users. Try again," he prompted.

It was like talking to a brick wall. He knew. His smug stupid face kept smirking up at me, and this whole mess revolved around him. Conall only latched onto me because Wolfram had me pinged as the weak link. Mortal-raised hung over my head. For users, it was pretty much a synonym for gullible and easy target.

And maybe they were right. "What do you want?"

Snorting, the mage rolled his eyes. "What do I want?" Wolfram's smile spread across his face like a knife. "Jordan has told you deals are important in the magical community. We could agree on my help for my freedom, but we both know the Daughters would love to interpret that as death, and I'm not partial to dying."

"I wasn't thinking about any of this."

Rolling his eyes, he pushed off the floor. "Genies weren't just inspired by deals with demons." He stretched and shook out his limbs. "I could ask for better food or it to be actually served at regular times rather than in an attempt to mess up by internal clock, but it could end up rotten."

"We aren't making a deal. I'm asking you what you want – not promising to give you it," I said, crossing my arms over my chest.

"You can't give me what I want."

"Wolfram…"

Away went the smile. "I want Conall. I don't care if the Erlkonig is dead or has simply abandoned him, but I want Conall broken and in this cell – nothing separately us. No walls, no chains, no glass, no spells – nothing."

"So you can kill him?" I asked. "Or screw him?"

His lips curled into a smirk. "Do you even care?"

"I think the Daughters would care," I pointed out, but as much as I wanted to pretend I didn't care, the idea of either of the two having momentary happiness bothered me. "Answer the question."

"I don't know. He kills me. I kill him." Wolfram paced the length of his cell. "Knowing would be better than not."

"Only problem is that if he kills you, Conall goes full demon."

Wolfram hummed. "Maybe."

"Yeah, that's never going to happen."

He shifted his weight from side to side, glancing down at his feet. "You asked."

"Do you seriously have a death wish?" I shook my head. "I don't know why I'm even asking you. You willingly went into Shiloh's void. Was that all for Conall?" Cocking a brow at me, he smirked, and I groaned. "And you call me an idiot?"

"Smarter than you – though I won't deny I have a tendency for the dramatic," he replied, leaning back against the far wall.

"Dramatic?" I scoffed. "You're not dramatic. You're certifiable."

Wolfram closed his eyes and let out a soft sigh. "Perhaps. After all these long *conversations* with the Jaegers, I'm rather exhausted." His dark eyes snapped open, flashing as they met my gaze. He seemed grounded in a way I hadn't seen even when he had played Wilhelm. "Conall is Conall. He'll make a choice, one way or another."

"You realize you won't win that, right?" I told him. "He's already picked the Erlkonig twice."

Wolfram shrugged. "Yet here I am."

"You honestly think you can win against the second most powerful demon in Hell? The one demon who could probably talk the Devil into apologizing to God if he wanted?" I scoffed. This guy was insane.

His lips peeled back into another bloody smile as his eyes slid shut. "Conall and I used to meet in this field outside the village. One day, this stag comes. Big enough to feed my whole family for weeks, but I hesitated. It was too magnificent. Conall didn't. He never did. I've dreamt about that field every night in here." Opening his eyes, he stared at me with eyes so black they almost looked like buttons sewn onto the pale fabric of his face. "Conall's unconscious. The last time he was hurt and alone...you're all he has. Convince him that he made a mistake."

"Now I know you're screwing with me. I'm not going to be your co-dependent frenemy's therapist," I retorted.

"The Erlkonig will expect him to kill me. Once he wakes up, he'll ignore you."

Pacing, I growled, "Great. That's some great advice. Last until he wakes up and the Wild Hunt comes back around. If you want even the hope of my help, tell me who released the draugr."

"It won't help."

"Just tell me!" I raged. Wolfram shrugged, offering me nothing. "A half-frozen Victorian will murder us all because you can't get over losing the gingered personification of manipulative narcissism to demon Genghis Khan!"

"Who?" he asked.

I gaped at him then threw my hands up. "Seriously? Nothing? You're absolutely useless. Why are they keeping you alive?"

Brushing the blood off his wounds, Wolfram clucked his tongue. "Pay attention to patterns." I narrowed my eyes, glaring at him. "The Wild Hunt bides their time. If they wanted to release a draugr, they'd wait until Conall was awake."

"I don't think the Wild Hunt let her out. I'm pretty sure an ex-mage did."

His brows furrowed. "If the draugr was rune-locked, only a magic user could let them out."

If Wolfram told the truth, Giuseppe either released the draugr beforehand or somebody else had done it. Considering the draugr hadn't struck in the last few days, waiting wasn't completely out of left field, so maybe she took some time to adjust first. Then again, it had been months since the summoning. Her effects froze everything. She

244

couldn't have hidden that long, and the yeth couldn't be a coincidence. Or they were. Yeth hung out in the Wild Hunt. Those hounds pretty much showed up everywhere. Maybe they could reproduce. That would explain why there were so many of them.

"You look constipated. I'm going to assume you're thinking, which means I said something useful, and you owe me," Wolfram concluded, wiping his hand through the drying blood, smearing it further on the glass. "Today's Thursday, right? I wonder if they'll hose this off before then." Rolling his eyes, he huffed. "I'd take a down payment in you letting me talk to Conall through you. Tell him there's nothing to forgive, and –."

"Screw this. I'm done," I spat, pulling the illusion tight back around me.

Unlike last time, Wolfram didn't call or scream after me. His fists went right back into punching the wards. Gliding right by Theda and Benny, I slid up beside Leta. "That was under five minutes, right?"

Helena sighed, pushing away from where she leaned against the wall to go and collect Benny while Leta and I headed back up the stairs. Running a hand through her hair, she asked, "You manage to get anything useful?"

"Wolfram's relationship with Conall is disturbing. Conall will likely ignore me once he's awake – which is really not helpful right now, and I still can't tell when he's lying or not. This was entirely a waste of my time and yours. I thought there was an off chance he released the draugr," I explained, rubbing my eyes with a groan. "He didn't, but he knows who did. Giuseppe wouldn't make sense – no magic, no runes opened right? But the Wild Hunt doesn't make sense either."

Leta snorted. "I think we learned something."
"Like what?"

Side by side, we headed up the stairs. Helena followed close behind with Benny who skipped up the stairs two at a time. "You knew this would be pretty much useless, but you came anyways."

"I thought he'd know something useful," I argued.

Helena let out a single huff of laughter. "Think about it harder."

My immediate instinct was to leave. I had come. Nothing useful had happened, and going home to eat my weight in junk food seemed the best option. A strange unease settled over me. Closing my eyes, I concentrated inward. Thoughts of my mother conflicted with my father. My go-to soul fuel festered, corrupted by reality until faith dwindled. My memory of Nonno Cataldo helped. A bit of a blaze shimmered, and grabbing hold of it, I stretched the shine as far as I could. The unease grew, and the desire to flee evaporated as did all the subtle rationalizations of why I had come. Wolfram had nothing to give. Exhausting myself, traveling over the havfine, none of it made sense.

"Crap." I had been played. The further I got from the wards, the strange headache didn't return; instead, a strange content feeling settled over me like when a cat settled in your lap when it avoided everybody else. "Seriously? This is how he influences me?"

"Conall sent his side piece to check his main squeeze," Leta joked as her sister handed Benny a chocolate bar and sent him off on his way.

"That's probably why Theda let you through. No point blocking you when Conall would probably make things worse," Helena informed me.

Of course, Theda had known I was there. I made all the same mistakes, thinking I was better than them. Better than the Daughters. Better than Jordan. Conall nudged, and like an arrogant brat, I ate up every second, believing I knew what I was doing. Rubbing my hands over my face, I groaned.

"I'm an idiot," I murmured into my hands.

Patting me on the shoulder, Leta said, "Maybe you should have Jordan check you out."

"We're not exactly seeing eye to eye lately," I admitted.

Helena crossed her arms over her chest. "I'd say go to Monday, but I'm betting you don't trust him more than Jordan." With a sigh, she gestured toward the top of the stairs. "Leta told you, right? You could join us. Three heads are better than one, and you've got more problems than one head – or even two can handle."

I had nothing but a shrug to offer her. The twins watched me. Judgment weighed equal to concern in their eyes, and I had little doubt a bit of their generosity had everything to do with wanting to watch the disaster unfold. They liked a good story just as much as Lei.

"I'll think about it," I offered. "And I'll talk with George."

Their eyes slid off me. Helena shook her head, and Leta's brows pinched as she said, "George isn't here anymore, Jon."

"What?"

"The Anastasius – the entire family in North America headed back to Greece after the draugr showed up," she explained. "Between that and the Wild Hunt, it was too dangerous for any sort of prophet – no matter how far removed."

"He couldn't have…I mean, he didn't…nobody…" I struggled for anything, grabbing at words to try to rationalize the panic settling in like it was making a second home.

I fumbled with my phone, but I couldn't even do that. I didn't have the cell plan to get anything in or out of Canada. A hunk of metal and plastic sat in my hand. No text to be found to explain why I had been abandoned again. I could think it out. George wanted to protect his children, his wife, and his whole family. Whenever possible, the Erlkonig hunted prophets. A family line would've been just too good to resist. Anything could happen, and nobody had bothered to tell me. Was I that insignificant?

"That's probably the safest bet, but all those prophets in one place…" I climbed the stairs as I continued, "If the Hunt decides to head that way, they might end up like Henrietta Scott's family."

"Who are the Scotts?" Leta asked.

"It doesn't matter. I'm sure George thought it through carefully -" when he left me in the lurch.

"I don't know. There was a call from the Elders, and everyone panicked because they couldn't reach George. Monday called Jordan. It was a whole thing," Leta said.

Before we reached the top, I pulled my illusion back up around me. Helena rolled her eyes, but plausible deniability was useful. The hall stood empty. Muffled voices filled the emptiness. Though hidden from view and cautious to keep my voice from carrying too far, being in the Grith squeezed tight around me like a vice.

"Maybe you should stay away for a while," Helena suggested.

Leta frowned. "Why would he stay away?"

"Just until he's figured out how to block Conall," Helena elaborated, holding her hands up as if to show she wasn't armed.

Annoyance flared in the back of my mind right alongside the buzzing, but assuming it was Conall, I flashed my soul, pushing him away until the annoyance simmered to reluctant agreement. Until I had my head on straight, my presence put everybody at risk. Even the illusion on my back picked away at Monday's wards.

With a sigh, I said, "You're right. You guys don't need to be worrying about me on top of everything else."

"It's not like they let us do anything. They've already sent every available Daughter to cull any weak links in the area to keep the Hunt from getting bigger. Jordan and Monday don't want anyone new between Toronto and Rochester, so we're stuck going south if we want any practice," Leta complained, setting her hands on her hips. "Do you know how many rivers I've cleared and re-cleared?"

Wrapping an arm around her sister's shoulders, Helena smiled. "We'll message you when we go on a hunt down your way."

"Same," I offered as they headed out through the gate.

If any of the other students were concerned about Leta's comings and goings, they didn't comment, and if they wanted to interrogate the twins afterward, they were both smarter than me and could lie well enough on their own.

Launching over Lake Ontario was more difficult without Conall motivating me. By the time I landed back in the States, Conall's smug primping over my discomfort lingered like bile on the back of my tongue. Storming southward, I followed the buzz. A British police box stood in the darkness of my mind.

Pulling out the phone, I growled into the speaker, "Do you mind?"

"Not at all," Conall cheerfully replied. "In fact, I'm so thankful for your assistance that I've decided to help you with your draugr conundrum."

"And how exactly would you do that?"

"Your draugr died on April 19, 1922," Conall informed me.

"Her name?"

"Unfortunately, I don't have that bit. My source happened to recall a wizard being killed and stored in the subway tunnels running beneath Rochester on that date. A mafia kill, I'm afraid, associated with a Mr. Porter and his demon companion, Lately," the copper-haired wizard explained. The box melted. A glass wall stretched between us with the phone wire coiled through where Conall stood on the opposite side. "I have it on good authority your bookkeeper has a journal from an alchemist in the area at the time of the murder."

"How can I trust you?" I growled.

Conall's lips curled into a smile, and the void of Hell expanded behind him. "I've got nothing to lose by telling you."

My eyes narrowed as I demanded, "But what do you have to gain?"

"Jonathan, you've seen what I can do with the dead," he said, pressing a long-fingered hand to his chest even as I flinched at the reminder of Gerhard. "Draugr are my specialty, and they are few and far between. The knowledge you gain hunting one is more than enough compensation for me."

Like pins pressing into my skin, the cold pressed against my defenses. Clay and metal - fragments of flesh scattered and burned, sinking into the ground. A letter almost formed a word, and the echoes would never stop ringing in my ears.

"I must be more sleep deprived than I thought to even consider listening to you," I spat, flaring my soul and isolating the connection in mind.

When my focus turned outward, my feet had taken me exactly where I hadn't wanted to go. There wasn't even a sign in the lawn marking George's home for sale. Just a large house with a picture-perfect green lawn, white picket fence ideal with a swing in the big tree in the front yard and the remnants of chalk drawings on the driveway. If I stayed too long, the neighbors would get nervous. I didn't want them thinking I was casing the place, but my feet stuck to the ground as if covered in cement. There was probably a German word for the feeling. Before me stood a house, which represented a dream - an ideal possibility and seeing it stand empty left me empty in return.

Shoving my hands in my pockets, I ducked my head and headed out. As small as the world could be with a single league step, Rochester towered over me. The shimmering surfaces of glass, metal, and stone loomed like giants, watching me spiral. Every part of my body ached, and I just wanted to curl up on my bed and never leave it, but if I hid there in the soft darkness, nothing would get better. Jordan twisted me around. The Grith and its occupants were too busy to deal with my issues, and even if they had time, their solutions ignored the point of my complaints.

I landed on the corner where Tyson and I had run into Giuseppe. The ex-mage hadn't showed up since. His appearance, however, couldn't be a coincidence. He had to have released the draugr. Not that that helped. Draugrs weren't demons. None of the books Jordan gave me had more than the basics: 1) draugrs were dead wizards; 2) until they decayed, heat worked, but light didn't; and 3) runes worked on them. If Jordan's library failed me, there was on either place I could go with the Grith and George out of the question, so I set one foot in front of the other and headed to the bookshop.

Entering the shop, I waved. "Hi."

"Good evening, Jon. Did you and Jordan have a lesson planned for this evening?" When I shook my head, he continued, "I'm afraid if you were looking for Jordan, you just missed him."

"I'm not here for Jordan."

Frowning, Solomon pushed aside the pile of books he had been going through. His brows furrowed. "Is something the matter, Jon?"

"I'm switching to biology or chemistry," I admitted.

Solomon cocked a nearly invisible white brow. "A rather significant change."

"Will you help me?" I asked. "Please?"

His long, pale fingers scratched at the side of his head, causing the whirlwind of white hair on his head to stand even more on end. He hummed softly. Bright blue eyes drilled into my skull, and it took everything to not flinch under the scrutiny.

"You're young, rebellious, and with a corrupted wizard on your shoulder. Anyone in the community would advise keeping you in the dark,"

Solomon drawled. He drummed his fingers on the counter top. With a curt nod, he smiled; his blue eyes twinkled. "I, as it happens, am no longer in that community."

"So, you'll do it?" I asked.

Solomon waved me to follow as he headed into the backroom. "Chemistry has its uses, and beyond the mystical, it is a rewarding field for exploration. To be frank, I admire this leap you're taking. Chemistry and biology will be far more useful if you intend to continue hunting demons." The old man waltzed around the room, pulling various books from his shelves. "There will be extensive texts. I expect you to treat this with the same importance as your lessons with Jordan and your other academic pursuits."

"Of course," I promised. "I've already picked out my next semester's courses, but Dr. Voigt won't let me change until the end of the semester"

Dropping a pile of books into my arms, he hummed. "That should give us time to ensure you're up to par. If all goes well, I would be willing to sign off on an independent study."

"What would I even tell him? Historical chemistry? Greek fire experimentation?"

With a chuckle, he crossed his arms over his chest. "I'm sure Charles would be fine with it being an introduction to experimental chemistry."

"Wait…you know Dr. Voigt?"

"I lectured at one time or another at all the local universities in the area at the request of my colleagues in the industry. I formed several connections during my thirty years at Kodak. I do have a PhD in chemistry, you know," the alchemist informed me.

Waving for me to follow him, Solomon led me into the back room. Jars lined the shelves filled with powders, liquids, and strange bits and pieces of creatures and plants. Textbooks and journals lined the far wall. Rows of shelves abutted a metal table with a ventilation hood. Everything was neatly organized and labeled.

"Don't mess with the containers. The liquids on the far end are highly flammable," Solomon warned. "Pick a few of the books out to start with – anything that catches your fancy and we can work from there once I finish closing up the shop."

Before he left, I reached out. "Thank you – for all of this."

His blue eyes twinkled. "My pleasure, Jon."

Left to my own devices, I scanned the shelf. The majority of the books were basic textbooks. I pulled out two introductory texts, setting them on the table before allowing myself to move onto the homemade journals which marked the separation into the magical. If Conall had been telling the truth, one of those journals had a clue about the identity of the draugr. He was probably lying.

Grabbing the first, I flipped through, but all the dates were in 1837-1839. The entire first shelf was 1800s, so I jumped down to the next. A detailed description of the use of table salt started off the 1900s. By the third books covering the right year, the scales tipped toward relief. Conall lying made sense. Unfortunately, on the fifth book, a familiar name and a strangely short entry caught my eye.

April 15ᵗʰ, 1922

Porter requested detail while at the Hotel.

Duration: 2 Weeks
Terms: Half up front
Add. : Lately

My heart dropped. This was it. Conall hadn't been lying. It wasn't exactly a diary as I would call it, but parts matched. The rest of the entries were more descriptive, but a second on the 18th was even shorter.

April 18ᵗʰ, 1922

Mason completed work.

While the pages were otherwise clean, a smear obscured the corner above the date for April 19th. However, the details weren't what I expected.

April 19ᵗʰ, 1922

Porter left earlier than expected. His man, Lately, left as expected. Button man chiseled like a grifter. Lately made Billy look like a sucker, but he sat for a picture. We thought

*he should try to blend in better. Lately
claimed shifting is bothersome. If he could
keep both eyes on task, the whole shindig
might've gone better.*

The names were there, but there was no mention of
a wizard, a murder, or anything that connected
Porter, Lately, or the book's writer to the draugr.
Flipping back in the book, the female name
mentioned popped up at the end of January.

January 29th, 1922

> *Dorothy Lloyd arrived from England. Billy
> got sent to the City. Porter won't be happy
> with H.F. Worse, H.F. delayed bonfire.
> Keeping logs on lock. If H.F. sinks, we sink.*

Solomon sauntered back into the room with
a flash drive in hand. "I thought you might like a
copy of my electronic article collection."

"I think I know who the draugr is."

His white brows jumped as he glanced down
to read over my shoulder. "Dorothy Lloyd? What
would make you think that?"

And my brain blanked. Sure, the details
Conall gave me matched, but there was no reason to
believe him. The draugr had an accent. It was
probably British, but that didn't mean she was a
1920s Brit.

"Her dress looked Victorian?" I offered.

"Victorian fashion era ended shortly after Queen Victoria's death in 1901."

Okay, so the draugr wasn't fashion forward. Or Conall lied. Setting the book aside, I admitted, "Conall told me."

Solomon nodded. "It should be easy enough to verify. The Daughters in the United Kingdom keep immaculate census records."

"Really? It's that simple?"

His bushy white eyebrows furrowed. Leaning in, he frowned. "Why shouldn't it be? In the end, if Dorothy Lloyd died elsewhere or wasn't a wizard, we'll know Conall lied. If not, we have a lead." With a pat on the back, he picked up one of the introductory chemistry books. "Why don't we see where we stand? I'll call around on Dorothy in the morning."

Chapter Fourteen

Friday's during the early afternoon left me alone with Joel. Joel hid in his room, and I had the kitchen table to myself. My phone sat amongst the mess of notes and textbooks. Solomon had promised to call when he knew where we stood on the Dorothy Lloyd front. The internet lacked any good information, so whoever Dorothy Lloyd was – if it wasn't a code name for some type of alcohol during prohibition – she hadn't been well known.

Shoving my phone out of my direct eye line, I glared down at my coursework. Buoying grades wasn't hard. Keeping them afloat – that would be the real test. Without anyone around, I laid out my upcoming readings. If I could just get ahead, I had a chance. Seclusion kept the itch at bay. Around anyone else, everything eventually tilted, and as much as I blocked out the strange influence of Conall's leechlike attachment, I couldn't silence it completely without giving up my magic. Conall likely got off knowing that.

Joel waltzed into the room as if he could sense I didn't want him there. Throwing himself onto the couch, he set his feet on the back, leaning his sketchbook to rest on his abdomen and thighs. Black dust covered his fingers. Wiping his hand on his black shorts, he flipped until he reached a fresh page.

Gritting my teeth, I waited for the buzzing to start. It never did. "Huh."

Joel glanced over at me. "What?"

"Weird headache didn't come when expected," I admitted.

With a scoff, he returned to his sketch. "Maybe Rochester's just not agreeing with you."

"Like I'm allergic?"

"Nah, like the atmosphere and what-not," Joel said. "You should probably just move back to Boston. You're struggling here anyway." Silence stretched, and he glanced back, staring at me with a frown. "Come on. You have to have been thinking about it. Schoolwork has you down. Jordan is unreliable. Best bet? You go back to Boston; join a community college and get your life in order. Cheaper than sticking around here and making yourself miserable."

Crossing my arms over my chest, I leaned back in my chair. "You're a dick."

"I'm the only one who's honest with you." When I rolled my eyes, Joel shrugged. "You were fine until Jordan showed up. You aren't giving up on that shit show, so the next best thing is giving up on U of R."

"He's my uncle," I retorted, and Joel's brows lifted.

Running his tongue along his teeth, he sat up with a frown. "What?"

"Jordan is my uncle. We're trying to locate my dad, who – as it turns out – doesn't even know I exist, so...no, I'm not giving up on this 'shit show,'" I snapped. Standing, I collected the readings into a pile, preparing to storm to my room and continue my studying from there. "It's not like

I'm doing drugs. I'm trying to figure out my life. You'd think you could appreciate that."

However, Joel stepped up beside me. "I never thought you were on drugs." He leaned against the table. "I'm not saying you don't have an addictive personality. I mean, you definitely are obsessive."

Gritting my teeth, I shrugged. "What do you want from me, Joel?"

"You have to admit that your relationship with Jordan is toxic."

And hello left field. I dropped the papers back on the table. "Okay…"

"I get it. My mom – she's the same way," he confessed, and all the fight drained out of me. Joel never spoke about his mother. "Doesn't treat you badly, not really. Just…forgets you exist until it is convenient or, more likely, when it's useful. She's a jerk to my dad, and my half-siblings are crap. They think they're better because their parents are married as if my dad hadn't raised them all for years before they found out they were the products of an affair." Running a hand through his hair, he sighed. "You had a life, and Jordan came into your life like a hurricane. It absolutely screwed up everything. You were doing well. Tyson told me all about it. You went from happy and hyper to a social recluse. It's not healthy. Just because he sticks around, doesn't mean you have to see him."

Finally, we got around to the point. "So – I should just give up on ever knowing my dad or his family."

"Yes!" Joel exclaimed.

Grabbing my supplies, I shook my head. "I can't, Joel. I need this."

"Can you even hear yourself? That's exactly what an addict would say! You're obsessing over something that's just going to destroy you and every single person around you," he yelled, slamming his hand against the wall to block my path. "If you stay here and stick with Jordan, you'll drag everybody down with you. I don't need that. Tommy doesn't need that. Tyson sure as Hell doesn't need that."

"Nothing I'm doing with Jordan affects you at all."

"Really? Cause your moody, broody self doesn't cause trouble?" Joel snorted. Gritting my teeth, I glared and shoved Joel out of the way with a bit more force than I probably should have, but even as he stumbled, Joel stormed after me – not letting it go. "You're switching majors. Is that even for you? Or is it all because of something Jordan said?"

"It's my life!" I yelled, kicking the door, but he caught it before it could slam shut. Dropping everything on my desk, I pushed against one side as Joel shoved against the other.

"What about that German kid? Moving children across borders – that's illegal! Do you want to get mixed up in something like that? Do you honestly think you getting involved in the goddamn mafia won't screw up all our lives?" he demanded, refusing to back down.

Electricity crackled around my fingers. They curled into fists, but I held back. Joel was mortal.

263

He had no idea who or what he was messing with. If I wanted to send him through a wall, I could. With barely a thought, I could take all the air out from around him. Throw him into outer space. Burn the whole complex down.

My forehead smashed forward against the wood. Blinking, I rubbed my forehead, glaring at the door. Joel gave up. Stubborn as me Joel just left. This had to be a trap. The second I let up on the door, Joel would come at it with a flamethrower. Wait, did Joel have a flamethrower? I was a flamethrower. A knock pulled me out of my thoughts.

"Jon?" Tommy called through the door. "You okay?"

I opened the door a crack. With his arms crossed over his chest, Joel glowered from behind Tommy. "I'm fine. I just need to study."

"Oh that is such -," Joel raged, but Tommy cut him off.

"You need to back off," Tommy commanded.

Joel grumbled beneath his breath, retreating to his room with a spat, "Users wreck everything."

"What did you say?" I growled, but Tommy stepped between us, giving Joel time to storm to his room and slam the door behind him. He had said user. Addicts were users. He meant to call me an addict. Joel didn't know. He couldn't know. It was just a word. "I'm fine. We just – we just don't get along."

"That's okay."

264

Rubbing a hand over my face, I sighed. "Is it? You've got PTSD because of me, and none of this is going away. Maybe I should leave."

"What? No," Tommy retorted.

"If I wasn't around, you wouldn't have to deal with it."

"Seriously, Jon? I'm your friend; I'm involved. We're stronger together. Joel just makes everything personal. His family is complicated," Tommy explained.

Shaking my head, I backed off. "Whatever." Tommy frowned. He held out an envelope toward me. "Here," he said. "It's addressed to you."

When I took it, he headed off toward his room. The slump of his shoulders ground into my gut, but I had nothing to say. Joel pissed me off. Still, he wasn't wrong. As long as I remained, everyone here would be in danger. In the end, they would be in danger anyways. Damnation hung over Rochester after the summoning, and that sort of stain took centuries to wipe away if the city didn't fall completely – another Atlantis lost to the sea. Waste and ruin encroached.

Flipping the envelope over, my heart stuttered. George sent it. I tore it open, tugging out the contents:

Dear Jon,

I'm sorry you'll have to read this in a letter. If I could, I would've told you in person, but as long as Conall has influence over you, I can't risk it. As you now know, my family has left the United States. The Daughters believe we've all returned to Greece. We haven't.

If nothing else, please know that it wasn't my intention to make you feel abandoned. I think of you like a little brother, and I wanted to help you and Jordan figure things out, but the Wild Hunt is too big a risk. I had planned to give up my magic; unfortunately, that's no longer a possibility.

You might be wondering why I waited to have this letter delivered to you. It wasn't entirely to hide our leaving. I knew you'd be afraid. After Wolfram, you've been spiraling, and Jordan can't give you the support you need. Please don't hold that against him. He really is trying. Anyway, I needed you to go to Solomon. He's a good guy, and of those in the know in Rochester, he's the best option. Trust your instinct on this one.

There's so much I had hoped to teach you. He'll be able to help with most. For those he can't, here are my main points:

1) Don't isolate yourself. You have friends. Trust them.

2) *Jordan cares about you. This doesn't mean you need to forgive him. You don't even have to like him, but I want you to have it in writing that Jordan cares about you. It's unfair of me to ask you to be patient with him. He's one of my closest friends, but he's a walking disaster. That doesn't mean he isn't knowledgeable or that he doesn't have things to teach you.*

3) *Don't let what happened with Wolfram cause you to doubt yourself. Conall might influence you, and you should question where that starts and stops, but if you believe in anything, trust that. You don't have a lot of faith in anything, so if you find it somewhere, hold on tight.*

4) *I've never met Jokul. I only know him through Jordan and others. Whether you meet him or not, do not judge your self-worth by him or his opinion. You are an enthusiastic, intelligent, capable young man.*

Call it an invasion of privacy, but I looked a bit into where you'd be when this letter could help the most. Joel does care, and you'll understand why he's lashing out soon. If you are unsure who to trust, take a walk in the abandoned subway tunnels. You know where.

*None of this was your fault. Giuseppe chose
Rochester. His actions attracted Shiloh, but
if it weren't for that, we might have never
gotten all those kids out of her void.
Wolfram was just one of many, and nobody
could have known about his connection to
the Wild Hunt.*

*You saved so many people. Don't let one bad
person make you doubt everyone.*

George

"It wasn't my fault?" I scoffed.

George took his entire family to
who-knows-where, running from the Daughters and
the Wild Hunt, and it wasn't my fault. Collapsing
back into my desk chair, I shoved the letter into the
top drawer. Giuseppe picked Rochester for the
summoning. He didn't know I was here. I didn't
bring him here. Didn't make him pick this city –
George's city.

Jumping to my feet, I grabbed the light-up
sword Jordan gave me and the journal from
Solomon, rushing out of my room. Both Tommy
and Joel were in their rooms, so nobody stopped me
as I flung on my jacket and tugged on my shoes.
From my room, my beanie flew into my hand, and
as the door locked behind me, I tugged it down
around my ears. Ice layered the city, but the heavy
clouds overhead worried me more. Sunlight was a
rare commodity in Rochester winters. Demons

thrived in the crevices of every gutter and alleyway. Down in the abandoned tunnels, every inch had hooks.

Fire risked detection. I had gotten lucky nobody had seen the wall I had created after G'ma Scott died. Though the tunnels might very well be empty, kids hung out there from time to time. Accidentally burning a mortal wasn't on my to-do list, so I ducked into the first cheap shop I could find, buying a bag full of light-up sticks, bracelets, and balls. If I kept on going on side quests, I had to get the name of Jordan's wholesaler.

Plastic bag in hand, I descended into the graffiti covered tunnels. A group of high school students hung within the first section, leaving against a wall with cigarettes in their fingers and smoke rising from between their lips. They fell silent when I drew near. Their eyes tracked me, whispering when I was out of sight. If I stole some electricity from their phones and watches, none of them noticed.

In the back of my head, Conall's influence rang, pressing against my nerves as he tried to reach out, but I flashed my soul, letting the stolen electricity dance about my fingers. I didn't need him. Walking through a tunnel wasn't hard. I had seen the runes before, and playing match-up between my phone and the pictures painted on the concrete settled the uselessness I felt. I could do this. Still, uncertainty itched at the back of my mind. When I reached the runes, I took a picture at the closest memorable section of graffiti and then another in front of the runes, sending both to my social media and to Jordan. He would probably ignore the text, but I hadn't seen a single demon, and George would be pissed if I got myself killed because of a grudge.

Carved into the concrete, the runes dipped in even, smooth strokes. Whoever had killed her planned this in advance. They had known she would become a draugr. What had inspired Dorothy Lloyd to come here? Why had she come? None of the journal entries suggested her reasoning. One page she existed. The next, she didn't. There was one mention in June 1921.

June 16th 1921

> *Increased buttons around the shop. One flashed a buzzer at Billy. H.F. asked for a fiend to be sent to the Hotel from the City. Worried we'll get nailed.*
>
> *Group of dames showed up, and H.F. asked for some Nevada gas. Though we should tighten the screws before rubbing them out, but H.F. had some hatchet men clean up the mess.*

A detailed map of Durand-Eastman Park followed. This was, just like the one mentioning Dorothy, had smeared ink, but unlike the other, there were three for this one. Three deaths and a group of women – they had to be a Daughter triad.

"Which means the Daughters knew…" I murmured.

Shoving the journal back in one pocket, I tugged out my own. Page by page, I scratched my pencil, pulling the impressions of the runes around the entrance. The stone doorway shifted up and down with ease, but runes lined the inside. With a grumble, I stepped half-way inside, continuing my work on the ceiling and walls before glaring down at the door.

"If I scratch a rune, we can't use it," I thought aloud.

Alternatively, closing the door risked getting stuck. Not my favorite. Small spaces didn't naturally freak me out, but someone entombed the draugr in the hole, and I wasn't about to be victim number two by means of stupidity.

Straddling the doorway, I reached my awareness out. Air shifted in the gaps. A delicate breeze traced the physical mechanisms which would align the stone and lock the warding in place. They blended into the rest of the structure; whoever did it had built the prison into the subway structure. If I kept just a bit of air between, I could get the runes.

Checking my phone, I sent a quick text to Jordan, Solomon, and Leta before putting my phone away. It would be fine. Worse case, Jordan would come get me. I would get a lecture, but I got those regardless.

The stone door slid into place. All the rules hovered beside one another slightly off track from where it ought to have been, but as long as there was that variance, I could still get out.

Brows furrowed and nose wrinkled, I hummed. "This had to take forever."

Someone had seriously not wanted her escaping. Knowing they were dead, I couldn't help but be a bit upset on her behalf. She would never have her revenge.

Graphite inverted the runes, and with each page, the puzzle made a bit more sense. Everything focused on keeping things in rather than keeping other things out. While most runes I had done focused on entryways to form barriers, runes covered every inch of the stone. A bit overdone in my opinion. Demons had to force through wards, and most didn't have the power, wouldn't bother or couldn't be bothered.

Lei could burn through the wards around Jordan's apartment, but he lived there too and the lazy jerk rarely bothered to burn up the void necessary to open the doorway - which was half the effort it would be to walk out it over the warding lines.

"Magic makes zero sense," I said with a sigh.

I set the page up a bit to align with the line on the opposite side of the door. Familiarity whirled around my brain, but the source eluded me. The number of warded places I had been wasn't that big.

Luckily, my lack of experience finally proved useful.

"Wait a minute," I muttered.

Lining up the runes, I read across the line. They matched. Whoever had done these had seen the Grith's dungeon and the identical warding engraved into what was now Wolfram's cell. Maybe the stone just wasn't in place correctly. Without thinking, I tugged the door further into place, and something within the walls thudded.

My heart dropped. "No." Grasping for the air, the wards shifted, pushing back against me as the mechanism clicked. "No-no-no!" I scrambled, nails clawing against the stone as it sunk immovable back into its space.

"It's not identical," I swore though I couldn't be sure. "Maybe…"

My magic whirled around me. Sparks crackled, and my shadow shifted. Hell tethered tightly to me. Plus side - still had magic. Down side - a demon could pop up and eat me. Real fire would eat up the air, and I'd suffocate while whatever evil sat back and twiddled its thumbs to pop back in when the shadows consumed me once more. Stupidest warding ever.

"Wait - don't be stupid." I smack my forehead. "She was a wizard. If Hell could get out from here, she could've just warped. So…" I pulled a glow stick from my bag. Cracking it, a dull green light spread across the runes. "This is fine. This is totally fine. She was dead. Maybe there's a living loophole…which I couldn't even find because I don't know anything about runes!" I roared, smashing my fists against the stone. My shield sizzled. Sparks jumped, but nothing changed.

I tugged my phone out of my pocket, and the lack of bars wasn't the first sign to catch my eyes. An unsent message blinked on my phone. Pulling up the texts between me and Jordan, I sighed in relief. Even if the text hadn't sent, the first of the two images had.

"Jordan knows where I am," I assured myself. Stuffing my phone back in my pocket, I measured the space with my arms. "I can turn around. Sure, no dancing here but plenty of oxygen for Jordan to get to me in time. He opened it once, right?"

Dread shivered up my spine. I need to be patient. Jordan would find me, and I'd be embarrassed but otherwise fine.

Why didn't they do complex math word problems about this? The average human used 'x' amount of oxygen per hour. Oxygen in one square foot of space was 'y' with the space being however big the hollow measured. How long could someone survive? No. Instead, we got questions about idiots buying truckloads of watermelon as individual buyers. Tyson probably knew. Maybe Joel too. Joel memorized morbid details like that, and Tyson studied anatomy and first aid.

Time hadn't permitted me to fully isolate Conall's connection before. Stuck in a hole in the ground seemed as good a time as any to start. Closing my eyes, I retreated into my mind.

Darkness spread in all directions. Meditation never made sense to me. Nothing existed inside my head but me; however, that was no longer true if it ever had been. My magic twisted. Pulsing and spiraling like a parasite lurking beneath my skin, the connection between me and Hell twisted around me. Somewhere in the writhing coils, a buzz hummed. It almost sounded like a phone.

The thought snapped the darkness into focus. An old fashion telephone hung in space. Wooden and rectangular, the phone had two metal domes nailed beside each other. On the right side sat a small crank. Hung up on the other with a wire attaching it to the workings within the wooden box, was a bell-shaped earpiece. Paired with the open-faced black speaker, it made for a strange image. I had never seen one in person, so the shape wasn't inspired by my own imagination. Magic coiled, flashing like a neon red warning light around it.

"You are not something I should mess with," I informed the phone as it rang. Each ring sent vibrations pulsating out through my mind. "Magic in my head probably isn't a good idea, but this is my head, so…"

I imagined smashing it with a baseball bat. As cathartic as the thought was, nothing happened. The phone stood unharmed. Fire failed. When I mentally tugged at the box, I tumbled as if I were attempting to move a tank.

Nobody could say I was a patient person. With a growl, I grabbed the earpiece off the hook. "Can you just shut up?"

"Hello?" Conall's lilting accent crackled. "Jon?"

"You are giving me a headache, so unless you plan on turning yourself into the Daughters - leave me alone!" I projected down the line.

Time stretched between us.

"But you haven't hung up," the wizard pointed out. His voice remained soft, echoing as if he were a vast abyss. Made sense. He was in Hell after all. "Your magic wavered, Jon. What happened?"

"Nothing."

Frozen, I wanted to hang up, but I couldn't bring myself to do so. Red pulsed behind the sound, and the metal domes glimmered like two gold eyes. My reflection glinted off them. Bags accentuated the dark circles beneath my eyes. Exhaustion showed up easily on me. A poor self-image didn't prove anything. I knew what I looked like. Most people could imagine their own faces, couldn't they? However, the graphite smeared across my forehead branded me, solidifying me even as I moved to wipe the mark away.

"I can tell when you lie to me," Conall said. Voices murmured in the background, but I couldn't pick up what they were saying. "If you tell me what's wrong, I may be able to help you."

Tugging the instrument from my ear, I managed to get it halfway to the hook before I

276

leaned forward to press it against my ear again. "Wolfram loves you." The words tumbled out in spite of me. "Like 'sail that ship' sort of love."

"Are you surprised?"

I scoffed because I wasn't. I wasn't surprised Wolfram could love. Conall wouldn't have been my pick, but the tension between them and the passion even when Wolfram wanted to kill the copper-haired wizard suggested more between them than I had ever felt for anyone. If they somehow managed a happily ever after, that still wouldn't shock me. Selfish people didn't know how to lose.

"Do you love him?" I asked. "He's hoping you two will get to share a cell for the rest of your lives."

A sigh whistled over the line. "Where are you, Jon?"

"Screw you," I spat and slammed the phone on the hook. Almost immediately, the bells rang. Opening my eyes, I leaned back against the warded cement. Conall could keep calling. I wasn't about to pick up the line again. "It'll be fine. Jordan will realize I'm missing. He'll see the weird wards like I did, and if I could open it up, so can he. It'll be fine."

The longer I waited, the less convincing those words became. My phone blinked. It was on its last bit of battery - over three hours later, and I cursed myself for not charging it. In my head, however, the stupid Hell-phone kept ringing. Ideas sparked half-formed in my head. They swarmed, pestering me. Maybe Conall would come if I asked. He kept calling, and he seemed to call whenever I got distressed, so he was in tune with the ups and down of my emotional state - or at least the flares in magic which accompanied them. Between life and death, life won hands down for me. Even if it was Conall to whom I would be indebted. I just wanted to live.

Holding my phone against my chest, I let my head rest on the cold stone. My eyelids drifted shut. Still in my mind, red neon blared. The phone box hung. However, the ear piece wasn't where I left it. From its cord, it swung back and forth off the line.

"…buried alive…a pleasant way…die," Conall murmured. Static scrambled his words. Each gap held crackles and pops, leaving me to parcel out the meaning. "Nobody…for you. He…not coming…there's still…if you asked." I grabbed the earpiece, and the static ceased. "Hello? Jon? Are you there?"

The ear piece slammed into the hook. Grabbing the domes, I clawed against the wood and metal, tearing the whole machine to pieces. When I looked up from the carnage, Conall sat in a leather chair. His legs crossed over one another, and in a dark turtleneck and slacks, all he was missing was a cat to tie the psychotic villain look together. A copper brow quirked at me.

"Are you done?" he asked.

"Get out of my head!" I screamed. Red blared so bright it was nearly blinding as it wove around my head, slamming into invisible barriers before coiling around him, but Conall kept his eyes on me.

"Wolfram has informed the Daughters of your...conundrum."

"How? You can't reach him," I reminded him.

He clucked his tongue. "Do you think you're the only lost boy I connected to myself? You and Wolfram are so alike. Do not, for a second, believe you are the only tool I have at my disposal because I am the only one you have."

My heart stuttered. Panic crawled across my skin as a cold sweat soaked my brow. "Who?"

"That information is need-to-know, Jon, and you don't need to know."

Grabbing him by his shirt, I hefted him up, but we were of a similar height, so even as I held him up, his feet remained mostly on the ground. Still, I growled, "Who else do you have in the Grith?"

His lips curled into an empty smile. "What will you give me in exchange?"

"I'll kill Wolfram for you."

"Who says I want him to die?" Conall retorted. A feral grin shattered the usual compose of his expression. "Maybe I've changed my mind. Maybe he and I want the same thing."

"And you think he'll let you keep whatever other lost boy you have? The Daughters will want to know how he got in contact with you if they trust his word at all," I said, shoving him back down in his seat. "Whatever little bird is running around, they'll figure it out. Either when I tell them or because they'll realize on their own that their wards wouldn't let you get through."

Conall tilted his head. Gold and kohl shimmered across his features, and the emptiness of his soul spread over him like a demon's void. It was like watching Bruce Wayne put on the cowl. The smiling, normal human was just a disguise that Conall's war paint washed away. Regardless of the state of his soul, Conall was a demon. Rising from his seat, he crossed to stand before me. His teeth flashed as sharp as daggers.

"You assume the 'little bird' knows."

Slamming his fists against my chest, he sent me out of my own head as the back of my head connected with stone. The runes around me glowed. Magic glimmered through them, and the stone moved.

Chapter Fifteen

Jordan and Ros stared down at me. Grabbing my arm, Ros yanked me out of the hole. Her eyes traced me up and down, assessing for injury as her fingers went over my head, messing up my hair even as I tried to wave her away. When she reached the back of my head, her fingers came away with blood.

"I'm fine," I grumbled.

Ros glared at Jordan. "He has a head injury. Wasn't he recovering from a concussion?"

"I barely tapped myself this time," I growled, and Jordan lowered a ball of glowing plasma into the hole where it lit up a smear of red against the rune-covered stone. "Head injuries bleed a lot."

"Lei can heal it," Jordan suggested. With a flare of his magic, Jordan sealed the hole.

Ros's nose wrinkled. "You're idiots. The both of you."

"Maybe we should be more concerned with how Conall's communicating with Wolfram," I said, and they both looked at me as if I had grown a second head.

"What are you talking about?" Ros demanded.

"Didn't Wolfram tell you I was here?"

Letting out a half-laugh, Jordan shook his head. "I keep a tracer on your phone."

"What? No way! That's an invasion of my privacy," I cried, and Ros chuckled, putting her hands on her hips.

"You've started the lone hunting phase of your training. If he didn't have some sort of tracking device on you, I would think he was a complete moron," she informed me. She glanced between the two of us. "I swear you two prove stupidity is genetic. I've never met two people so idiotic in the same way."

Wrapping an arm around either of our shoulders, she guided the two of us out of the tunnels and across town to a dive bar, refusing any attempts either of us made for an argument.

The bartender's brows furrowed, looking from me to Ros and Jordan. "Licenses?"

"They aren't drinking," Ros assured him. Sliding into a seat at the bar, she smiled. "Whatever you'd suggest, that's on tap for me."

"Water," Jordan requested, taking a seat beside her.

I sat down beside him. "Coke, please."As the bartender set down our drinks, I added, "If we're doing this, should we go to a corner or something to talk in private?"

With a snort, the bartender headed down toward the other end of the bar, giving me a pointed look as she did so. Ros chuckled. Her hands wrapped around the glass, obscuring the golden color of the beer within it.

"Where do you boys want to start?" she asked. "With the draugr's hole? The two of you constantly fighting? Or should we skip to finding alternative arrangements for you, Jon?"

"Or how about how nobody told me George was gone?" I retorted.

"He asked us to wait," Jordan informed me.

"For what?" I growled. "His letter? Me to ask?"

Ros's lips twisted into a frown. Laying a hand on Jordan's shoulder, she insisted, "Why don't you take a walk? I can handle this one."

Sliding the glass between his hands, Jordan shook his head. "No. This is on me." He shifted in his seat to face me directly. "Your personal feelings matter to me. They matter to Ros, and on a good day, they might even matter to another handful of people you've met in the community, but the reality is, between your feeling abandoned or taken advantage of and the welfare of the majority in the community, a good hunter always picks the community."

"Oh, yeah, and how's that worked out for you guys so far? Chebar Culling wasn't for the good of the majority," I returned.

Jordan sighed. "Ezekiel Ostairius is always a shit show for the community. His lack of punishment connects directly to his privilege as a male wizard capable of producing high level magic users. Honestly, if he'd had half a dozen already, Solveig would've killed him by now."

"Ah, saved by vasectomy," Ros murmured, lifting her class in a faux salute.

"Greed saved him. By running away, Jokul and I removed ourselves from the line of inheritance. Jukka inherits everything – including the house and land taken by Ezekiel from our mother's family. Solveig isn't about to let anyone stand between her and that. When she's ready to give birth again, I'm sure Jukka will get a brother," Jordan explained, glaring over his shoulder at Ros, who smiled as she ordered Buffalo wings.

"Point being, you want to be an Ezekiel?" she asked, turning back to me. "You're a warlock, so a few magicless Daughter lineages might want you."

With a groan, I buried my face into my arms. "This is not how I expected this conversation to go."

Running a hand through his hair, Jordan stared down at the moisture gathered on the bar. "We're a finite resource. More Daughters are mortal than user, and that difference grows every year. It might've been God's plan, but as far as anyone on the ground can see, we're losing. Hell isn't slowing down. Urbanization has done more against demons than we have."

"Then what's the point?" I demanded.
"It's a question of free will," he said.

When the world went insane, Jordan went philosophical. This was just another in a line of write-off excuses where no matter how hard I argued, the picture was always too big. Simple answers weren't popular with magic users. While

Ros didn't say anything, her concentration wasn't entirely on her beer.

"Why does it always come down to a question of security or freedom?" I asked rhetorically. "Free will is just a fancy way of saying people would rather other people die than them not doing whatever they want. How many magic users are corrupt? Use their magic to steal and kill just because they can? They're probably doing more damage in the end, right? If all the tech and lights keep the demons away from mortals, then aren't we doing more harm?"

"Probably," Jordan admitted.

Swallowing the last dredges of her drink, Ros clucked her tone. "We're getting a bit too nihilistic for my tastes."

"The opposite, frankly," Jordan argued, leaning back in his chair as he glanced between us. "I'm saying the failure of the Daughters or any organization to uphold moral principles shouldn't be used as reason to believe that they don't exist at all. People are flawed. People fail." Jordan shifted to face me directly again. "George needed to leave for his family. He didn't abandon you, and even though he knows that, he'll probably still struggle with guilt because he knows how bad everything will get for Rochester. That's his problem. You need to focus on you. On forgiving yourself for your mistakes, learning from them, and determining whether this is actually a life you can stand."

Crossing my arms over my chest, I slouched against the counter, glaring as the bartender dropped a plate of wings in front of Ros. "I can't be held to higher standards than the Daughters. They're supposed to police us."

"But that's the point, isn't it?" Ros asked. She gestured at the wings, sliding it my way, but I waved off the offer. "Power corrupts, and corruption magnifies like toxins in a food chain. It isn't about a higher standard. It's the same standard with the expectation that failure on one end doesn't ensure failure on the other."

Dr. Voigt's words echoed in my ears. This wasn't a battle I wanted. No matter what I said, Jordan couldn't afford to take my side, and neither could Ros. Railing wouldn't change the Daughters. Magic users trusted them. Kasimira and Theda believed in them. They were Daughters. Ros and Monday worked for them too even if they both seemed to be a little less enthusiastic in their support recently. Revolution took time and dedication. Dedicating my life to that cause was a solid no go for me, which meant I had to find a way to live with it.

"I'm overwhelmed," I admitted.

Jordan ducked his eyes, bowing his head. "As long as you're connected to Conall, everything will get more complicated. I know we've had our problems, so if you need another option, I'll find one."

Wiping off her hands, Ros said, "Kasimira has taken over the older students. Most of hers are fourteen to seventeen. She's got most heading elsewhere, so having you join shouldn't be a problem."

"We don't really get along," I replied.

Jordan ran a hand through his hair. "You like most of her other students well enough. Leta? Helena?"

"They don't like her either. They also are leaving soon, so not really much motivation to join." I ducked my head, playing with the laminated menu. "I'm good where I am. You good with me?" I asked, and Jordan nodded. "Then we're fine."

If they didn't believe me, the two of them didn't say. Leaving Ros with her wings, Jordan escorted me back to my apartment in companionable silence. With a nod, he vanished with a step, and a growingly familiar weight slid back into place on my shoulders as I trudged up the stairs to my apartment door. A trill pulse rang in the back of my head. Creeping down my spine, it flared in the sparks which skittered down from my fingers when I opened the door into the dark and empty living room. Tossing my jacket over the counter, I toed off my shoes. Collapsed on the couch, Tommy snored.

A flick of my wrist sent a blanket over him as I walked by. Tyson sprawled across the bed across from mine. A sight I'd spent over a year seeing, but as I stood in the doorway, the world splintered in the strange shifting of a dream. Crawling into bed, I slid into the depths of my mind. In the dark, a payphone stood. The ringing grew, and when I picked up, Conall's voice crackled

over the line: "You're welcome." Even after I
slammed the phone back onto the hook, it
reverberated around my head. Imagining a wall
built, brick by brick between us softened the noise,
but like a chill, it lingered in my bones.

Chapter Sixteen

Safety meant waking up in my own bed. Despite this, panic pulsed like a warning in my blood, and my magic shifted restlessly beneath my skin, bringing the whispers from the living room to my ears before I could even decide if I wanted to know.

"He's not ready," Tommy insisted.

Joel snapped his tongue against the roof of his mouth in a disapproving noise. "He'll never be ready. As far as that idiot knows, he'll get cut off the second he lets someone outside the community know."

"Jordan was cool with me," Tommy replied.

My stomach churned, and the warmth of being in my own bed, safe in my apartment, fled like startled crows. They knew. How could they know? I had been careful, hadn't I? Sure, I flashed my soul multiple times a day, but magic shouldn't be their first conclusion. Tommy covered for me, didn't he? I had to be misunderstanding. They weren't talking about magic. It had to be something else. Like my trips to Toronto. There were so many options. I had other secrets. All of them involved Jordan in the end. It could be any of them.

"Jon can't get into trouble if nobody else knows we know," Tyson suggested, and my tongue went dry when he added, "He's got magic, so what? It isn't like he's being tracked, right?"

"No. The Daughters expect the mentors to do that." And how the hell would Joel know that? He didn't have magic. Jordan would've told me. I would've known.

Tommy sighed. The chair creaked as he stood. "Then we have to tell him."

"We should have told him from the beginning," Tyson grumbled.

Slamming his feet on the ground, Joel stood. The even pace of his strides giving him away as he stormed around the corner of the room, ignoring the call for him to wait – to let me sleep. Even with the warning, I could only stare – unblinking – when he threw open the door to my room. He stretched across the doorway, blocking it with his long limbs and towering height. Staying on Tommy's good side motivated me not to annoy Joel before, but he had never actually intimidated me physically. We were of like height. He had more muscle, but with my magic, that wasn't a threat. Face to face with him – knowing that he knew and that I had no idea how – he was horrifying.

"You heard," he demanded.

I nodded as Tyson came up behind Joel, shoving him to the side. The second his eyes landed on me, Tyson crossed the room, and the need to disappear throbbed in my head so hard I almost flared my soul thinking it might be Conall trying to mess with me again.

"We're not angry," he told me.

Joel scoffed. "Speak for yourself."

Tyson glared over his shoulder, but when he looked back at me, his expression relaxed like I was a cornered, injured animal. "I know it's confusing right now, but this is a good thing."

"A good thing?" I echoed, and his lips pressed into a thin line.

"Everybody knows now, so you don't have to lie. If something comes after you, none of us will screw up the warding or open a window without having you reinforce it. This is a good thing," Tyson repeated, holding up his hands in a placating gesture that felt anything but.

Shoving the blankets off me, I swung around, standing – counting my exits – debating the cost of shoving them all aside. Even if I raced around the room at full speed, I couldn't collect my stuff fast enough to get out of here without causing damage. People made packs for this kind of situation. Earthquake evacuation kits – they would've been a good idea.

Tyson stared at me. Tommy and Joel shadowed the door, and my head screamed sirens, but I couldn't move. There were too many possibilities, and I hated every outcome. My words caught in my throat. *God, just make me disappear. Let me wake up – please, god, let this be a dream.* But no matter how my pulse raced – the room bending round me like a warp – they just kept looking at me.

"Stop that," Joel demanded, shoving me back. Stumbled, I sat down the second the bed hit my thighs. Joel glowered down his nose. His hands held tight to my wrists. "So much for half-breed."
"What did you say?" Tyson growled.

"You know what I mean," Joel spat, but he never took his eyes off me. "If his mother was a mortal like us, he would be a warlock tops."

That made no sense. My mother was mortal. I was a warlock, but I couldn't find the energy to argue, and Tyson seemed content to argue for me. He elbowed Joel away from me. Standing between us, Tyson straightened his shoulders. Though broader in the shoulders than Joel, he was the shortest of the four of us.

"We've met his mom. She doesn't have magic," Tyson reminded Joel.

"Then how was he opening a warp?" Joel demanded. "Only wizards can do that."

"I wasn't…" I couldn't have been. There was no way I opened anything. The room had stopped spinning when Joel pushed me back, but I couldn't have been opening a warp. A tingle in the back of my head reminded me why I could've been. "Shit."

All eyes turned to me. Tommy worried his bottom lip, glancing between Joel and me. "They know, Jon. It's okay. You can talk to us."

But I couldn't. Joel acted like I was dangerous even without knowing a rogue had wormed his way into my head. If they knew about Conall…I flashed my soul, stopping the thought in its tracks. The worry didn't go away. Instead, resignation slid into the gaps where panic had resided.

"A rogue wizard formed an empathic connection with my connection," I murmured, avoiding their questioning gazes.

My eyes didn't have to be on Joel's face to know he was sneering when he said, "Of course. Because you're a freaking train wreck."

"I didn't let him," I snapped. "He formed it Hell side."

The bed creaked, shifting as Tyson settled beside me. "So you are a warlock?"

Covering my face with my hands, I groaned. "Yes."

"Was this rogue wizard the guy you tried to fry when G'ma died?"

Spots danced in my vision. My extremities tingled. "You saw that?"

Tyson snorted. "You're not exactly subtle."

At that, Joel cackled. "You're lucky he was the only who saw."

"I spent the majority of my week away making sure nobody else saw anything. My family probably thinks I'm crazy. Christmas is going to be fun." Tyson nudged my shoulder with his. When I didn't respond, he patted me on my back. "Man, we're all good. Just means I'm the Froggy to your Murdock."

Sitting up, I frowned. "So who told Joel?"

"Joel told Joel," the man in question announced. "I might have no magic, but my half-siblings and mom are all psychics. Dad used to be too before Chebar."

My brain spiraled, attempting to connect the dots. "But you're the youngest."

"Yep." Joel sat back on Tyson's bed. "Mom felt the need to give Dad a kid before she admitted to her continuous infidelity and ditched him for his still a magician brother." Crossing his arms, he sighed. "On the bright side, you're roomed with the ultimate demon hunting support team. Between his network and Rochester know-how, Tyson's got the mortal side down. I've got magic knowledge on lock, and Tommy can whip you into fighting shape. Best pit crew ever."

"See," Tyson offered. "It's good."

Good. My roommates discovered I was a warlock, but that was fine. Only two of them were my fault. If Joel's family was a magic lineage, I couldn't be blamed for him knowing. Tommy was a fluke. Jordan already knew, so that shouldn't get me into trouble. Tyson was one hundred percent my fault. Wolfram messing with my mind didn't excuse the excessive force I used.

All three of my roommates waited for me. A chill raced down my spine. A pulse ran through my brain, picking up, but it wasn't mine. Swallowing, I forced myself to relax. Maybe Wolfram had gotten out. This could all be an elaborate illusion. He hated me enough. A glow to double check - nothing. I turned with my hands out.

"I know you didn't expect this, and we weren't going to rock the boat, but you've got to admit, you've been a mess lately," Tyson said.

Cocking a brow, Joel stretched. "Don't lie. This was going to happen sometime. You honestly thought Tommy brought me in because I was the nicest guy for this crap? My mother's a Daughter. I've got connections that'll help. I think we've all realized Jordan's in over his head."

He was right. Jordan never learned to trust outside of my father, and we all saw how poorly that went. More often than not, I enjoyed complaining about Jordan, but he was my uncle. I had reasons to talk badly about him. Joel only had whatever his biased, lying freak of a mother said.

Anger pushed out anxiety and refocused on this new target. "You have no idea what you're talking about."

"Really? Because I think you're completely out of your mind. He lives with a demon, Jon! Or do you think that roommate of his is just a weird transplant?"

Point Joel. Arguing Lei wasn't a demon was futile. "And you really think a kid could be responsible for the Chebar Culling? Oh, let me guess, your mother told you that. How far up the Daughters' ass is she?"

Joel's shoulders relaxed. One side of his mouth tilted up into a smirk as he leaned against the wall. "There you are."

"What?" I demanded.

"You're not cowering anymore. Now we'll get somewhere," he replied. "You honestly think I give a shit about Daughter politics? If I did, I would've let myself be recruited like the other 'sorry-I-had-an-affair' null

296

children from Chebar marriages. My mother's a bitch. Siblings aren't much better, but I bet what I know about the magical world runs rings around you."

I frowned, but the cat had escaped the bag. "How old are your siblings? Chebar was like thirty years ago."

"And I'm twenty," Joel said with a shrug.

True, ten years between the first and last wasn't too big, but the idea hadn't ever struck me. People my age had been affected by Chebar even if indirectly through nullified parents. I pressed my lips together, ignoring the concerned expression on Tommy's face.

Tyson bumped shoulders with me again. "You've got to keep us in the loop. When I saw the wards, I thought Jordan recruited you for a cult or something. I get they're keeping us safe, but we're not always here.

"And wards don't do shit when you invite evil in." Joel added.

My brows furrowed. "What are you talking about?"

Tyson leaned back, looking at Joel. "Yeah, I'm with Jon on that one."

"German kid."

Rubbing the back of his head, Tommy glanced at me then back to Joel. "A demon pretending to be a German kid?"

My gaze dropped to the ground. Wolfram. Biting my lip, I shook my head. "No, he means Wolfram."

"Who?" Tyson asked.

"Wilhelm," Joel corrected.

Tyson's nose wrinkled. "What? No. That kid was a mess."

"Exactly - a mess of lies. Could practically smell the crap he was spewing," Joel stated. He cocked an eyebrow at me. "You can't even see through illusions, can you? I'm a null, and I didn't even need to use wards or tricks to burn off the mist on that one."

"I know better now. I thought…he was from Hamelin," I offered when no other explanation came to mind which fit.

Joel's eyes widened. "Shit."

"Great - now I'm lost again. Is this what it's going to be like?" Tyson demanded. "You and Joel have this whole secret world, and Tommy and me - we're just out of luck in the dark. Not what I signed up for."

"Pied Piper," Tommy murmured.

Tyson looked over his shoulder. "You're kidding me." He turned back to me and Joel. "Are you kidding me? Grimm's fairy tales?"

"Most stories about anything," I told him.

"Pied Piper was a demon." Tyson grimaced. "Not that the story was happy anyways."

"Shiloh. Jordan destroyed her, but I got a bunch of kids out of her void first. Wolfram disguised himself as his younger brother Wilhelm. He - it was a mess. People got hurt, but the Daughters have him in custody," I explained, rubbing the bridge of my nose. This conversation was exhausting.

Joel hummed. "Probably torturing him."

Tommy and Tyson looked to me for confirmation - or maybe they wanted a denial. They had only seen Wilhelm after all. Wolfram likely wouldn't have inspired such concern - especially if they knew what he had done. Another question I didn't want to know the answer to because I was a coward. This time, however, I couldn't avoid at least saying something.

I sighed. "That's what they do."

"Torture?" Tommy whispered.

298

Studying his hands, Tyson murmured, "I don't know what I expected, but it wasn't that."

"Magic users are just as screwed up as mortals," I said because arguing the point wouldn't have made sense.

Joel snorted. "Probably worse."

"Well, yeah, not like there are any other big groups keeping them in check. It's a global network all run by the Daughters. Those who aren't in…" I slid a finger across my throat, and Tyson's jaw dropped. "That's why people hunt. You hunt or give shelter or you…just don't exist anymore."

"You can't stop…" Tommy sat down beside Joel. "That's messed up."

"No magic, no problems," Joel joked then winced. "Well…not exactly true. They go after null kids all the time. Like it's a family affair.

"They went after George's kids - his wife's mortal. His kids are mortal," I sighed, leaning back against the wall, sliding down until I sat on the floor.

"Null," Joel corrected. "They won't be considered mortal until two or more generations removed. Like - my kids will be mortal, but they'll probably still try to recruit them."

Tyson exhaled slowly. His eyes trained to the ceiling. "Secret societies are messed up."

"Know what's worse?" Joel asked. "We're supposed to be diluting it. That's the whole redemption scheme on a platter. Reduce by marrying mortals - have kids with mortals - dilute the magic until it's gone, but it's like some Harry Potter bull. Pure bloods and keeping it in the community."

"Dr. Gersh would call that bottlenecking," Tommy murmured. "Not good for survival."

299

"Magic isn't good for survival," Joel retorted.

"Ever think maybe that's why I didn't want to involve anybody else? Tommy was in the wrong place at the wrong time…and he…" I bowed my head. "It gave you nightmares. You're a mess because I couldn't keep you safe."

Brows furrowing, the big guy claimed, "I'm not a mess."

"You aren't sleeping. You aren't eating," I listed.

"Nearly took off Scott's head at practice," Tyson added.

With a sigh, Tommy rubbed his palms against his knees. "I just…feel so useless." He shook his head. "Demons came out of nowhere, and I haven't seen another since. It's like getting a peak behind the curtain, but not knowing where the edges are. What if it lifts up again? What if I'm not ready? I get that they don't go after mortals most of the time. I understand that my soul means I'm safe. That my family is safe too because of their souls, but…what if?"

Bowing my head, I drew my knees up, resting my feet on the edge of the bed frame. "Jordan wants me to keep my mom in the loop, but how can I do that? I don't want her to be scared all the time again."

"You're her kid," Tyson pointed out. "She's going to always be worried about you."

"How much do you guys know about the summoning that took place last spring?" I asked, and Tyson glanced at Tommy.

"I told them what I knew, but it wasn't much," Tommy admitted.

"My mom reached out after that – around the same time Tommy asked me to move in with you guys. She wants me to stick close to you, so that if the time comes when Rochester needs to be cleansed, you wouldn't get in the way." Joel smiled ruefully. His fingers clenched into Tyson's blanket. His gaze met Tyson's then moved to Tommy. "That means they'd evacuate the city and burn it down. Like Sodom and Gomorrah style."

"And they won't wait to make sure everyone's evacuated," I added.

Looking to me, Tyson asked, "That's why things are intense, right? The summoning left a stain, and now we're like a beacon for bad?"

"It's like dominos. The summoning brought a lot of demons, including Shiloh. Shiloh brought Wolfram who's got a love-hate relationship with a rogue wizard, Conall, who is in league with the Wild Hunt. Our latest problem – well, we're not sure what happened there," I grumbled and then sighed. "There's a draugr – like an undead wizard – who's freezing the city."

"Shit," Joel whispered.

Tyson leaned forward. "Then what do we do?"

"No idea. Everybody wants to just kill her, but I think…" I trailed off, pulling the journal to me to show him. "I think she's trying to find her dead daughter."

"No way – the Lady in White is a zombie!" Tyson exclaimed.

Joel ran a hand through his hair. Unlike Tommy and Tyson, he understood the implications of a draugr. Probably even better than I did. However, of all the times for them to confront me, Dorothy didn't seem interested in harming anyone but Jordan, so as long as they didn't try to get in her way – which they couldn't do anyway as mortals – then they were safe. It was whatever came next that we had to worry about, and as long as there was a stain of damnation on the city, there would always be something else coming down the line.

"So we're looking for her daughter's grave?" Joel asked.

Tommy's brows furrowed. "Would she stop if she found it? If they want to kill her, there's probably a reason."

"Jordan's distracted. As far as I know, nobody's directly confronted her yet, and the one time she attacked, Jordan didn't seem motivated to take her on full power, but maybe that's because I was there," I pondered aloud.

"Or they aren't actually in agreement." Tyson shrugged when I glanced at him.

"Draugrs mostly go two ways. Either they were rogue before and there's not much choice, or they stuck around for a particular purpose. If she stuck around to find her daughter, this could end without anyone getting killed. She'd just self-immolate after," Joel explained, slouching back to lean against the wall. "I'm cool with going with it. Where are we on research?"

"I've got a name, some dates, and maybe a location in Eastman-Durand Park, but she was locked in a draugr hole in the abandoned subway. I feel like knowing who put her there is important. For what comes next," I explained, handing the journal to Joel, who flipped through, scanning the pages.

"I've got nothing on this. 1920s Rochester is Tyson's turf," the quarterback returned and tossed the journal to Tyson.

"We'll figure it out," my roommate assured.

Crossing the room, Tommy wrapped his arms around me, pulling me into a tight hug. "It's okay," he promised, patting my back as I tried not to sob like the mess I felt bubbling up inside of me. "You're not in this alone. Even if you just need to talk about it, we're here."

"And we're ordering pizza!" Joel announced. He jumped off Tyson's bed and headed toward the kitchen.

Stepping back, Tommy gave me one last clap on the shoulder. "You good?"

"Yeah, I'm good."

He shuffled off, leaving Tyson and I alone. Holding up his fist, he cocked a brow. Knocking my fist against his, I smiled. A familiar weight dissolved, leaving me loose and content. "Thanks. For everything."

"We're best friends," Tyson reminded me. "We're going to figure this out."

"And whatever comes next..."

He smiled. "That too."

Chapter Seventeen

Dorothy Lloyd, 1921, and the Rochester mafia – not exactly nothing, but the trail was definitely growing colder the more I looked. Keeping the information to myself might have been Conall's influence, but the idea of figuring everything out and saving the day appealed to me. Jordan would be proud. Frustrated, probably, but definitely proud. Not my goal, by any means. I didn't need him to be proud. Sure, if it made up for the whole Wolfram situation with the Daughters and helped make my life easier, I could live with Jordan being proud of me.

While magic users weren't recorded in Rush Rhees outside of the fiction section, there was plenty to go on about the 1920s and the mob influence around the city. If there was a hotel under mob influence, I would find it. Even if it took me days of sitting at the microfilm reader going over the dates in the journal one by one, I could do it. Matching up just one event would help. The closest I had managed was a few articles stemming from a jailbreak. The first mentioned a New York City businessman named James Porter and his associated, Ansaldo Segreti. The latter had been seen about Rochester and was believed to be connected to the break and the police raid which had the five escapees arrested in the first place. Four of the five ended up dead in the next article.

Porter could be the same one mentioned in the journal. The rescue only to kill the criminals could've been him cleaning house. None of it mentioned Lately, anyone with the initials H.F., or a hotel.

"Are you done yet?" Tyson asked, glancing back from his book.

Sighing, I pulled out the microfilm and set it back. "Sorry, this is going to take a while."

"And why are you looking up newspapers from the 1920s?"

"Personal project."

With a scoff, he shoved his book back into his backpack. "Come on. I bet if you tell me, I could find whatever you need to know quicker than you."

"I really don't need you to be a better researcher than me, thanks," I retorted, bringing up the next page. All the while, Tyson's eyes drilled into my back. "Fine! I need to know about a hotel operating in 1921 which was a base for mob activity. Preferably associated with someone initialed H.F. or with the name Porter."

"Got it," he cheered, slinging his bag over his shoulder.

Crossing my arms, I demanded, "If you know something, just tell me."

"No, no – you chase this down your way," he encouraged. "See you tonight!"

"Hey!" I called.

With a mocking salute, he left me to make my way through the stacks, hoping to find something. Abandoning the microfilm, I headed back to the shelves. A few students milled about, but it wasn't hard to find an empty aisle. Hidden behind the stacks, I leaned against the cold metal of the library shelf. My breath curled in white plumes as the temperature dropped. Ice spun patterns along the floor. Black shadows shifted along the walls and floor. Soot scattered as claws clattered, and a hound of Hell prowled the shelves.

Flammable seemed a mild word for my surroundings. Books - paper and perhaps some cloth - surrounded me. If I drew the lighter from my pocket, I risked burning Rush Rhees to the ground. Light worked against demons, but against a draugr, I needed heat.

Over my head, the lights flickered. Two aisles down, a light buzzed. The light grew lighter and lighter. With a crack, the bulb shattered, and the whole casing fell to the floor, raining glass and sparks down. Nothing caught fire. Nobody made a sound.

There was no way I was the only person in the Level 3 stacks. For all that I delayed, other students procrastinated too. Somebody else had to be here, which meant I had to protect them. Tilting my head back against the metal, I glared at the ceiling. Great power, great responsibility - great ways to die.

"Screw it," I grumbled. This was why Jordan gave me the stupid light-up stuff.

Rolling to my feet, I threw my hand forward. Wind slammed down the row, knocking the yeth off its feet. The demon clawed at the ground. Its long tails clacked against the floor, but for all it might have been made for the cold, even the best predators slipped on frictionless surfaces, and the ice had left the floors slick.

Spider-Man had a mask. I had vapor. Pulling it around myself, I shifted the light until my reflection showed a familiar red and black. My clothes were basic enough nobody should take notice, and if they saw my hands, there were enough kids with my skin tone and height in the city that I'd be fine. Hidden identities hallmarked superheroes after all.

From my backpack, the LED yo-yos streamed through the air. They slipped around my finger. Blinking, they spun through the air, leaving streaks of light in their wakes. One skimmed along the void beneath, and the light above our heads exploded. Both shadow and void vanished. Snapping its sharp teeth, the yeth collected the strings in its maw. With a growl, it tore them from my hands.

"You're my least favorite demon species," I spat.

Spitting the toys out, the yeth lowered its head. Rows of white canines flashed. I made the wise decision to run. Light after light exploded. Glass and sparks rained down on my shield, which fanned out above my head like an umbrella. Though the yeth didn't need to breathe, it panted and snorted, crashing into the shelves whenever I turned down another row. Desks lined the walls, and maybe it wasn't the most heroic to duck under and call Jordan, but I didn't see another option. With my lighter, I had tossed the rest of my light-up gear into a box beneath my bed. I couldn't have known Jordan wasn't being a superfluous jerk when he said I'd need them. Who fights demons with toys?

I slid to hide under the desk, but as I glided across the floor, vapor burst around me. The lights stopped flickering. A quiet buzz of activity returned, and at the desk in front of me, a student sat with their head bowed over a book.

Cursing, I pulled up a cyclone with one hand and swept an illusion up with the other, bending light to hide me. I wasn't skilled enough to instantly mimic the hall behind me, but if she had hidden herself and the yeth in a section of the library, her illusion might just cover my mistake. Flipping back around, the wind tossed me back through the wall of vapor, which sealed neatly around me as the student startled and glanced around.

The yeth growled, leaping with its open jaw, but as my feet tumbled over my head, I sent myself to the ceiling. Empty pits tracked me. Claws skittered across the floor, and as it slid closer to the barrier, the illusion shifted, jumping back almost to a foot away from the desk. Running over its head, I scrambled back. Both the hound and the illusion followed.

The illusion glimmered and jumped from one aisle to the next. Every time I slipped out, other students came into view, and I had to tightly wrap myself as I passed. If Jordan needed training ideas, this was an absolute terrifying trial by fire.

Jumping along the shelves, I pulled light where I could, but the yeth's shadow shifted in and out of the illusion. Somewhere in the stacks, another one lurked. They pawed at the ground. The click of their claws was the only sound in the illusion that wasn't my own. Light bent around me. Like a kid with an anthill and a magnifying glass, I focused the light. Tilting its head, the yeth snorted. Up and down, it chased me. Running in circles up to the ceiling then down one shelf in a spiral as the hound pounced, I threw heat and light around like marbles, but nothing could trip the demon up.

"A plan, a plan, I can think of a plan," I chanted to myself. The door stood at the end of the frost-covered hall. No telling what lurked behind, but there was a chance.

When the door snapped open, my heart nearly jumped out of my chest. A pair of students entered. Everything stilled. Around them, the illusion bent. On one side of the doorway, I clung against the upper corner of the ceiling and wall above the shelves. I crouched, barely breathing. The yeth froze. Its ears rose, and cocking its giant black-furred head, it tracked the mortals as they passed.

"I'm telling you, that's not how Cockney slang works," one of the young women said.

The other scoffed. "I don't care how it works in England. I'm saying there's a reason we don't have it here."

They walked on, comparing notes on American dialects. By the time they were two shelves away, the illusion sealed, and off we went like a greyhound and hare. Launching off one shelf, the yeth clawed near my legs, but my shield held.

"We both get this is a wild goose chase, right?" I raged at the beast as I plastered myself against the ceiling to avoid its gnashing jaws. "You aren't going to hurt the mortals. I'm not her main target if you haven't killed me already, so why don't we talk this over?"

Between the shelves, the hound circled. Ice spread from its every footfall. Dark eyes stared up, and gaps in its fur twisted with each turn to reveal the charred bones of its spine. From above, the yeth looked like someone had skinned a wolf, dug out the flesh from the bones, and then tried to tie the pelt back in place.

Scooting closer to the door, I frowned. "Can you even talk? Or are you too shattered?"

The yeth sat, blocking me from opening the door. If the demon could communicate, it clearly had no plan to do so with me.

Taking advantage of our temporary stand-off, I slid my phone out of my back pocket, clicking Jordan's contact as the yeth sat and watched.

"What?" Jordan demanded.

"Hello to you too," I grumbled. "I've been cornered in Rush Rhees. Haven't seen the draugr, but I'm pretty sure the yeth currently eying me isn't responsible for the illusion that's been moving around with us."

The jerk had the gall to sigh. I couldn't practically see him pinching the bridge of his nose in annoyance. "What floor?"

"Level 3."

"Body count?"

"A lot of mortals? Can't count unless I burn the illusion. If I burn the illusion, the yeth might be difficult to explain." Stretching, the aforementioned demon laid down. "Now that's just rude."

"What?"

"Nothing," I replied. "Just, can you warp me out of here or something?" "Warping should be kept to a minimum," Jordan informed me.

I ground my teeth. "You warp all over the place."

"I'm not currently attached to a wanna-be demon wizard," he retorted and promptly hung up.

Resting its head on its forepaws, the yeth huffed, sending soot flying all along the bottom edge of the door. In three directions, the illusion stretched. Books, which were tumbled and torn, decorated the floor. In the center, coldness spread upward from the hellhound. Ice crawled up the walls, filling in the edges of the door.

"Oh no you don't," I growled.

The hinges creaked. The door nudged the yeth's claws, and the ice continued to spread. Barely the width of my arm, I couldn't hope to sneak through without stirring the demon to chase once more. My feet slipped against the ceiling.

While architecture wasn't my major, I had a basic idea of structural integrity and engineering. A hole above the doorway shouldn't affect anything. Pressing one hand on the ceiling, I shifted a layer of force like a second skin to catch the mess as the demon snuffled below. Burrowing through the ceiling wasn't hard. Illusions weren't my forte, but I managed to keep one across the top and bottom to hide my actions from view. Shifting the wires and metal left me with a gap no bigger than my fist into the floor above.

Frost caked the hole, but light buzzed right above the gap, so as long as I kept an illusion around me, I had a chance at making an escape. Bit by bit, the space increased. Wires shifted until it was wider than my shoulders. Still, the yeth beneath me reclined. Its head remained on its forepaws.

Reaching up through the gap, I held the illusion, letting it expand around me like a bubble as I peaked up through it. On the next floor, nobody was in view. My shoulders relaxed and I pushed myself half-way up when a growl caught my ear. Glancing back down, I swallowed hard at the still resting yeth beneath me.

Half-between, I had to go forward or go back, and back had no clear escape, so up I went, and though the growling continued, not a single hound stood in my view. Sealing the floor beneath my feet, I kept low and hidden from view. A single yeth wouldn't have been able to move its void like the one I had been facing. If there was one on each floor, my new goal would be to get them all together.

A black demonic hound barreled toward me. Leaping, I shifted my shield like a gravitational field to drop me on the ceiling. While the other had contented itself in cornering me, the next yeth growled, snapping its jaws as it knocked against the shelves trying to grab hold of me.

"Going down?" I asked, and opening the floor beneath its feet, I cheered as it fell down on top of the sleeping yeth.

The two tumbled over each other, growling first at one another before turning their ire upward. Sealing the floor, I dropped to the ground, racing to the stairs. As I took the stairs three at a time, I whistled, hoping the demons would follow if I pissed them off enough. When their howling echoed up the stairwell, the grin splitting my face might have bordered on manic.

I bounced off the wall. With a backflip, I landed, but the second my toes touched down, the shadows shifted. My breath puffed out in clouds. The light shattered, and two hounds emerged from the shadows.

"I forgot you could do that," I admitted.

They charged, and I jumped to the ceiling as the light sparked. Frost spread from the doorway like vines, and as the pair chased me in and out of their shadows, a third tugged the door open and trotted out to watch from the upper level.

My life had become a game of Frogger. Except, instead of obstacles traveling in straight lines, the yeth popped in and out of every nook and cranny, defying the laws of physics to switch and jump along the ceiling. It busted my ego. The one lazy hound could've gotten me the entire time if it had been motivated. Then again, gravity seemed to be an on-again-off-again affair, considering I had managed to drop one through the floor.

Standing on the rails, I stared up at the ceiling. I guided the cement, wires, and pipes. Piece by piece, they separated. A gap grew. Snow drifted down - gliding down in a single beam of white, crystalline light. Shield like a bullet, I shot myself through to the roof. Prowling there, a pack glowered up, and the largest of them - black with gnarled knots in its fur, released a sound like a blizzard hitting deadwood.

They charged, and the looming clouds thickened overhead, darkening until not even a glimmer of unadulterated sunlight perforated to reach the campus below. I fell and dropped back through a new whole which ended on the top floor. The beasts followed as I sunk into the icy territory of the yeth posted there. It uncurled from the stairway door. Bone and sinew stretched in the cracks between its flesh and fur.

Kicking the yeth in the side, I skidded across the shelf, sliding down through the floor around pipes and wires to the floor below. The gap remained open just long enough for the hound to follow. Floor by floor, I gathered the beasts. Their barriers collapsed one into the other. Each illusion crashed into the next, and the temperature crept lower and lower.

The second my feet touched down, I launched toward the stairwell. Weaving in and out of the shadows, the pack followed. Without lungs, they panted. Their breath spread the ice; frost crept up along each bit of metal even as I leaped through the door, sending the pieces of it scattering in all directions to float. Up I went once more. The metal railing bent. Students milled about from one floor to the next, and nobody noticed the tunnel of hellhounds charging up the middle and through the ceiling.

"Come on!" I called.

With a cold front at my back, flying through the ceiling didn't startle me much. Low and cold, the wind howled. My eyes honed in on the Genesee. The water brewed beneath a thin layer of ice. It wasn't much, and there was a chance I'd make as much mess as I had at Tyson's, but it was a chance I was willing to take. The hollow groan of dead wood snapped under my power. Tinder floated a foot above the water, waiting for me to set the match as a barricade of illusions block my design from the yeth and any passing mortals.

Taking the familiar weight of a cheap lighter from my pocket, I set blasts back, egging the demons on. The river rose. I jumped. Fire caught on the dead wood, and the whole line went up in flame. Magic magnification hit natural tinder. Flames raged, spitting at me and tossing me off course as I careened toward the opposite side. I scrambled, shooting magic every which way trying to catch myself, but flying over the river, I stuck the landing.

"Suck it!" I cried and spun with my fist in the air.

White rushed down, foaming and freezing until my wall of hidden fire was completely extinguished. Through the fanning vapors, she glided to hover just far enough off the ground to look down on me. At her heels, the hounds prowled. The hints of singe around their paws and maws faded with each step as the chill settled back into their bones. Ash trailed in their wake.

"Warlock Blythe," she called.

"Wizard Lloyd?" I offered, and she bowed her head in return. Even if Solomon was getting the runaround, I had my answer.

Biting my tongue, I stepped back with each step she took forward. "You know, stalking me seems like a bad idea. Ninety percent of my life is mortals, so...not the greatest idea."

Pausing in her approach, she watched me from beneath her veil. "I have no intention to hurt any mortals."

That held. The hounds hadn't gotten near the other students, and the illusion kept them away. "So...are we going to fight?"

"No, Jon. We are not," she informed me. "I have no desire to harm an innocent. Attacking you before was a mistake. One, for which, I sincerely apologize."

"Thanks."

She bowed her head. Lowering to the ground, she ran her fingers down the side of her dress. "Your master...he is problematic."

"Most people are."

"I request you separate yourself from him until I've completed my task," Dorothy requested.

"On the list of bad ideas, killing the Source seemed pretty high to me, but I've been wrong before." With a shrug, I drummed my fingers. "I'm guessing the whole 'no harm' bit doesn't extend to me if I stick by Jordan. Can I at least get an idea about why you want to kill him?"

Tilting her head, she studied me. The weight of her eyes slid from my shoes to my head. Every bit of me weighed before she said, "I hesitated once to kill a man like him. My daughter died."

"You realize you're a draugr, right? Kettle, pot."

She sneered. The torn edges of her veil flaring to press against her mottled skin. Death painted her lips blue. Around her cheeks, the skin shimmered under its own swollen puffing, but in the hollows, it stretched like wicker beneath the bones. As quick as the anger flared, it drained until the almost alive glimmer in her eye dulled like fog on a mirror.

"Do you know how the Daughters cleanse cities after a summoning like Mammon?" she asked, not even pausing for an answer before she said, "They burn it to the ground. The same is done when a Source becomes corrupt. People are corrupt. Magic users more than any, or did you not think it odd that nobody came to train you? We expect child soldiers. You – you were raised mortal. Do you not understand how destructive that was? How much danger did he put you in?"

Probably not. I could measure could-haves and should-haves and all the what-ifs in the world, but the Grith showed me enough. My life would be spent in service to people I couldn't be sure were worth protecting in a war better served if there were no magic users. Mortals had invented their way out of the dark ages. Given enough light and being left alone, who knew if they could even defeat whatever blight Mammon had brought down on their heads. Hell, without a magic user, they wouldn't have had to worry in the first place. Not that I wanted to be mortal, and wasn't that the rub?

With a shrug, I gave her the only answer I had. "I got a childhood. I'm not really upset about that."

"And when you die because you weren't trained?"

"I'll end up in Heaven."

And she fell back. Her hands twitched at her side in aborted gestures, but no magic followed. "He has failed you. If he truly cared for you, he would have taken your magic the moment you were born." The yeth retreated first. Their shadows shifted, voids returning from a pair who had maintained them at the back. One by one, they descended into Hell. "I should have taken her magic the moment she was born," Dorothy whispered. Around us, the blizzard worsened, and she flickered in and out of my view, but she wasn't really seeing me when she murmured, "Then she wouldn't have died."

Trudging back to my apartment, I called Jordan. My phone rang only once before proclaiming the number I was calling was not available. Because him being available would have been too easy. I texted him what I'd found out, and if my pleasure at being right verged close to vindictive, the frustration was well earned. Dorothy Lloyd rejected death to avenge her murdered daughter. Couldn't exactly hate her for that, and convincing her to pass on nicely probably would go as well as the Hindenburg. Snow covered and frustrated, I stormed up the stairs to my apartment. My key made it into the lock before my eyes caught the shimmer of a coin taped to the front of my door. I peeled it off, and a small folded piece of paper fell into my opposite hand.

Consider this a sign of my good intentions.
– G. Farro

Chapter Eighteen

Flaring my soul produced no hooks. The coin was just a rough circle of metal with an imprint on it. One side showed a building and an address: 1005 North Clinton. On the opposite side, there were two crossed keys. Glancing down the hall, I stretched my shield, but still – nothing. Maybe it was a stupid idea, but I unlocked the door and stepped inside, ditching my coat and reinforcing the wards at a touch before I headed to my room. Pulling the address up online, there was an empty lot with a barbershop adjacent. A hotel popped up in the website history. In a single article buried five pages in, there was a report of the Schröter Hotel burning down post-World War II. Police suspected arson. The odds of it not being the hotel in the journal seemed ridiculously low. This had to be another setup. But what did Giuseppe gain through this?

"Hey," Joel called, leaning against the door. "Where's Tyson?"

Shit. I had ditched him – again. "Library?"

Crossing his arms, Joel sighed. "We need a jar. Dollar for every time you run off without telling someone." His lips curled into a smirk. "You'd be broke in a week."

I wanted to avoid an argument, so I tugged out my phone and sent Tyson a quick text. He walked off first. Not that Joel would care. Holding up the screen for Joel to see, he shrugged and continued into his room – kicking his door shut behind him. Flipping the coin, I passed it from finger to finger. Going back wasn't exactly an option. If I showed up, the draugr might too, and while I could handle a sudden blizzard, the rest of the university shouldn't have to. Most of the out of the out of state freshman didn't dress right for their first winter anyway.

The front door slammed. Stomping to our room, Tyson glared. "You ditched me."

"You ditched me first."

Still bundled, he dripped water onto the rug. His boots and hat were covered in snow. Chucking his bag onto his desk chair, he waved me to follow. "You owe me like a thousand coffees."

"For ditching you?" I scoffed.

Reaching into his pocket, Tyson slapped a printed page down on my desk. "Because I'm a freaking genie – never had a friend like me level of awesome."

On the page, a black and white picture took up the bulk. A line underneath labeled it as being from 1923 and listed the individuals' pictures. There were two which immediately caught my eye: James Porter and Ansaldo Segreti. Segreti stood in the back right corner of the backmost row. Porter sat in the middle. Dark hair slicked back, he wore a slick suit. One arm wrapped around the back of the man next to him. I almost choked on air as Lei's put-out expression stared up at me from the page.

"See, that's Porter," Tyson said, needlessly pointing to the man before sliding to Lei. "And that's his left hand, Lately."

"That's Lei."

His forehead wrinkled. "What?"

I glanced up at him with a sigh. "Lately is Lei."

"Shit – well, that makes my next fact make more sense," he informed me. "James Porter came over from Iceland at fifteen and worked his way up, but his original documents through Ellis Island have him listed as James Ostairius. Guess Lei's a family man."

No wonder the draugr hated Jordan. The Ostairius line kept getting more dangerous. If Dorothy recognized the relation, she might not care if we located her daughter's burial. Fear of death inspired most draugrs, according to lore. She didn't strike me as the type. Her unfinished business could have been revenge as much as it was finding out what happened to her daughter's triad.

"Well? You going to just let me keep dripping here?" Tyson interrupted my thoughts, holding up his arms.

"What? Oh, sorry."

Magic whirled around the apartment. Water went to the drain as Tyson stripped off his coat, tossing it into the air just to cheer as it flew out of our room to hang beside the door. He kicked off his shoes. Eyes sparkling like a kid on Christmas day, he fell back into his chair laughing as they marched off after his coat.

"Seriously. This is a misuse of my power," I intoned as I crossed the room, taping the wards to reinforce them. We weren't under siege like the Grith, but it was a good habit.

"You found anything? Or did you ditch me before the storm hit for no reason?" he asked.

Passing the coin to Tyson, I waved a hand at my computer screen. "I think I also found the hotel. Apparently, it was a speakeasy back during Prohibition. Patrons presented the coin and got into the hidden bar."

"Schröter Hotel – owned by the Friedrich family," Tyson read off the page. "Makes sense. The stuff I found on Porter talked about a German-Italian syndicate of rum runners around Lake Ontario."

"Rochester is way more interesting than I gave it credit for," I grumbled.

Tyson pulled a book from his bag, slapping it out on the desk. "You've got the journal of Segreti the Slicer."

"I get a feeling I don't want to know why he's called that," I intoned.

"He was a big-time fixer in the area. Disappeared right before World War II hit. Nobody knew if he was taken out or fled. When the police started rounding up some of the gangsters in the area, he'd already split, but his tally books sent a bunch of guys to the chair."

"Shit," I murmured, staring down at the journal.

If Segreti had turned in his tomes to the police, leaving this one out made sense, and the way the dates jumped forward made more sense too. As a fixer in Rochester, the bulk of his work had to be non-magical. Anyone in the know who wanted to keep evidence for whatever use would be smart enough not to bring the magical into the mortal. There was no telling if the journal in my possession was the only one he had on the magical world. Segreti kept his writings vague enough magic didn't factor; however, there was a change Segreti knowingly handed over the mortal books and kept the magical ones back. A chance he had left his employers high and dry.

"Do you think he was a snitch?" I asked.

Tyson half-shrugged, half-nodded. "Probably."

"But just the books? Why would that help? He gives dates, but locations are broad and a lot are pretty vague. He uses 'Hotel' for the Schröter, and if H. F. is a Friedrich…"

"Heinrich Friedrich was the top dog at the hotel," Tyson noted.

"Fine, if initials were used, there's got to have been other guys with the same initials and other hotels. That's not exactly solid evidence. They had to have something else to corroborate, right?" I asked, glancing at Tyson, who nodded along with my train of thought.

"My cousin's on the force. I texted him, so we'll see," he offered with a shrug, tossing to me.

"Thanks, man, I couldn't have done this without you."

Tyson grinned. "Course."

My eyes fell back to Lei's face, which smiled up at me from the printed page. "Want to help me figure out how to tell Jordan?"

"I'm not that nice."

I hummed as my eyes scanned the other faces in the picture. They fit the 1920s New York mob image in my head. The same sort of suits on each of them although Porter wore the nicest. Split into three rows, none of them smiled except for one. A cold chill raced down my spine. Bright eyes and a feral grin stared back. Even back in the day, he had his trophies strung around his neck.

"Oh no – now what?" Tyson demanded, tugging his chair up beside mine.

I tapped a finger against the grinning face. "See that guy?"

"Yeah…" His eyes narrowed.

"That's Mammon."

"Well, shit."

Chapter Nineteen

Sitting down in my regular chair, I shoved the food from the table. Black tendrils pulled them close, and one darkening eye turned in my direction, but Lei failed to complain, keeping silent as I laid the scanned photographs out on the coffee table. Each slap of paper against wood had him setting up straighter. One by one, the screens paused then fell entirely black. Setting the last in the center, I sat back. No accusations. Nothing but those black and white photos making my claim for me.

As if he were mesmerized, Lei floated. Extending a pale finger, he traced the edge of the man's face. Though he had no need to breathe, he released a choked whimper. His jaw clenched.

"Where did you get these?" the demon asked.

"Everything's online nowadays," I lied. Nobody needed to know Tyson was in on the secret. "You were part of the New York mafia crowd."

"Turn of the century - contracted."

Leaning with my elbows against my knees, I pointed to Mammon. "Him too?"

"Yes."

"Strange, I thought it took five at least to keep someone his level in line, and I saw how not well that went, so why was he playing nice for this?" I retorted.

His brows rose before his eyes slid shut, and picking up the photograph, he sunk back into the couch and tugged his blanket tighter around him. "I like being told stories. I don't like telling them."

"Fine," I growled. "Then I'll tell the story, and you tell me if I'm wrong."

He pressed the photograph against his chest. Black eyes slid to Jordan's closed door, the runes shimmered, but nobody was inside. Wherever Jordan had run off to, he wasn't here, or I wouldn't have gotten away with interrogating Lei this long on my own. Pulling his knees to his chest, Lei sighed then nodded.

"Mammon likes killing humans, and he's not supposed to kill mortals, so having a magic user around asking for it gave him an out to do so - one his father couldn't complain about, so eating whatever corrupt souls got chucked his way - Giuseppe style - from that Godfather guy was fine by him even if he didn't get a full soul out of the deal. Possibly even better because it didn't just piss his dad off, it pissed you off, and I can't begin to guess that backstory, but it mattered," I suggested, and Lei hummed, giving no denial, but he offered no confirmation either. "And you-you like being told stories. Your favorite stories are adventures - ones where the heroes aren't really heroes."

"Within reason," Lei offered.

I gestured at the picture he held to his chest. "You'd get a lot of good stories staying with the head of a magical mob, and you obviously liked him. I mean, you're sticking by his relatives right now."

Lei glanced down at the photograph. "They don't look alike. Maybe around the eyes, but that one was...healthier, happier."

"Eviler?"

Lei glared, wrapping the blanket around the photograph as if to hide his memories from my scorn. "I'm a demon, stupid-me. Evil, to me, is subjective - personal."

"And he hadn't done anything to hurt you," I finished for him. Shaking my head, I ran my tongue along my teeth, grounding myself amongst the exhaustion stretching out in my bones. "Did you kill her? The draugr? Her daughter?"

"No."

"Did he have her killed? Either of them?"

Lei nodded. He listed sideways, collapsing into the couch cushions. "The other killed the three. When she came around, they wanted help. Covered it all up. She kept looking. The other reminded them of what she could become." Lei's voice dropped as his void crawled up and around him. "He decided she needed to be contained. Thought she might be useful later."

"Would the Daughters have known?"

Shaking his head, Lei drifted, becoming almost invisible within his void. "The other knew. I knew. Two others."

"The other is Mammon, so if Giuseppe knew before the summoning, it had to be one of the other two. Giuseppe has connections, so if I can figure out who has connections to the original leadership, I should be able to figure it out," I considered, but Lei reformed, slamming and the photograph on the table and glaring down at me. "What?"

"Does it matter how he knows? He knew. The other murdered them. She won't have revenge here. The End!" Lei roared. "Nothing more to it. Boring story."

Growling, I slammed my hands down on his table. Magic shot around the room, upending his snacks and turning off his screens. "Not to me," I spat. "And not to Jordan. Seriously, Lei! If you had told us from the beginning, we could've taken care of this weeks ago!"

"How?" he hissed.

"We'd have an idea of where to start. We would've known about Mammon. Jordan's good at reading between the lines. You could've told him about his mafia relative's involvement, and we could've reached out to her – offered to help locate her daughter's remains – something, anything!" I exclaimed.

"And what then?" Lei demanded. His face stuck out like a pale mask against the shroud of his void and the empty darkness of his eyes. "What if she does not treat? What if she already knows?"

"Then we deal with it."

Rising from his void like a puppet pulled up by its strings, Lei floated – a clash of whites and blacks like inked paper. "You may be willing to risk your life – his life," he cried, pointing toward Jordan's door. The air crackled as he fought to speak clearly. "I am not."

"Then you should have told us from the beginning. This never should have fallen on him or on me, but you followed the stupid story, Lei, so here we are," I retorted, refusing to stand or back down as he loomed above me.

He reared back as if struck. "I didn't – I never intended –"

"Nobody cares what you intended, Lei. This is what we're dealing with."

His hands pressed over his pitch black eyes. White blotting out black until, like a marker pressed into a glass of water, color returned, spreading across his skin. Retreating beneath the couch, his void dimmed. With his knees pressed to his chest, he curled in upon himself. Shoulders shook. His nails dug into his forehead, blocking out his sight, but there was no blood to draw out from beneath his skin.

"I will go. If Source-me agrees to this, I will go with you," he intoned. His claw-like nails dragged down his face, cutting his skin, but it stitched itself back together, following the trail down his cheeks. "If it needs flesh, it takes mine."

Lei might have cared about Jordan. Maybe he even cared enough that he would allow characters he disliked or bad plot lines to sneak into the mix, but he still saw us all as stories in the end. Nobody fell on their sword over a book. Especially not a demon.

"You mean you'll swallow her whole and see if you can stomach her?" I retorted.

His brows lifted and fell in a strange facial shrug. The thrill of seeing him fall to pieces as I picked away at the illusion of calm he displayed drained. A flare of my soul failed to incite even a flinch. Not that it mattered. Slithering around my head – feeding me emotions, Conall tested the edges of my strings. I slipped before. This time, I had to be sure this idea was my own.

When the distrust remained, I pressed, "I need to know, Lei."

Holding out his hand with his thumb up and level with the floor, Lei sneered. "Do not rest your plans on me, boy. I am a demon. I will do what I want when I want it. If it means you die…" He shrugged once more with his face – a shift of brows and lips – and held up the page. Stretching up from his fingers, his powers distorted the paper. Age and decay reduced it to ashes on the floor. Eyes flicking to the door, he sighed. "But this time – we'll do it your way."

The lock clicked, and the door swung open. Jordan's brows rose the second his eyes landed on me. "What's going on?"

"I know how we're going to take care of Dorothy."

His nose wrinkled. "Who?"

Chapter Twenty

Leaning against the stone wall, Jordan huffed and crossed his arms. "I'm not saying this won't work. Just keep me in the loop next time."

"I brought you in before I did anything stupid," I reminded him.

Jordan rolled his eyes. His soul lit, spreading out over the area, but there were no more demons here than there had been when we arrived or the other six times he had flared his soul between then and now. The intention, after all, wasn't to cleanse. Dorothy Lloyd didn't have a phone, and while weather radar might've given a hint to her general location, tracking a cold front was harder than having her come around to us. Luckily, her target sat on Jordan's back.

"Temperatures dropping," he murmured.

"That's good, right? She'll be here soon."

"I'm not entirely sold," Lei grumbled from where he lounged like a cat on a wide tree branch. His void wrapped around him like a blanket. "She could sense me and not come."

"Or she could sense you and ignore Jordan – I think that'd be a fun time," I retorted, spiraling fire around me quickly to warm up the air.

Large snowflakes twirled around us. Dark clouds lumbered overhead, and a wall of dispersed ice crystals loomed with shadows shifting as if behind a veil. The yeth came first. They prowled forth, bowing their heads and hunching their shoulders. Winding their ways around stones and trees, they sprawled along the slope of the hill and gathered beneath the tree where Lei reclined.

"Wizard Lloyd," I called. "We're here to parlay."

"Parlay?" Her shadows grew, spreading like a giant's across the veil. "What could you possibly offer me?"

Jordan pushed off the wall and said, "I've found your daughter's grave."

Ice crawled along every surface. Each inch which froze spurred the cold faster across the field. Black so dark that it shimmered purple flashed, catching the light before a dive interrupted as the draugr cast the void of her reach deep beneath the cresting edge of the hill. Though a hoarse shriek vibrated up from the depths, her eyes remained on Jordan. They flashed red beneath her veil, and all along the field, the Yeth pawed at the snow. Their breaths curled. White mist rose from their mouths through the gaps in their sides showed no movement in their lungs - if they even had them.

"They didn't even leave her bones." Her voice trembled, echoing like wind through hollow branches. "No ash or even a trinket to bury. Just the Source's word - Radhika's word that she'd died. Only the certainty that my daughter wasn't coming home."

Licking his lips, Jordan sighed. "She lied."

Shaking her head, the woman waggled her bony finger. Dark gray clouds sunk overhead. The static built between them. When she took another step, a stain remained where she had stood. Black and viscous as ink, it pooled, running across the rough surface of the frozen river, pooling in the crevices and reaching out like tendrils.

"Radhika wouldn't have lied to me," Dorothy retorted.

Lei slid down from the tree like molasses oozing out of a bottle. Around him, the yeth backed away, but they weren't fast enough. His void spread out. Tendrils snaked around, swallowing them as he sauntered over to us.

"She lied," he affirmed. "Informed them after three came. Buried in the park."

"Ansaldo Segreti was supposed to dispose of your daughter's triad, but he didn't," I informed her, stepping aside to show her the gravestones.

Three stones stood side by side. Before we had arrived, two had names and dates – perhaps the Daughters had thought it a reward when the mother of those other two girls accepted her daughters' deaths without question, but they had left one gravestone blank. Carving the stone hadn't been too difficult, and Margaret Lloyd deserved to have her name back. Backing away, I joined Jordan as Lei paced, consuming all the yeth who did not flee. If Dorothy noticed him, she gave no sign.

Crossing the distance, her eyes remained on the grave. Though she had no need to breathe, her chest stuttered. A wheezy hiccupped inhale broke the drumming of the rain. Falling to her knees, Dorothy reached out. Her hand shook. Mottled skin pressed to stone. Her entire body collapsed. Shoulders falling as she fell forward to sob outright into the cold ground although her body could no longer shed tears. Drenched, the shroud clung to her. The towering phantom became a small woman. Thin and decayed by centuries. Her gray nails traced the letters of her daughter's name, and as she trembled, I turned my eyes to the sky. Tears disguised by the rain.

"No," she whispered. Her voice cracked. "No."

Rogues took her daughter from her. Margaret 'Peggy' Lloyd died. The Daughters knew and hid it from her. They had known Peggy had died in a strange country after being kidnapped and tortured, and no amount of blood could wash that truth clean. Years caught within the shroud couldn't temper a mother's thirst for vengeance. Hatred fueled her, but love did so too. All the fury came from love. Every cruelty she'd almost visited – and those which she had – grew from the understanding that the men hadn't been punished sufficiently, and Jordan had created that and worse for others – for me. My fingers flexed at my sides. The second this was over, I was calling my mom. She needed to know I loved her. All this danger. All this sadness. I should have been telling her every day.

Kneeling beside her, Jordan bowed his head. "It's really not, is it?"

Dorothy stretched, wrapping both arms around the stone which marked her daughter's grave. "I am empty. She has gone on, and I am still here."

"You can still follow. You led a good life," Jordan offered.

All the dark and quiet shattered. At least, the illusion it was silence broke. Hail slammed against the ground. Small craters dented the earth as if meteors slammed against the frozen ground, but the shards spiraled upward rather than burning upon impact. Winds howled, but the screaming in my head roared above the deafening gusts. Dorothy froze. Her pain overpowered her, poured right out of her, leaving rage to fester in the crevices it failed to reach.

"And her killer?" she whispered.

Jordan shook his head. "Mammon."

Gritting her teeth, she pulled back. "Then Farro was right.

"You let her murderer go. Mammon's summoning, the city's damnation - that is all because of you," she intoned. Her darkened fingers pointed at Jordan as she stalked toward us.

A headache itched up the back of my head. It spread down my spine and fanned around until my ears pulsed. An indescribable urge came over me. She was dangerous. Even if Lei did as promised and jumped in, the blast radius would be catastrophic. If I opened a warp – twisted the fabric between Earth and Hell, I could escape. Sweeping down through Hell, I could grab Conall and make a run for it.

I slammed the break on that thought, throwing it aside and burying the idea down into the depths of my mind. Conall wanted to fall. He made the decision to go with the Erlkonig. If he regretted his actions now, I wasn't about to risk myself or those I cared about to save him. Not after Gerhard.

"If you want to punish Mammon, go to Hell. Burn him up down there," Jordan suggested. "I have a student to consider."

Her dark eyes darted to me, but he had played the only card she had admitted weakness to herself. Even side by side with Jordan she refused to attack me. The hail bounded off Jordan's shield, but it never even came close to me. All on Jordan's other side, the yeth prowled. They hung about in a semicircle, avoiding getting any closer to me.

"You are the Source," she accused, but she shook her head as if dismissing her own argument.

"If I swear to kill Mammon if I come across him again, will it appease you? By the time he makes it back to Earth, Jon should be trained," Jordan noted. Ten years and counting. Good to know the time scale wasn't an eternity for me then.

Ajith jumped on the deal, but Dorothy stared unblinkingly through the shredded remains of her shroud. The sharp bones of her face protruded from the tight leathering of her cold mummified skin.

"Everyone at fault is dead and long buried. My daughter is dead, Source, and this agony tears me apart. Heaven and Hell offer no rest. This rage inside me won't die," she whispered, running her fingers along the runes which glowed beneath her touch like a threat, binding her tightly within her decaying body. "Trapped in that hole with only my memories, there's nothing left of me but this. As

341

long as I exist, this pain will, and I can't - I can't continue. Not from this. There's nothing else." She swallowed, and though face scrunched up as if to hold back tears, the shine across her bones was just the stretch of her skin. "This place is infected. I need to be nothingness. I need to stop."

"You can't come back from that," Jordan warned.

My throat tightened. Self-immolation, as she descended into Hell, would cut into the damnation marking the city, but while nobody knew for certain how conscious souls were in Hell or if any ended up in Heaven, burning up her entire being as she sunk into Hell meant she would cease to exist. Knowing we had hoped she'd make this choice made it all the more bitter. We had guided her into suicide – worse than because she would erase herself entirely. No afterlife, no thoughts, nothing.

She sighed. Her body sagged against the stone, and for a moment, I thought she had gone. Then, she sat back on her heels. "I have mourned my daughter for so long. I do not know if I remember how to die, but I will go. Bury me beside her? Place me here." She pressed a hand to the earth. "And when you meet that demon again, strike him down."

Jordan nodded. "I will."

Tilting back her head, she gazed at him through the dull, stained veil. "There is only so much darkness you can consume for another. Live better."

Frost curled along her cheeks, chasing the tears until a layer of ice formed over her decaying eyes. Digging her fingers into the frozen earth, Dorothy leaned forward. Her lips brushed against the stone which marked her daughter's previously unmarked grave. Ash had long ago melded with soil, and the reeds which sprung stone hurried the transformation.

A sob wretched its way from her throat. The dark mottled flesh of her hands oozed, and even downwind, my stomach turned at the memory of the stench. Parting her cracked lips, she slid to lie curled in the fetal position on the ground. Her soul swirled around her. As tarnished bronze lit the marsh, Jordan raised his shield, and I followed suit.

The encroaching ice stalled. All along the tree line and water's edge, the yeth slunk back; their ice melted below their feet. While their instincts warned them to run, they were smart enough to not retreat to Hell nearby. Howling, they raced northward. They likely would reunite with the hunt.

Darkness arose beneath her. A warp unfolded, but there was no other side. Hell's sharp cold spread upward, climbing against the swell of heat and light gathering tightly around her. Closing her eyes, she sunk into Hell, burning. A patch of green grass rose where she had been, but the frost inched its way back across the softened blades. Winter remained in Rochester, and if she did as she promised, if she ignited - a self-emulation in Hell, I had imagined a more overt change, but the shadow of Mammon's summoning hadn't altered much.

"Maybe the Daughters will back off now," I murmured as we both let our shields tighten and dim until they hid invisible around our bodies. "Her soul was pretty bright, right? For a draugr. So she could've taken out a lot of the damnation, wouldn't she? So no need to raze the city."

Jordan shook his head. "This won't change anything."

"Then what's the point?" I demanded.

"Minimizing as long as possible. Think of it as a loan. We're paying the interest and whatever else we can," he intoned as Lei strode down the hill to join us.

Like an optimistic fool, I asked, "Do you think it will be enough?"

Jordan glanced at Lei before he said, "No."

Chapter Twenty-One

We showed up, exhausted but luckily not bloody, on the doorstep to the Grith a few hours later. Helena and Leta waved us inside, and Phuong checked us over at the second, but the Grith no longer had enough users within its walls to guard each corner of its barricade. The yard stood empty. No footsteps echoed with shushed whispers once we ended. Nobody came to greet us, but some banging of pots sounded from the kitchen, and Monday sat within his office, grading papers. Benny curled up on the window seat reading, and Theda leaned against the desk across from Monday. Shadows cradled her eyes, and when she glanced up, she sighed, sinking further into her seat.

"I don't care what Kasimira said. Take out the draugr on your own. You aren't an acolyte. We don't need to witness every hunt," she groaned, rubbing her hands over her face. "Crap, wait...what day is it? Are we redoing the wards?"

"We can if you want, but the draugr self-immolated," he informed her.

I piped in, "She took out some of the damnation too."

Monday put down his pen. "The Elders called her earlier today. They wanted to know why we were looking into the death of Dorothy Lloyd – a wizard who went rogue almost a hundred years ago. Was I correct in assuming that is the name of the draugr?"

"Yeah, she was looking for her daughter, who had been killed, along with her triad, by a mafia group out of New York City," I explained, shifting Benny aside to sit beside him in the window seat. He immediately sprawled across my lap. "We found her grave."

"Jon found her grave," Jordan corrected.

I preened at the acknowledgment. Tyson might've had the connection with his cousin at the Rochester Police Department, but nobody needed to know that. Frankly, my magic would be on the line if they did. However, while I believed we had done something pretty fantastic, Theda sighed and sunk down as if she might slip right out of her chair and onto the floor like a pre-tantrum toddler.

Jordan demanded. "What?"

"I hate being lied to," she complained. "So she wasn't unreasonable? Mad with loss over an understood risk?"

"Margaret Lloyd died because the rogues in question were protected by James Porter – my great uncle," Jordan told her, shoving his hands in his jacket pockets.

Theda rubbed her hands down her face once more. "Tell me you didn't label the grave."

"We didn't label the grave," Jordan deadpanned.

Taking Benny's book away, I cut off his protests. "That's your cue to leave."

"I was here first," the kid argued.

"Benjamin," Monday intoned, and the kid slid off me and stomped away with his book in

347

hand. At the door, he gave one final pout toward Monday, but the man crossed his arms, and Benny merely huffed before closing the door behind him. "We can now be sure everyone will be eavesdropping."

"They realize it'll weaken the wards," Jordan said as if that made a difference.

Theda and Monday didn't argue. The twenty or so remaining wards were a creative and stubborn bunch. If they wanted to spy on Monday's office, there was a good chance a technological means bugged the office already. As if he knew we had arrived, Wolfram stared directly into the camera. Symbols scrawled in blood framed his face. Most were wards, but the others seemed like half-formed words, and even as I typed them into my phone to look into once I could reactivate the data plan on my phone, I had the feeling it wouldn't tell me anything. I flashed my soul quietly, ensuring Conall wouldn't get to see them in case it was a code especially for him before pointedly looking away.

"They're only so many children left," Monday stated. "We might as well let them know if they're able."

Jordan shook his head. "It doesn't matter to me."

"First, you can't tell us anything. Second, the Elders will want you to swear to take whatever you learned to your graves," Theda informed us. "The Daughters don't acknowledge their work – historical or present – with rogue syndicates. Any evidence to the contrary is buried."

"Literally," I grumbled.

Crossing his arms, Jordan sighed. "I'm not making this harder on you than necessary, Theda. I'll agree to whatever you need me to."

Theda reached out, squeezing Jordan's elbow. "Thank you."

"Regardless, Hikmat wants to speak with both of you," Monday said.

Running a hand through his hair, Jordan glanced at me. "Fine. Give us a call when she decides the time. Try for the weekend. The kid doesn't need to be up late on a school night."

If it were for any other reason, I might have reminded him that I was eighteen and could go to sleep whenever I wanted, but losing sleep to get lectured by an Elder wasn't my goal. Pushing off the seat, I stepped up beside Jordan, expecting to head out. We neared dinner time, and Jordan never let me stay; however, Ros threw the door open. In a striped cream and green apron with denim pockets, she stood with her hands on her hips, blocking Jordan from making any sort of escape.

"You are staying for dinner," she announced.

Theda snickered, pushing out of her seat to clap Jordan on the shoulder. "Let her feed the boy. It'll give us time to talk about what's coming."

"We have a call scheduled with Hikmat tonight. It would be prudent if you stayed and handled this now rather than later," Monday intoned as he set aside the papers he had been grading into two piles. "I have a few more pages to get through."

Ros hummed. "You can take the second shift with Kasi." Reaching out, she grabbed Jordan's upper arm, guiding him toward the dining room. "I know you're partial to breakfast food. If you don't like anything you see, I can whip up some crepes or something."

"I'm sure whatever you've cooked will be fine," he assured.

Theda waved me through the door and walked at my side, following Jordan and her sister. Her exhausted gaze slid to me. "If your friend recognizes the writing, email me."

"I'm hoping not to involve him," I returned, but she laid a hand upon my arm, stopping me in my tracks as she let Ros take Jordan further down the hall before she turned to face me completely.

"Show him."

Pursing my lips, I fought against the knot forming in my brow. "What? Isn't that exactly what you guys told me not to do?"

"Ros mentioned you were concerned about another leak at the Grith. Someone connected to Conall. If that's true, we'll want them to make a move. If that writing means what we think, it'll give them a chance to coordinate which will put a target on both their backs. Turning the Erlkonig against Conall is our best bet," Theda said, and there was frustrated desperation in her eyes which assured me this was a calculated risk. One she wasn't entirely pleased to take.

Saying Conall was chaos simplified him too much. He had a plan. We were all just dominos, and for all that his injuries seemed like the result of an emotional act – one of passion inspired and out of the context of his usual logical, predatory thinking – I believed Wolfram in this at least. Emotions served as weapons to the wizard. His help came with strings. He parceled honesty like gold, paying out just enough to draw his prey close enough for him to strike.

Someone might have been able to keep up. Maybe my father had the cold, analytical ruthlessness needed to trick Conall like he spun Jordan round. Joel would have done a better job of this than me. I didn't have it in me to go up against that. I wasn't smart enough. My magic fell significantly short of the task, and even though my lying improved, I still invested too easily. If nothing else, I could see myself clearly now.

Rubbing the back of my neck, I shook my head. "I can't, Theda."

She opened her mouth, but no words came out. Snapping her jaw closed so quick her teeth clacked together, Theda inclined her head. All desperation drained from her posture. Her eyes focused ahead, and when Ros went straight, she ducked to the side, heading upstairs. The request was probably due to sleep deprivation. She would be glad I had refused when she woke up again.

"We have to eat in rounds," Ros was saying when I joined them in the dining room. "Originally, there were just too many kids, but now…" she waved out the window toward the walls. "Leta and

Helena will be in shortly. They received some news today that I'm sure they're excited to share."

"They'll be upset if you give away the surprise," Meinhard stated, setting a bowl of roasted sprouts on the table. A roast sat in the center, surrounded by carrots and onions.

Ros laughed, smiling as she promised, "I wouldn't dare."

"I want to sit next to Jon!" Benny shouted.

He raced around the table, slamming so hard into my leg I nearly fell over. Grinning up at me, the young wizard tugged me toward the opposite side. Windows lined the wall. Though the hair on the back of my neck rose at having my back exposed, I sat where he instructed.

"Who else is still here?" Jordan asks.

He didn't sit; instead, he leaned against the back of the chair across from me as if talking his way out was still an option. Meinhard returned to the kitchen, and as the door swung shut behind him, his sister's voice carried. Ros's fingers twisted the tablecloth. Her eyes shifted to the door.

"Meinhard and Adalheidis, of course. Leta, Helena, and Roderich – for a bit longer. Conrad, Phuong, and Benny have refused several placements. There's a psychic in Sri Lanka who offered to take Phuong. It's a friend of her aunt's, so I'm hoping she'll go, but…" she trailed off with a shrug. "Ajith and Indra are here for now. Ajith wants to go to the Sons, but Indra said he would, but he hasn't been completely sold on the idea, so

Ajith has been dragging his heels until he can get his cousin comfortable with the idea."

While I sat on my hands unsure whether to serve myself or wait for whomever else, Benny stood on his chair. He piled potatoes and several slices of roast, pointedly avoiding the vegetables until Ros paused. Her gaze settled on him. She crossed her arms, and with a huff, he added carrots to the mix. Pleased, she returned to listing out another half-dozen more names. Most of which, I honestly had no idea who they were. All in all, the total came out somewhere south of twenty. Not being the one in charge of that, I enjoyed droning the conversation out in favor of grabbing food for myself until the doors opened. Leta and Helena stomped in with Phuong right behind them.

"Awesome! You're actually getting food!" Leta cheered as she slid into the chair on my other side.

"Contrary to popular belief, I can feed myself," I assured her.

Helena rolled her eyes. "Our food is better."

"True," I agreed, sniffing the sprouts.

"Conrad, Roderich, Luka, Ajith, and Indra have the next shift on the walls, but Harald and Wei should be down. I'm going to check on Meinhard and Adalheidis," Ros said as she headed toward the kitchen. The door flapped behind her, and she leaned back out, holding it open. "Since you're staying, why don't you do Harald tonight rather than wait?"

"I could do it right now if you need," Jordan replied.

Ros shook her head. "I want him to confirm what he wants directly to you."

When Jordan nodded, she left, letting the door swing shut behind her. Pulling out the seat across from me, Jordan sat down. Phuong sat beside him. The three teens dished out their dinners while I awkwardly waited for everybody else. Benny had no such qualms.

"Heard you have some news," Jordan said, leaning back in his chair.

"We do!" Leta nearly dropped the serving fork for the roast in her enthusiasm. Grinning, she looked to her sister, but if she wanted them to speak together, she didn't give Helena enough time before she exclaimed, "We got into the University of Rochester!"

My brain careened like a train flying off its track. The nice, clean line between the Grith and Rochester shattered. Inhaling, I forced a smile. "That's awesome!"

"There's a safe house in Fairport that the Daughters are letting us take over. There are three rooms if you want one," Leta offered, but before I could turn her down, she kept talking. "It's got a yard with a fence. There's no swimming pool or anything, but I've always wanted a dog. We considered staying in Toronto, but we're not technically citizens. Dad was American; Mom came from Greece, so..." She weighed the two in her hands with a smile. "We lived in Greece until we were ten, so we thought – why not? Our dad always wanted to show us his birth country, but Texas is just hot."

"You're not letting anybody else talk, Leta," Helena cut her sister off on an inhale.

Leta huffed, but she sank back in her chair and mimed zipping her lips shut. Jordan chuckled. "We'll be glad to have some help around the city," he assured them.

I kept a smile firmly in place. "It's a great university."

"And we'll make friends on our own. You don't have to big brother us," Helena promised, but the way Leta rolled her eyes, I didn't believe the twins would give me space for an instant.

"No, it'll be nice to have other magic users on campus. Though…I don't think I'm up for being your third – roommate-wise or hunting-wise," I said.

If either of them met Joel, I would have to play the fool. Joel probably would have a plan to deal with them. He and Tyson could think up something. The instinctual panic drained at that thought. I wasn't alone in this. My friends knew, and I had people I could rely on when I got ahead of myself.

Leta frowned. "Don't say no just yet. You haven't seen the house."

"I like my roommates."

Meinhard came back in with a basket of steaming bread rolls. Adalheidis followed with gravy. They both took seats with Adalheidis taking the head of the table. She glanced around; her brow furrowed. "Did you tell them already?"

"Yes. Jon doesn't want to live with us," Leta replied.

Phuong giggled, and Benny's little brows furrowed. "You don't want to live with me anymore."

"It's not that we don't want to, Benny. We're going to university," Helena said.

Benny grumbled under his breath, cutting bits off the slices of roast as he glared down at his food. Jordan leaned back in his chair. Like the awkward adult at the kids' table, he stared at the door until Ros returned with Harald and a tall girl who I guessed was Wei. They sat down at the table, and once everyone else had served themselves, Jordan filled his plate.

Meinhard stirred his food around his plate, smothering everything in gravy as he scanned the table. "Are we all going to pretend this is normal?"

"We've got a call with the Elders later," Jordan explained.

"And you should get used to this," Ros added. "Jordan has volunteered to lead the trainee hunts."

"Hunts in Toronto? Or hunts in Rochester?" Wei asked.

"We'll keep north of Lake Ontario," Jordan replied.

Wei's eyes slid to Phuong who shrugged. "Exciting. Not many people can say they trained with the Source."

356

"It's a thrill," I drawled, earning Leta's elbow in my ribs.

"He's doing this for you," she hissed as the others continued their discussion on Jordan's future in teaching.

I rolled my eyes. "Sure, this will totally get the Daughters off our backs."

"Not everything is about the Daughters," Leta scoffed.

All around him, the others asked him questions. Jordan fielded them calmly, but the middle finger on his right hand rubbed against the handle of his fork, worrying the metal.

"If we're taking hunts on, who's going to take care of the walls?" Wei asked.

Jordan kept his shoulders relaxed, and when he looked at her, it wasn't with the same condescending expression which crept onto his face whenever I asked something he considered stupid, but his nail pressed against the metal. "As I'll be up more, I can reinforce the layers of warding. I can carry the difference. Also, if we hunt more frequently, the Hunt will have fewer demons to throw at the shields."

"Do we get to pick the groups?" Adalheidis gestured toward her brother with a knife. "I don't want this idiot going anywhere without me."

"You're not smarter. Just louder," Meinhard retorted.

Jordan smiled, and while it was a good fake smile – the kind of person only could get by practicing for years, I recognized the dullness in his eyes. He kept it firmly in place as he said, "I'll take you guys out in groups of three."

"You'll still take my magic away, right?" Harald asked.

Jordan set down his silverware, focusing all his attention on the boy. "Ros said you wanted to become a baker."

"My elder brother's descendants run a bakery back in Germany. They've got children my ages, but they're mortal. The last psychic was three generations back," Harald explained. "They want to take me in."

"Did they make giving up your magic a condition of that?" Jordan's voice remained bland. Any trace of judgment pushed as far down as he could manage.

Harald shook his head. "No, but I don't want them to be in danger, and..." Shoulders sagging, he sighed. "I like cooking. I want to be a chef. I don't want to spend my life hunting demons."

"This is a one-way street. You can't change your mind," the Source forewarned.

Harald set down his own silverware. "I want you to remove my magic."

Everybody kept eating. Nobody said a word. Adalheidis glanced between her brother and Leta as she chewed, but Meinhard pointedly kept his eyes on his meal. Ros smiled. While the expression started off as encouraging, the tight lines around her eyes grew as her gaze flicked to Leta whenever she opened her mouth, even if it were just to take another bite.

358

Jordan nodded. A pulsating ache throbbed in the back of my head. If Conall hadn't been attached, I likely wouldn't have felt the tether between Harald and Hell cut off. With the rogue wizard watching from the opposite side, I only could compare it to the shifting pressure in a shower when somebody else turns on the water. The steady drum – each going through pipes to different people shifted, growing just a bit stronger before returning to normal. Harald's eyes widened. Squirming in his seat, he turned a bit green.

"There you go," Jordan informed him.

Wei frowned. "That's it."

"That's it," the Source confirmed.

"I thought we'd feel something," she muttered.

Meinhard hummed. "Harald looks like he felt something."

"The more magic users involved, the more noticeable it becomes for those not involved," Ros explained. "As Harald is the only one having his magic removed, you'd have to know what to look for to feel it."

Everyone watched Harald as if expecting him to lurch away from the table or vomit, but his breathing evened out. Within a few seconds, the color returned to his face. "It's not so bad."

"You're crazy," Leta muttered. Receiving a reproachful glare from Ros, she huffed, but before she could speak, a figure turned around the corner, ducking into the dining room.

Glancing around the table, Conrad said, "Ah, sorry to interrupt, Hikmat's elected to call early. Monday asked me to tell Jordan and Jon to come to his office."

"We'll be right there," Jordan assured.

He moved to grab his plate, but Ros stopped him. "We'll handle that."

"I miss washing dishes with magic," Adalheidis lamented.

Conrad waved. "I'm raiding the kitchen. Roderich's stomach was growling before he hit the wall, and I don't want to deal with him if he's got to stay up there without eating anything."

"I put bags together in the fridge," Ros called after him as he left.

Leta rolled her eyes, grumbled, "He wouldn't be hungry if he ate his lunch."

"Not everyone is used to eating three meals in a single day," Meinhard stated.

Silence fell over the room, and Jordan pushed out his chair, summoning me to follow with two fingers. Saying my goodbyes quietly to Benny, I excused myself and followed him out of the room. Chatter started soon after we left. Leta saying something about guilt cards and the Hamelin children having to adapt or get left behind. Her sister was quick to refute from the sound of things, but whatever else was said was lost behind closed doors.

Jordan and I headed back down the hall. "I'm proud of you," he said. "Leta and Helena will be a good influence for you."

"I'm pretty sure I'm a horrible influence on them."

He reached out, pausing in the middle of the hall. "I'm serious, Jon. I'm proud of you. The Grith won't be like this for long, but the kids who are still here need some help learning the mortal side, and I think it would be good for you. I'm going to be up here anyway. If you have time, you should come up here."

"Okay."

With a pat on my back, he nodded and walked away.

***

In a magical community smaller than most colleges, I wasn't lucky enough to get lost in the shuffle. Despite Jordan's best attempts, Hikmat glared at me. Every silvery slick scar across her skin intensified her glower and the near black brown of her eyes. An Elder of the Daughters – fierce and experienced. She probably could kill me a hundred ways with her pinky. Even if they had made a mistake, pointing it out screamed 'dangerous.' Once Jordan finished explaining, she sat in silence for five painful seconds before speaking.

"You should exterminate the creature regardless," Hikmat intoned.

Jordan clenched his fists. "I'll kill Lei when the Daughters publicly admit fault for the handling of the trio sent to Rochester, Dorothy's follow-up and betrayal, and the resulting draugr. Giuseppe's decision to summon here would be the Daughter's fault as well."

"Which means the rise of Shiloh and the proximity to the Grith falls on the Daughters too," Ros pushed, causing her sisters to gawk. "We cannot hold fault for Wolfram; however, his release may have gone better or worse if at a different time which would have delayed or quickened the issue of the Wizard Conall."

"So…we are to admit fault for an endless string of events?" Hikmat clucked her tongue.

"No," Jordan retorted though they had expected the same of him. "I hold some responsibility, and my decision not to level the city remains on me. Regardless, the decisions up to Giuseppe began with the Daughters knowingly protecting rogues and allowing their members to be killed without retribution."

Waving her had as if to brush the topic aside, the Elder sighed. "You could have just refused, Source."

"No, I couldn't. The Elders saw to that."

Her lips pressed together, but the daggers flying from her vicious gaze kept the almost empathetic expression hard. "One fisherman cannot empty a river."

"Your point?" Jordan asked.

"You cannot contain the damage. It may not spread, but until you cauterize the wound, it will bleed. The draugr may have minimized the damage, but the fact remains." Hikmat eyes darkened. "Burn it to the ground, or we will." Before anyone could reply, her video feed cut.

We all sat, staring at the black as if it would reveal everything as a joke. Monday bowed his head. Crossing the room, Ros stood at his side. Her hand rested on his arm as he glanced up. Wrapping his arms around her, the wizard pulled her close. Their foreheads pressed together. While my inner ego cheered because I was right, I kept my mouth shut. So did her sisters.

Shifting in their seats, both were lost in thought. Ros had made her decision. No point in arguing with her. If the Elders didn't change their mind, Rochester would go the way of Gomorrah. Burned and ruined. A pile of ashen nothing.

Bile rose in my throat. Tyson's family needed to be warned. Thousands of people lived here. We had to do something. "We can fake a nuclear disaster or-or make a lake hurricane, right? Earthquakes? Something to evacuate the city, right?"

Jordan rested his elbows on his knees. His face pressed into the palms of his hands. As his fingers dug into the hell-bleached blond of his hair, my hope withered. With his back arched, the hanged man peeked out from his collar. Like a pendulum, the earth swung back and forth beneath my feet.

Worse came to worst, we had the Source. He could take everybody's magic in one fell swoop. Maybe the demons hanging around would still cause trouble, but hundreds of thousands of lives would be saved. The idea of doing nothing tormented me.

"Dorothy minimized the damage," Ros murmured, pulling back from Monday.

Kasimira shook her head. "Not nearly enough."

"But what if we gathered all wizards to the area. Warped in as many as possible to blaze out the damage," Ros suggested. "Her soul wasn't pure, yet her self-immolation managed to seal off at least two to three percent of the rift. If we can get the damage down to less than sixty percent, it will push it outside the bounds of the order."

Sitting up, Jordan twisted around in the chair to face her. "Wizards have more magic, but their souls aren't more powerful. Twenty magic users of any sort could do it."

"The more wizards the better," Monday retorted. "We'll need to be ready to warp everyone out of the damage as it shrinks."

"And to handle the demons gathered there," Kasimira added.

"The Hell-side of an infection is always worse, and with the Hunt nearby, they could swarm the second we go down there," Theda warned, but glancing around, the hardened faces told me that didn't matter.

With a sigh, Jordan nodded. "It's worth a try."

"A gathering of wizards," Monday hummed.

Thank you for reading Lady in White! If you enjoyed this book, please consider leaving a review!

Or sign up to our newsletter!

Other books by Eli Celata:

Warlock of Rochester Series
High Summons
Grimm Remains
Smoke & Mirrors

Kasmai Cycle
A War of Brothers
The One That Lives
The One That Remembers

Scifi Horror
Conquest Rising

YA Sports Romance
Getting to Go